CHASING NORMAL

CHASING NORMAL

A Chip Fullerton/Annie Smith Sports Novel

T. L. Hoch

iUniverse, Inc.
Bloomington

Chasing Normal
A Chip Fullerton/Annie Smith Sports Novel

iUniverse books may be ordered through booksellers or by contacting:

iUniverse
1663 Liberty Drive
Bloomington, IN 47403
www.iuniverse.com
1-800-Authors (1-800-288-4677)

ISBN: 978-1-4697-5148-1 (sc)
ISBN: 978-1-4697-5149-8 (hc)
ISBN: 978-1-4697-5150-4 (e)

Library of Congress Control Number: 2012901861

Printed in the United States of America

iUniverse rev. date: 02/21/2012

To Louann, Abby, and Jessie

Preface

This story has been a joy to write. It has taken several years of sporadic effort. I always thought the story had merit, but the writing needed improvement. After way too much deliberation, I decided to just finish it and let the reader be the judge. A good deal of the story came to me while bike riding along the Mississippi River and swimming at the local "Y." Characters came and went, as did name changes. Ralph became Riley and Chet became Luke. My wife and two daughters all had their say, and I believe the story improved as a result of their efforts. I am currently working on book number two of the series: *Discovering Balance.* I promise a speedier delivery on this one.

Note to coaches and players: I understand that there are several ways to coach and play the game. Through Annie, I am conveying what I believe is a solid approach to the game, but by no means do I believe it is the only way to play.

I would like to thank the following people for their help and their support: my wife, Louann, and daughters, Abby and Jessie. They were diligent readers and editors. Additional readers and editors included Missy Hartman, Sharon Law, and Judy Schreiber. Hilary Handelsman did an awesome job on the final editing. Also, thanks to Alan Perrin for his information on the Texas State Basketball Tournament. Special thanks to Heather Houzenga for her sketch, which appears on the back cover.

Contents

Chapter 1

New Girl

Annie Smith followed her mom's car as it passed the sign indicating they were now in Reston, Texas. She had one major goal for her new life in Texas—to live the life of a normal teenager. She was looking forward to not being hassled by the media or her teammates. *Life is going to be totally different in this quiet little town*, she thought.

She reached over and turned down her CD player, which was playing some serious Led Zeppelin. The people in this small town were probably all country music lovers, and she didn't want to get off on the wrong foot. The brake lights on her mom's Buick came on ahead of her. She downshifted her Ford Ranger into third gear and looked to her right. About forty boys in football practice gear were hard at it, just east of a very modern-looking building. The western end of the school was two stories high and threw a huge shadow over the practice field. Knowing how serious Texans were about their football, Annie wondered if the school was designed to provide shade for early-evening practices. The summer Texas sun can be brutal.

What a nice school for such a small town, she thought. *That tall portion must be the gym. I hope the locals won't mind a new face on the basketball team.* Two blocks later, her mom turned into an area filled with fairly modern ranch homes. At the end of Jefferson Street sat a nice two-bedroom, split-level house that Annie recognized from the picture her mom had shown her three weeks earlier. But she hadn't told her the best thing about the house—no neighbors! There was a vacant lot on either side of the house and a field behind it. She wouldn't have to worry about bothering the neighbors when she turned up her music. This was a nice start to a new, normal life.

* ◆ *

Two days of unpacking and moving furniture around was enough to last Annie a lifetime. She sat on her bed and looked at her reflection in the mirror on the closet door. Her shoulder-length hair was somewhere between blonde and brown. She always felt that her features, except for her eyes, were fairly normal—just the way she liked them. Her green eyes seemed to have a perpetual sparkle in them. Her mom and dad always told her that her eyes were the reflection of her inner goodness. She liked that, and the fact that her dad had written a song about them. He was still working on that song when he died. Below the neck, Annie was different from most teenage girls. She stood about 5'7" which, by itself, wouldn't draw any special attention. However, her broad shoulders and lean body had "athlete" written all over them. The muscles on her arms and shoulders, which she usually kept covered, were well-defined. To the experienced eye, it was obvious that she had spent some time in the weight room. She gave herself a little wave and the girl in the mirror reciprocated. The simple gesture conveyed a feeling of guarded anticipation. School, sports, and friendships were all huge question marks now.

Annie looked around her room and gave a nod of satisfaction. A queen-sized bed was centered against the right-hand wall as you walked through the door. Two monster Electra-Voice speakers occupied the corners on the opposite wall. Two guitars leaned against the wall to her right, and her stereo system was within an arm's length to her left. The guitars were special to her. The bass was hers, and the other one was one of her dad's. He had been killed in a plane crash just before she started the eighth grade. It had been a rough year for her. She threw herself into basketball and softball, which laid the foundation for the player she was today. The six-string was autographed by her dad, Eric Clapton, and Kim Simmonds. She was pretty sure it was worth a lot of money, but that meant little to her. Her dad's memory could not be bought for any price.

A big box of trophies and a scrapbook of her softball and basketball exploits were already tucked away in the back of her closet. She just knew things would be different here in Texas. It was a huge state, easy to get lost in. There were probably hundreds of female athletes better than her in both sports. That was fine with her. That would mean no reporters to bother her and no weirdo teammates to make life miserable.

* ◆ *

Annie lay back on her bed and relived her freshman year back in Arkansas. The basketball season had been stressful, but it had been nothing like the softball season. You wouldn't think throwing three consecutive no-hitters would be a problem, but it was. Annie and Sally Phelps were supposed to share the pitching duties for Franklin High School. Annie actually lived in Jones Ferry, a little town of about 900. Franklin High was in DeWitt, about twelve miles away. Each school had its own basketball team, but they had to coop to field a softball team. Sally lost the first game of the season 3 to 2, even though she pitched a good game. She was fairly fast, with good control. She also had an excellent sinker that caused the opposition to hit a lot of playable grounders against her. With some fine-tuning, she would probably have a chance to pitch at the junior college level.

Annie started the second game against a weak team and threw a five-inning no-hitter. The game was stopped because Franklin was ahead by more than ten runs. Her second no-hitter came in the second game of a double header. She had all the pitches: blazing fastball, sinker, change-up, and a fantastic rise-ball. She was also experimenting with a hook that started out at the right-hand batter's box, and then curved across the plate. Most batters just froze, wide-eyed, when that pitch came at them. She didn't throw it often, but when she did it was very effective. Her catcher, Darcy Turner, had names for three of her pitches. "Godzilla" was her fastball, "Bad Boy" was the hook and "The Sleeper" was the change-up.

Her third game of the season was against a pretty good team, and it was Franklin's first home game. The Lady Cougars from Charles City were conference champions from the previous year. Annie wasn't playing high school softball then, but she did remember them from the basketball season that had just finished. They played real rough and even dirty at times. It was obvious that they were coached that way, but the players seemed to like it. She wondered if their coach had the same philosophy in softball as he did for basketball. Annie didn't like them—not even a little bit. She was throwing her warm-ups to Darcy behind the equipment building as usual. It was a nice secluded spot where no one could see or bother you. It was obvious that she was upset about something. The conversation came back to her as if it happened only yesterday.

"What's up with you today?" asked Darcy as she walked up to Annie holding the ball.

"I don't know," replied Annie. "I just get all worked up when I see those Charles City girls."

"Yeah, I know what you mean. They're real sweethearts, aren't they?"

"Why do they have to act that way?" asked Annie. "Sports isn't about trying to humiliate the other guy. It's about playing hard and pushing yourself—with a little fun mixed in."

"These girls don't know that," said Darcy. "All they know is you scored thirty points against their fresh/soph basketball team, and they want revenge. So be careful when you are up to bat. They just might throw at you for spite. Anyway, have you noticed anything different?"

"Like what?" asked Annie. "Are you getting taller?"

"Not hardly," said Darcy. "I'm destined to be a shrimp for the rest of my life—just like my mom. I'm talking about your speed, girl. I've never seen you throw so hard. Matter of fact, I've never seen anybody throw so hard, even in the big city tournaments. My hand would look like the Hulk's if I didn't have my bandana stuffed inside my glove. When you get riled, you can really bring the smoke."

"I do feel like I've got a little something extra today."

"Well, it's a good day to have it. These Charles City prima donnas really suck."

"You know I don't like that kind of talk," said Annie as they walked shoulder to shoulder around the shed into the view of the players and fans.

"Loosen up. That's not a bad word. Now go ahead and say it."

"Say what?" asked Annie.

"Say, 'I hate these guys.' You know you do."

"Let's just say they are not on my Christmas list. Maybe we can have a little fun with them, though," said Annie with a mischievous look in her eyes.

Before Darcy could respond, they saw Coach Hargraves waving at them from the dugout. They broke into a jog and went out onto the field, where their teammates were putting the finishing touches on their pregame infield practice. As Annie reached the mound, the umpire threw her the game ball. He held up seven fingers to indicate how many warm-up pitches she could throw. She nodded and threw the first one overhand as though she were pitching a baseball and not a softball. Darcy pegged the ball back to her with a flick of a wrist. After her fourth overhand toss, she switched to underhand and continued to lob them in. Darcy's mask hid her huge grin as she began to chatter at her pitcher.

"That's it, rag arm, nice and easy. Don't show them the good stuff right away. Tease them a little."

Annie's last pitch was a weak effort that barely got to the plate. Coach Hargraves started to come out of the dugout, but Darcy waved him away and jogged out to the mound.

"This is the fun part, right?" asked the catcher.

"Yup, the fun has started," replied Annie.

"Let's stick with the Godzilla and just a few Sleepers," said Darcy. "We don't need to get too fancy with this crew. They're more noise than they are dangerous. They won't know what hit 'em. Remember what good sports they are, so don't hold back."

As Darcy turned and jogged back toward the plate, Annie felt her eyes tearing up. They sometimes got that way when her emotions ran high. Darcy had seen that look before on the basketball floor, but this was the first time it had shown up on the softball field. She looked over at Charles City's dugout, and their whole team was standing at the fence, shaking it and chanting. It wasn't a chant to get the team fired up. It was meant solely to razz the opposing pitcher.

"Hey!" hollered Annie after Darcy had taken only a few steps. "You're right. I really don't like these guys."

Darcy was smiling as she turned back to face her battery mate. "And—"

"And they—they stink," blurted Annie. "Godzilla on the second pitch. Be ready."

Darcy ran back to her position and started to chatter. The Charles City dugout was even louder as the first batter stepped in. Brenda Stevens was a sophomore and played guard on the fresh-soph basketball team. She was the type of player who would hold you and slip in an occasional elbow when the refs weren't looking. Annie looked in at her catcher, who was going through all sorts of crazy signs and talking nonsense.

She let the first pitch go—high and soft. It looked like something you would throw in a slow-pitch game. It came in shoulder high, and Brenda actually swung at it. Little did she know, that pitch would be her best chance at making contact. Nevertheless, she still whiffed by a foot.

"Come on Brenda," hollered the Charles City coach from the third base coaching box. "Just be patient. When she's done messing around, we'll show her what a good hitting team can do."

Darcy pegged the ball back. Annie caught it and rubbed it up with both hands. The laces felt as though they were more pronounced than usual. New balls might feel the same to the other players, but to a pitcher they all felt different. She liked the feel and smell of a new ball. She wiped the sweat from her forehead with her sleeve and looked back in at her catcher. Coach Hargraves was standing in the dugout opening with a quizzical look on his face. Darcy kept flashing her index finger between her legs where only Annie could see it. Send it in. Annie grinned and nodded. This would be her first real pitch as a high school varsity player on her home diamond. She wished her dad were here to see it. He would not have been disappointed.

Annie wound up and unleashed Godzilla. To say the crowd of about seventy-five fans was stunned would be an understatement. The ball came in like a rocket. It cracked into Darcy's mitt with a crisp, sharp sound. She had the knack of making even a mediocre fastball sound like a smoker. This was not a mediocre fastball. It was the fastest pitch the Charles City girls would see for the rest of the season. The batter never moved. The umpire just stood there with his mouth open. He finally raised his right arm to indicate a strike. The fans milling around the sidelines and behind the home plate fence just stopped what they were doing. Varsity high school softball pitchers were supposed to throw the ball fast, but what they had seen was nothing short of phenomenal.

The visitors sat down on their bench and didn't chant another word as Annie threw her third straight no-hitter and opened up a whole new bag of troubles.

After the game the coach gave an interview to the local paper. He said Annie would be pitching every game from then on. Annie thought that was unfair to Sally, the other pitcher. She was only a junior, and with some improvement, she might have a chance at a college scholarship. Also, if Annie pitched every game and turned an ankle or something, Sally would be pretty rusty from lack of action. It might also make some of the upperclassmen resent her. How could the coach be so stupid! Coach Hargraves had only one goal with his softball team. Winning every game was all he thought about. Putting a solid team together at every position, with intelligence, sportsmanship, and great attitudes didn't even enter his mind. He had a real racehorse, and he was going to use her to the max. Since he wouldn't listen to reason, Annie took it upon herself to fix the situation. After eight games and four no-hitters, she claimed her pitching arm hurt when she threw underhand. Overhand, she claimed, was no problem. It wasn't a popular decision, but once she made it, she stuck by it. Anyway, Sally finished out the season as the number one pitcher and had a great season the next year, (with help from Annie who hit .520 and played right field as though she owned it), and she was getting some scholarship help to pitch in college.

◦◆◦

Annie shook her head and brought herself back to the present. *Things will be different here, I just know it,* she thought. *I'll play it nice and cool. No one will be mad if I play right field in softball and average ten points a game in basketball. I'm gonna be so laid back, it's going to be hard to stay awake. How tough can it be just to fly low under the radar?*

Melinda Fullerton was practicing three pointers between games on one of Reston High School's outdoor courts. She only stood five feet four inches, but there was a lot of ability and desire in her little frame. Her shoulder-length brown hair was tied up into a ponytail with a pink hair tie. Brown eyes and thin nose gave her an elflike quality. Her face was usually lit up with a big smile—that is, when she wasn't talking at a pace that challenged the listener. Melinda was enjoying her high school years as Reston's top female athlete. She was the starting setter on the volleyball team, the point guard on the basketball team, and the starting shortstop on the softball team. Needless to say, her life revolved around sports. Her friends, and most everyone else, called her "Chip," which was short for microchip. She was well known around the area for her skills, sportsmanship, and her hard play. With all this going for her, she still had two unfulfilled wishes. Wish number one would probably never happen. She had always wanted to be taller. She had grown exactly one inch since seventh grade, and now she was a junior, so unless a miracle happened, she was destined to be a semi-midget. Her other wish looked like it would also go unfulfilled. Most of the Reston teams that she had played on in high school and junior high had only moderate success. A couple of games above .500 was the best they could do. Just once, she wanted to be on a really good team. Her teammates tried hard, of course, but the skill and knowledge just weren't there. She also had to admit that their lack of ambition was part of the problem. Chip had no idea that her ticket to wish number two had just arrived in town.

Chip's teammates hardly ever practiced a sport when it was out of season. She loved to throw the softball around or shoot some hoops, no matter what time of year it was. She really didn't blame them, though. Athletics were her passion. Boyfriends and parties took up a lot of her teammates' time, but she just wasn't into those activities. She had a lot of guy friends, and she enjoyed playing ball with them, but she never thought about seriously dating any of them. Well, there was this one guy, Luke. He was her best friend. They had a lot in common, since they both loved sports so much. Luke had one small problem when it came to sports. He had absolutely no talent when it came to any athletic endeavor. The boy was six-foot-two inches of athletic mayhem. It was painful to watch him shoot a basketball and utterly horrific to watch him try to throw a baseball. Luke stayed close to the things he loved by writing about them. He was the sports editor for the *Reston Talon*, the school newspaper. Any time a school activity called for participation as a couple they went together. They had had this arrangement since they were in eighth grade. Any time Chip needed someone to hit her grounders or to rebound for her, all she had to do was call Luke, and he would be there. Their relationship was very practical.

"C'mon ya'll," hollered Chip to the guys lying on the benches that lined one side of the court. "I know you've got one more game in you. I know this for a fact, because you've been doggin' it on defense since you got here."

"Give it up, Chip," said Bobby Sims with a wet towel over his face. "It's too hot, and don't you have dance practice or something?"

"Volleyball practice doesn't start for another hour," replied Chip. "Ya'll are wimps. You're gonna get creamed every game this year if you don't show some ambition."

All she got for an answer was a few groans. An orange car pulled up beside the courts with Luke behind the wheel. He honked and waved at her. She turned and threw the ball at Billy and hit him in the leg. He didn't even move.

"Later," she hollered and jumped into the front seat beside Luke. All she got was a couple of halfhearted waves.

"Was that Slowinski?" asked a voice from under a wet towel.

"Who else has a car that sounds like that?" asked Chet Stevens.

"At least he's got a car," said Gary Sturgis, the team's starting center.

"Yeah, a car and a girl," quipped Al Radford.

"They're not like that," said Billy. "I bet they don't even—"

"Don't even what, mister dating expert?" interrupted Chet.

"That's why you don't have a girlfriend, Mr. Smart Mouth," said Billy. "All you can think about is sex, and most girls aren't like that, at least the decent ones. I was gonna say they don't even hold hands, dork."

The guys all sat up and looked at Billy.

"Jeez, what set you off?" asked Jimmy. "Hey, you got the hots for Chip? Wait till I tell her."

Billy retrieved the ball and started toward his car. It was too hot, and he was too tired to match wits with these nimrods.

"Later, morons," he said waving back to them.

• ◆ •

"Hi Luke," said Chip, sliding into the front seat. "How's it going?"

"Not bad," responded Luke. "Why are you playing basketball before you have volleyball practice? If the coach catches you, you're gonna get it. What happens if you jam a finger and can't set for a while?"

"I've never jammed a finger, silly, and from the way the team looks, I don't think it would matter if I was setting or not. We're just awful! We're tall enough, but we just can't hit. I had a perfect set for Tammi Olsen yesterday, and she timed it so poorly that she spiked it straight down. She almost shot herself in the foot—ha!"

"You're kidding," said Luke, reaching into the backseat and handing her a towel. "Then what happened?"

"Some of us started laughing. No one from her little group of followers thought it was funny, so we're kinda feuding already. It's going to be a long season. It's too bad Tammi isn't more like her twin. Jenny is easygoing and likes to kid around. Tammi is always trying to find a reason to be mad at someone. If she doesn't have a reason, she makes one up. I feel sorry for Jenny. She has to live with her. Hey, where are we going?"

"A couple of days ago there was a moving van sitting in front of a house a couple of blocks away, and I want to drive by to see who is moving in. My uncle works for the moving company, and he said it looked like the kid was a good athlete because there were a couple of boxes marked "Trophies" in their stuff. If this guy is still in high school and a star athlete, I might want to interview him for the school paper. It never hurts to do your homework."

"What if it's a girl, and she's a star athlete? Why do you always assume it's a guy? She could be a super volleyball hitter, a high-scoring center, and a power hitting catcher."

"Don't get all hyper on me," cautioned Luke. "My uncle thought it was a guy because of all the stereo equipment, plus a couple of guitars in the kid's room. Anyway, if this person is high school age, we should stop by and introduce ourselves. It's tough to relocate at any age. We'll tell him we're the Reston Welcoming Committee."

"I know you have good intentions," said Chip, "but you are also the snoopiest person I know. I suppose that's what makes a good reporter— sticking your nose in everyone else's business."

"Darn right. It's the house at the end of the block. We'll just drive by slow and see what we can see."

It took three trips around the block before the occupants of the orange Topaz got a glimpse of the new kid. She was stretching in the driveway along the side of the house. It looked like she was getting ready to go for a jog or something.

"Ha!" exclaimed Chip. "I told you it might be a girl. Drive on. She doesn't even look like an athlete. Look at that goofy headband she's wearing."

"Wait a sec, I still want to talk to her," said Luke stopping the car. As he walked up the driveway, Luke checked out the new girl who looked to be about his age. Her shoulder-length hair was somewhere between blonde and brown. It was kept out of her face with a red bandanna. Her features were plain enough. She appeared to be about five foot seven or eight, but it was hard to tell if she had an athlete's body. She was wearing an oversized T-shirt and the type of shorts that a jogger would wear. When he got closer, he noticed her most striking feature, her eyes. They seemed to be smiling at you even if the rest of her face wasn't. They made you want to smile back.

"Hi," said Luke, offering his hand to the girl with the cheerful eyes. "I'm Luke Slowinski, sports editor for the *Reston Talon*, the school newspaper. I thought I'd stop by and welcome you to Reston and find out a little bit about you. You know, what sports you play, and stuff like that."

Annie took his hand and gave it a firm shake—maybe a little too firm. She wasn't terribly fond of sportswriters, if this guy really was one. It would be a long time before she could forget their rude behavior and their invasion of her privacy. Midnight phone calls, false allegations, and quotes out of context seemed to be the weapons of choice for headline-seeking sportswriters. At least that was the case with the ones she had come in contact with over the past two years. They would pretty much do anything to get a story. Maybe this guy was different. She decided to give him the benefit of the doubt. Anyway, she had been thinking about going by her initials instead of her name and this would be the perfect time to try it out. She actually liked her name, except when they put all that crazy stuff in front of it—"Freight Train Annie" and "Fast Annie Smith" were names that the press made up. She considered the sportswriters back in Arkansas her enemies. They would never leave her alone, and they were constantly printing things without checking the facts. A lot of stuff they wrote only served to make her teammates mad at her. Because of this, she'd decided to be a totally different person here in Texas. Not that she was a big secret or anything, but it sure would be nice to be just a regular high school kid for once.

"I'm B. A. Smith, Luke," she said making up her mind about the initial thing. "Who's your friend in the car?"

"Her name is Melinda Fullerton, but everybody calls her Chip, 'cause she's so short. She acts like she doesn't like the name, but I know she does. She is by far our school's best female athlete. Do you play volleyball? I'm taking her to practice, and maybe you'd like to come along."

B. A. decided right away that she liked Luke. He was a smooth talker but seemed to be genuine. She didn't have much time for phonies.

"No, I'm not much of a volleyball player," she answered. He had a look of disappointment on his face, so she volunteered, "But I am thinking about going out for basketball."

"That's great," said Luke. "We can use all the help we can get. Chip carried most of the scoring load last year on the varsity, as a sophomore. A taller guard who can pass would really complement her in the backcourt."

"Actually, I'm a forward, Luke. I've never played guard."

"Oh," said Luke, suddenly at a loss for words. "Well, we can use a quality player at any position." Before Luke could go on, his horn honked. He turned to see Chip waving at him and pointing to her wrist.

"C'mon, Luke, I'll be late for practice," hollered Chip, leaning out the window. "Hi, new girl," she added.

B. A. waved at the girl in the car as Luke turned to leave.

"We'll talk later, B. A.," said Luke as he turned to leave. "Where are you from, anyway?"

"Arkansas," answered B. A.

"Annie," called Martha Smith from the kitchen. "Where are you and what are you doing?" She said it the same way she used to say it when Annie was little and out of sight in another room.

Annie looked through the back door window and into the kitchen. Her mom was drying her hands and looking down the hallway toward Annie's room. Martha Smith was a forty-two-year-old who looked like she was twenty-five. She was Annie's height, but about thirty pounds lighter. Her brown hair almost reached her shoulders, which was considered the proper length for a "woman her age," as Annie often reminded her. She had a warm smile, with two of the biggest dimples imaginable. Recently, Annie had been telling people that she was her sister. Martha didn't protest too much because it was good to see her daughter finally return to her old self. Joking and making fun of each other had always been a big part of the Smith family. Now that there were only two of them left in the household (her older daughter, Margie, was away at college getting a master's degree), they had to rely on each other. Maybe this move to Texas would be everything she hoped it would be.

Annie let herself in quietly. With two quick strides she was halfway across the kitchen. From there she leaped into the air and landed heavily on both feet right behind her mother. Her mom was startled, but before she could react, Annie had her in a bear hug, easily lifting her off the floor.

"You losing weight, Martha?" asked the teen as she set her mom down.

"You're just getting stronger," replied Mrs. Smith. "You better go easy on those weights. I don't want you straining anything. I'm not even sure how to get to the hospital from here."

"Well, you better figure it out if you're going to start work tomorrow. Fort Worth is a pretty big city. I'm going for a run to check out the neighborhood. Maybe I can find you a nice, good-looking accountant or a lawyer with a cool dog. A lab would be nice. You would get a guy friend, and I would get a dog friend."

"Don't even think about it," said her mom. "I'll start dating when I feel comfortable about it. On second thought, maybe I'll look up the basketball coach to see if he's single. Wouldn't that be fun? You two could have some great discussions around the dinner table."

Annie just gave her a disdainful look and headed for the back door. She danced down the driveway like a boxer, throwing left and right jabs at an imaginary opponent. Her mom opened the window and hollered at her.

"Don't cause any trouble, girl. This is a new setting for us, and they might not be ready for someone like you."

Annie stopped and turned around with a shocked look on her face.

"What do you mean 'cause trouble—someone like me'?" she asked, feigning hurt feelings.

"You know what I mean," said her mom. "I know you threw the first punch that started the brawl at the football game last year. Just don't do anything that you might regret later. We're new here, and people will be watching us."

"Mom, an allegation like that becomes fact only if it can be proven in a court of law. And I doubt that you could prove that your little girl hit anybody, even if he was slapping his girlfriend around at the time and totally deserved it."

"Just the same, tough guy, don't touch anybody."

She waved to her mom as she started to jog toward town. *I'll be good*, she thought. *What kind of trouble can you get into in a little town like this?*

Martha went to the refrigerator to find something for supper. She shook her head and smiled.

"I hope this town is ready for you, Annie. It should be an interesting year, one way or another."

* ◈ *

Annie ran through the streets of Reston checking out the houses and businesses. The town seemed friendly enough. The few people she passed on the street said "Hello" and then stared at her after she passed by. They couldn't believe someone would be out running in the afternoon heat. Annie had already decided that her next run would be in the evening when it had cooled off some. Ninety-five degrees was too hot to run in, especially when you hadn't run in almost two weeks. She prided herself on staying in shape. In fact, she couldn't remember being out of shape since she started playing basketball in the seventh grade. Her conditioning and her strength were big assets in basketball and softball. Basketball was her true love because it involved a lot of running and an endless variety of situations. The softball thing just sort of happened.

She remembered the first time she threw an underhand pitch. It was to her dad in the front yard. She was eleven years old. They were playing catch before dinner just as they always did. Her dad traveled a lot with the band, but he did his best to get home as much as he could. He squatted down like a catcher and said, "Hum one in here, big girl." She wound up imitating her big sister and let it fly.

"Man, that was fast," he said excitedly. "I'm going to get your sister to start working with you. You've got a strong arm and pretty good technique for a little dude. Sorry, I meant dudette."

Annie loved working with her sister on her pitching. Margie was six years older than Annie, so they didn't do much together unless you counted babysitting. Margie was the star pitcher on the high school softball team and was destined to play college ball. Pitching to her sister was probably Annie's favorite thing that summer. Margie knew her stuff when it came to pitching. She wasn't big on some of the current fads and told Annie that slapping yourself with your glove or making loud noises when you released the ball was for showboats and didn't serve any real purpose. Annie was a natural and quickly picked up the basics. Her velocity picked up as she grew and got stronger. Her sister rarely got to see her pitch, as she left for college the next year, spending her summers at school working and taking extra classes.

Annie's thoughts of the past stopped abruptly as she realized she was heading west out of town. She stopped under a big tree at the last house before the road headed out into grassy fields. She was puffing pretty hard and thought about sitting down for a few minutes but didn't want to give in.

"Come on, sissy-girl," she said out loud. "What's the matter? Are you soft and out of shape?" She picked up the pace and started back into town. Two blocks later she began to feel light-headed, and she knew she would have to stop. She was disgusted with herself as she slowed down to a walk. She decided to sit down on the grass for a few minutes. Halfway down her legs buckled and she wound up flat on her back on someone's front lawn. *This is not good*, she thought. *Man, it sure is hot.* She threw her arm over her eyes to block out the sun and promptly passed out.

• ◆ •

In her mind, Annie was back in the parking lot by the football field in Jones Ferry. Everything looked hazy and surreal. She was walking between two friends, Riley and Tank. They were about to get into Tank's old beat-up Mercury when she looked over her shoulder and saw Billy Crenshaw slap a girl across the mouth. Through the mist, Annie saw herself walk over to where Billy and a few of his sleazy friends were standing. It was obvious that they had been drinking. Tank and Riley, the two best athletes at Jones Ferry, were trying to pull her back to the car. They were saying something about not getting in trouble and being ineligible for sports. Everything became crystal clear when she saw Billy's grinning face. She was talking to him, and he just stood there with that stupid grin. Stepping forward, she caught Billy flush on the jaw with a hard right. He went down to the pavement in a state of shock.

Now she was standing several yards away, and everything was foggy again. Riley and Tank got into a little scuffle with some of Billy's friends. It was hardly a brawl, as her mom had described it. A few punches were thrown, but no one was hurt. The drinkers had enough of their wits about them to know better than to mess with Riley and Tank. Mr. Barnes, the history teacher, came over when he saw the commotion. Tank told him that Billy had slipped on some oil and hit his face on the car mirror, and he and Riley had gone over to see if Billy was okay. Mr. Barnes just smiled and walked away through the fog. She remembered hiding her hand from her mom until the swelling went down. She didn't see much of Billy for the rest of the year, and his poor footing in the parking lot wasn't brought up again.

• ◆ •

Annie's breathing was back to normal, but she now felt sick to her stomach. As she lay on her back, looking over the edge of her arm, she saw a big shade tree that she hadn't noticed before. *Got to get under that tree*, she thought. *This sun is murder.* She pushed with her hands and feet to move herself along the ground. After moving herself a couple of feet, the tree moved and started to talk.

"Are you all right?" asked the tree, which turned into a giant person right before her eyes.

"I'm not sure," she replied. "I was running and fell onto this nice carpet."

"You're losing it," said the giant. "Come on up to the house. You need to get cooled down."

Rod Martin, all six foot seven of him, bent down and scooped up Annie as though she were a little doll. She was heavier than he thought she would be, but it mattered little to his muscular, 250-pound frame.

"I'm not supposed to touch anybody," she said softly. "I'll get into trouble. Don't need any more trouble. It's awfully hot here." She put her head on the big guy's shoulder as he carried her across the lawn toward the house.

Rod turned the knob and kicked the front door open. The air-conditioned room felt wonderful to Annie. He laid her down on the big sofa and stepped back to look at her. Her hair was kind of brownish-blonde. It probably looked better when it wasn't plastered all over her forehead. Her facial features appeared to be in order. Her nose wasn't too big or too small, and her chin looked normal. Her eyes were half-closed, so he couldn't tell what color they were. He guessed her to be about average height for a girl, but then again, everybody looked small to him. She sure did weigh a lot for her size. Girls were supposed to have more body fat than guys, but she looked pretty lean. Rod decided she was nice-looking. Not drop-dead gorgeous, but reasonably attractive.

"Could I have a glass of water, please?" asked the girl.

Rod was a little startled when he heard her speak.

"I'm sorry," he said. "I was just thinking about what I should do."

"You were staring at me like I was some sort of alien."

"I wasn't staring at you," replied Rod as he went into the kitchen for water. "I think I should call Doc Rupert to check you out. What were you doing before you passed out on the lawn? It looked like you were jogging or something."

"I wasn't jogging," she said sitting up on the sofa. "I was running. Jogging is for people who can't run but are trying to make it look good."

Rod came back into the room with a glass of water for her and a big diet soda for himself. He handed the glass to the girl, who was now sitting and smiled at her. He decided that he liked her. She was kind of feisty. He hoped she didn't have an attitude to go with it. He didn't know many feisty girls who didn't have some sort of attitude. Heck, he didn't know many girls at all. He was a little on the shy side, and his size was a detriment when it came to getting dates.

"I mixed a little warm water into this so it's not too cold," he said, handing her the glass. "It's not good to drink ice-cold water. Don't drink it too fast. It might come back up."

Annie drained the glass without coming up for air.

"I told you to go slow," he scolded her. "You better not yak that up all over the carpet."

"Nothing's coming up," she said smiling. "I feel a lot better. Can I have a sip of that soda?" Rod handed her his soda, and she drained that too.

"I know how you feel," he said as he headed back toward the kitchen. "When I used to come home from football practice, I'd drink everything I could get my hands on. You stay right there. I'm going to call the doc. What's your name, anyway?"

"My name's B. A. Smith," she answered as Rod came back into the room after making his call. "I just moved here from Arkansas. Who are you?"

"Rod Martin," he said, taking her outstretched hand. He was surprised at her strong grip. "I called the doc's office, but he's not in right now. You should go over and have his nurse check you out. I'll drive you if you want."

B. A. got up and headed toward the door.

"Thanks for helping me out, Rod. I feel a lot better. My mom is a nurse. I'll tell her what happened." She put her hand on the doorknob and looked back, smiling. "Thanks again. I owe you a soda."

"See you around, B. A. Next time do your running in the morning or evening. This heat is rough on Texans. It must be murder on someone from a northern state like Arkansas."

"No kidding," she said as she headed toward home.

Chapter 2

New Friends

B. A. sat on the bench next to Reston High School's outdoor basketball courts. She was watching Chip and seven guys play. She liked the way Chip played. She was real quick and could get her shot off even against the guys. She also looked like she was having fun and not taking it too seriously. The play was hard, but not too rough. The guys were actually playing the game and not trying to show off. Put a few more girls on the sidelines watching, and the style of play would probably change. B. A. wondered if guys everywhere were like that. *No doubt*, she thought with a smile to herself. One of the players went down with a twisted ankle. They helped him off to the side and stood there taking a breather.

"Let's just go three on three," said one of the guys.

Chip looked over at B. A.

"Hey, how about the new girl?" she hollered.

None of the guys would look at her.

"Well, how about it?" Chip asked again, only louder.

"I don't know, squirt," said Bobby. "She doesn't look like much of a ballplayer. We'll just sub in and play with six."

Chip looked at B. A. and shrugged her shoulders, trying to communicate that she had tried.

* ◆ *

B. A. was hot. They would actually rather change the game than let her play! She turned to leave with tears in her eyes. So this was what it was like being a "normal" kid. She wasn't so sure she was going to like it. She walked briskly toward the parking lot. As she was about to get in her truck, she saw a familiar figure walking across the street. At 6'7" it was hard to miss him.

"Hey, big guy, what are you up to?" she shouted.

"Aw, my stupid car broke down about half a mile up the road," answered Rod as he crossed the street to B. A.'s side.

"Hop in. I'll give you a ride," said B. A.

"Thanks, I could use one," said Rod as he got in. "Could you make a left and take me back to my car? I have some things to get out of it. By the way, how's the heat treating you?"

"I'm okay. What are you going to do about your car?" asked B. A. as she pulled out onto Reston's main street.

"I don't know. Tow it over to Chuck's Garage, I guess. I hope he can get it fixed right away. I've got a ten o'clock class tomorrow at the University of North Texas, just north of here in Denton."

"I heard you were a big football star here and at UNT," said B. A.

"*Were* is the key word there. I blew my knee out in the final game last year, so my football career is over."

B. A. looked at his scarred left knee and winced.

"It's probably all for the best," said Rod. "I get to keep my scholarship, and I'll get my degree. I can do just about anything on this knee except play football and maybe ski. I've never skied before, so that's no great loss. Being able to walk like a normal human being when I'm forty will also be a plus."

When they got to Rod's car, B. A. whipped her truck around and pulled right in behind it.

"Here's what we'll do," she said. "You get in and turn the key on so you can steer. I'll push you over to Chuck's and that will save you the tow charge."

"What if a cop sees us? We could get a ticket."

"No problem," said B. A. with an air of confidence. "If I see the town cop, I'll just tap my brakes and let you go. You just put your arm out the window like you're cruising down Main Street. Don't worry, I've done this before."

Rod wasn't sure about the plan, but B. A.'s confidence convinced him. After a smooth push job, Rod jumped back into the passenger seat of B. A.'s truck. He had a basketball and a gym bag with him. B. A. sat looking at the ex-football star. His features were chiseled and angular. Soft brown hair came almost down to his ears and, surprisingly, neither one had a ring in it. His brown eyes were also soft-looking, and when she looked directly into them, he turned away. She could tell that he was still somewhat shy around girls. Well, he would have to get over that, because she had just picked him to be her new best friend.

"Thanks, B. A.," said Rod. "Chuck would have charged me at least fifty bucks to tow my car. Would you mind dropping me off at home?"

"It depends on where you were going with that ball and if I could tag along. I don't know many people here yet, and I'm kinda bored. Oops, forget I said that word. It's outlawed at my house. My dad, before he died, always said if you were bored you were lacking the imagination to entertain yourself. He was an energetic person and couldn't stand it if we were just lying around doing nothing. I guess it rubbed off on me. I'm not much for just sitting around, either. It feels like such a waste of time."

"Your dad sounds like a pretty cool guy," said Rod with a concerned look on his face. "How long ago did he die?"

"A little over three years ago. And you're right, he was a cool guy. The best dad a girl could have."

"Sorry about your dad. It must have been tough."

B. A. just nodded in agreement. Rod figured she didn't want to volunteer any more information about her dad, so he didn't say any more on the subject. He didn't know why, but it was awfully easy to talk to this girl. There weren't a lot of girls he considered friends. His size intimidated a lot of them, and his shyness didn't help, either. Of course, he had his share of dates, but the relationships never lasted very long. It only took a couple of dates to figure out whether the girl liked him or his status as a star athlete. This girl seemed different, though. Heck, didn't she just save him fifty bucks by pushing his car to Chuck's?

"To answer your question, I was going to the university to play ball with some of the guys. We play every Sunday afternoon if the weather's decent. It will take us at least a half hour to get there, depending on the traffic. And yes, I would like you to come if you don't mind watching a bunch of sweaty guys running around pretending they're NBA all-stars."

"I don't mind," said B. A. with a grin. "I just have to stop at my house for a minute and get some things."

• ◆ •

B. A. jumped out of the truck and hustled through the back door. She yelled back at Rod, who was a little slower extricating himself from the small truck. He didn't quite hear all that she said, but he did make out something about grabbing a couple bottles of soda from the fridge because she owed him one. Sodas were the only luxury that he allowed himself when it came to nutrition. Even then, he usually drank diet ones. He always watched what he ate and drank a lot of water. When he did splurge, it was usually a reward for finishing off one more grueling set of incline presses or squats. Lifting weights was his passion now that he couldn't play football anymore.

B. A. came into the kitchen with a gym bag over her shoulder and a red bandanna rolled up like a headband tied around her forehead. Not only did it keep her hair out of her eyes, it also kept the sweat out of her eyes. She tended to sweat a lot when she was working out or playing ball. And she intended to play ball today, with the big boys! She scribbled a fast note to her mom, in case she came home from work early, and turned back to the big guy who was standing in the middle of the kitchen watching her.

"Let's go," she said heading for the door.

Oh no, thought Rod. *She thinks she's going to play! There's no way the guys are going to let a girl play. It gets pretty rough, and sometimes the language isn't the best. What am I gonna do? This is a big mistake.*

Rod gave his driver directions and turned to stare out the window. He didn't mind letting her play, but Reyes and Jonsey would definitely be against it. They'd complain about her dropping the ball, and they all would have to worry about knocking her down and hurting her. And she might be one of those girls that he saw at one of those three-on-three tournaments. They were the ones that grab and hold all the time, then cry "foul" if you barely touched them. She didn't seem to be the type, but you never know what someone is going to be like when they step on the court. What a mess he was in! The best he could hope for would be even numbers and that she would be understanding about it. He was concentrating so hard and looking out the window that it took him a while before he realized she was talking to him.

"I'm sorry, what did you say?" he asked sheepishly.

"I said—can I ask you a couple of questions about weight training? You do a lot of lifting, don't you? A body like yours just doesn't happen naturally. It looks like you take your workouts seriously."

Rod was a little self-conscious about the way he looked. He always drew stares if he had a tank top on or if he had his shirt off. The attention was something he could do without, but he wasn't going to give up lifting for anything short of an injury. And even then, he would try to work around it. For the rest of the drive to UNT she quizzed him on lifting techniques and different exercises. He was surprised at the depth of her knowledge. She was interested in strength training and not bodybuilding. He actually worked out with both in mind. The conversation flowed back and forth, and before they knew it, they were at the courts. Rod felt bad. When she found out that she couldn't play, she was going to think that he had used her just for the ride. He made up his mind as he got out of the truck—he was going to get her into the game even if the rest of the guys didn't want her to play.

• ◆ •

Rod was surprised when his buddies made no objection to B. A.'s participation. And they were all more than surprised at what they saw. B. A. hung around the perimeter until she was familiar with the style of game the guys played. Once she was used to the larger ball, she picked it up a notch. Going hard to her right, she took a hand-off from Rod at the free throw line. After a quick dribble with her shoulder down, she hit the brakes and banked a soft jumper off the board. Her defender was lagging behind, thinking he would catch up to her on her drive with his superior quickness and jumping ability. Terry Funk, the guy who was guarding her, took some ribbing from his teammates. He decided to tighten his defense and not let this high-schooler score again. Two plays later, she had the ball on the right baseline. She took two smooth dribbles with her left hand toward the free throw line and then jumped at a ninety-degree angle past Terry's shoulder toward the hoop. The six-foot college freshman was fooled by the move, but he recovered quickly. He jumped high in the air with both hands above her head, intent on smothering her when she shot. After jumping by him, B. A. was not about to make the mistake of sticking the ball back in his face. She held it out in front at arm's length and banked it in.

After Rod's team won their second game, 15 to 13 on B. A.'s jump hook, the players took a break. They sat down with their backs to the fence that surrounded the courts. B. A. dug two water bottles out of her bag and gave one to Rod. It didn't matter that they were warm by now, as long as it was liquid. The rest of the guys got up and headed toward the tennis courts, where the water fountains were. When they passed out of earshot, Rod looked at her with a sweaty grin.

"Man, you sure are smooth. I mean, you're the best girl basketball player I've ever seen, and that includes college players."

"Thanks," said B. A., somewhat embarrassed. "And thanks for letting me come with you. Your friends are nice guys."

"Yeah, they're pretty cool," said Rod. "I can tell they like you, because they cleaned up their language. I'm a little surprised. Most guys our age just say what they want no matter who they are with or where they are. It's pretty sad that even educated people, which is what we're doing at this university, getting an education, think that it's okay to use bad language."

"I know what you mean," added B. A. "All that nasty language doesn't impress anyone. In fact, it's one of my pet peeves."

"If you're such a good basketball player," asked Rod changing the subject, "why didn't you go out for volleyball?"

"Well, besides not liking the sport, I'm awful at it. I can block spikes pretty good, but I can't serve, pass, or hit worth a darn. And how do you know that I didn't go out for volleyball?"

"I heard it from my cousin. She was hoping you would be the answer to her prayers. She's a cocky little thing who is just dying to be on a good team for once. The Reston girls' athletic program hasn't been very successful lately. She's all they've got, and she's rather disappointed in you because you're not a volleyball player."

"How can she be mad at me? I don't even know her. What's her name, anyway?"

"Melinda, but everyone calls her Chip, 'cause she's so short."

"I guess I do know her. I was watching her and some other guys play before I saw you today. They wouldn't let me play."

"Well, it was their loss," laughed Rod.

● ◆ ●

The two were sipping from their water bottles and laughing like old friends when they rest of the group rejoined them.

"Are ya'll good for one more?" asked Victor Reyes with a smile. "We want revenge."

B. A. jumped up and offered Rod her hand. Rod took it and acted like she was pulling him up. He had never met anyone like this girl, and he was really beginning to like her. He wondered if she had any more surprises in store for him.

It only took a couple of plays into the third game to figure out this one was war. Victor and his teammates did not want to lose three games in a row to a team with a girl on it—a high school girl, at that. The score was tied at four when Victor drove hard along the baseline and ran right over B. A., who had come over to help out. Rod felt his blood rise. Victor was his friend, and rumor had it he was once in a gang. But at this moment, he felt very protective of B. A. It was a feeling that he had never experienced before, and he wasn't sure what it meant. He would need time to sort it out later.

Before Rod could come to her aid, Victor helped her up.

"Sorry, Tigrita," which was Spanish for "little tiger." "It was a charge."

"Good call," said B. A. as she slapped him on the rear.

The rest of the guys broke into laughter. Even Rod had a big smile on his face. His basketball buddies had accepted her and obviously respected her too. The last play of the game would have made a Luke Slowinski headline. Rod's team was up 14 to 13 and B. A. was in the air with the ball on the right side of the court. She was in the process of shooting the game-winning jumper when she figured out that she wouldn't get it over Victor's outstretched hand. She held on to the ball until she started to come down and then tossed it one-handed over him high on the backboard. Rod, coming in hard from the left side, caught the rebound at the top of his jump and slammed it through for the winning bucket. It was a thing of beauty.

Victor stood in the middle of the court with the ball. He slammed it down hard with two hands, which got everyone's attention.

"Okay, Martin," he hollered. "You aren't leaving until you answer some questions. Who is this girl? She can't be a high school player like you claim. How come we've never heard of her? C'mon, man, we just want some answers."

"She just moved to Reston from Arkansas," said Rod, trying not to laugh. "And she is a junior in high school. That's all I can tell you about her, except that she has a twin sister that's even better than she is."

"Yeah, right," countered Victor with a big grin. "Bring her back next week. And bring her sister too. It was fun."

As they walked to the car, B. A. did something that Rod had never seen anyone do before. She grabbed a few pieces of trash, bottles, and some food wrappers lying on the ground, and ran them over to a trash receptacle.

"I don't like it when people don't throw their trash away," she said as he stood watching her. "It's another one of my pet peeves."

* ◆ *

The ride home was enjoyable for both Rod and B. A. They talked as if they had known each other for years. B. A. was surprised at how knowledgeable Rod was on a myriad of subjects. He seemed to have a sensitive side too. She found out that he was a tight end for the UNT Mean Green and had started as a freshman. After he hurt his knee he had been depressed for a couple of months. He had always worked hard at being the best athlete he could be. The physical therapy that he had to go through after his knee operation was a real eye-opener. It was during this time that he decided that he wanted to be a physical therapist or an athletic trainer. He hit the books really hard the next semester and made the dean's list. In order to keep his scholarship, he had to do some janitorial work and other odd jobs for the school. A lot of guys who used to be star athletes would consider this a demeaning task, but he attacked his duties with vigor. Most college athletes don't make the pros anyway, so if they are smart, they'll find a way to make good use of their other skills. Rod was one of the smart ones. He understood this fact and did not try to hang on to past glories.

B. A. liked Rod's attitude. He seemed really positive about things, and he appeared to be someone she could trust. He'd better be, because she had plans for him. Back in Arkansas, after she had faked her arm injury, she still continued to pitch secretly. She just had to keep pitching. It was a great way to vent her frustrations, and she loved everything about it, from the smell and feel of the ball to the crack as it hit the catcher's mitt. She got an adrenaline rush every time she threw.

• ◆ •

Back in Jones Ferry, Tank Johnson was two years older than Annie and was the perfect battery mate. The big, easygoing football player was also the catcher on the baseball team. He would catch for her anytime she wanted. She had learned a lot about pitching strategy from Tank. He was the one who told her to throw her change-up on the inside part of the plate or even tighter. That way, if the batter did wait for it and put a good swing on it, it usually went foul. The Johnson farm was an ideal place to throw because no one could see them behind the barn. After their first clandestine session, Tank installed a pitching rubber and a plate. They had a lot of great times together behind that barn—talking, listening to the radio, and playing catch. Their plan was almost foiled one day when Riley Buelow walked around the corner of the building and surprised them both. They had the radio turned up and didn't hear him when he pulled up in his old junker. He promised to keep their secret and even caught Annie a few times when Tank was sick or too busy with chores. She was going to miss those two. She remembered the tear that rolled down Tank's cheek when they said their good-byes. They still e-mailed each other frequently, but it wasn't the same as being there.

* ◆ *

B. A. was toying with the idea of asking Rod to catch her when they pulled up in front of his house.

"Pull around back, through the alley," said Rod. "I've got something to show you."

She gave him a quizzical look before she started the engine. Rod saw her look and was immediately embarrassed.

"I'm sorry," he said, looking at the floor of her truck. "I didn't mean anything by it. It's dark, and you don't know me that well."

This was a side of him that B. A. had not seen yet, and she liked him all the more for it. He usually had an air of confidence about him, but now he was flustered and somewhat sheepish.

"It's okay," she said, putting her hand on top of his. "I think I can trust you. I was even thinking of letting you take my truck to school tomorrow if your car isn't ready. If that's not trust, I don't know what is."

"That's great," said Rod, perking up. "I really do have something that I'm sure you would appreciate. It's around back in the garage if you have time."

"I've got time," said B. A. as she started the little truck.

Rod unlocked the side door to his garage with B. A. right behind him. He reached over and flicked on the lights to his private domain. It was a two-and-a-half-car building, and most of it was filled with weights, benches, and other lifting machines. Most things were homemade and of top quality. It was a weight lifter's dream. B. A. walked around and inspected each piece of equipment without saying a word. She hopped up on the leg extension machine and looked at Rod with an eager expression. He came over quickly and put a ten-pound disk on each end of the bar. B. A. leaned back and grabbed the handles and did ten easy reps.

"I don't put a lot of weight on this machine," said Rod. "I've talked to some docs and physical trainers who aren't too keen on this exercise, so I use it as a warm-up or a cool-down.

"This is some really cool stuff," observed B. A. as she stood up. "Did you make all of this stuff yourself?"

"Yup. I started in metal shop when I was a freshman and it just kind of got out of hand. I bought some of the weights, and the chipped ones I got from the university. They were going to throw them away, so they said I could have them."

Rod spent the next half hour telling her the history of each piece and how he had made it. He was almost like a little kid with his toys.

B. A. pulled into her driveway a few minutes before her mom got home from work. They sat at the kitchen table and talked about their daily adventures. Martha Smith was an emergency room nurse, so she always had interesting stories to relate. When it was B. A.'s turn, she babbled on about playing ball at UNT and about Rod, his weight room, and his car troubles. Martha marveled at how quickly her daughter made friends. She hoped that tomorrow would go smoothly for her. The first day in a new school could be a traumatic experience. Well, whatever Annie, or B. A., came up against, she was sure her daughter was up to the task. She was very mature for her age. Martha thought the early maturity came partly from losing her father at such a young age. It would have been easier to regress or to sulk around feeling sorry for herself. Instead, it seemed to strengthen B. A.'s mental toughness.

After fifty crunches and twenty push-ups, B. A. jumped into bed. She reached over and picked up her phone, hoping Rod wasn't sleeping yet. If his first class was at ten, he should still be up.

"Hello," said Rod. They had exchanged numbers in case he needed to borrow her truck the next day.

"Hi, it's B. A.," she said, marveling at how natural the name sounded after only using it a few days. "I just wanted to thank you again for letting me play today, and I wanted to tell you that my truck will be in the school parking lot with the keys under the floor mat."

"Thanks, B. A., I just might take you up on that if my car can't be fixed right away. Come along next Sunday, I mean, if you want to. The guys seem to like you, and you're not half-bad."

B. A. said her good-byes and hung up. In five minutes she was fast asleep. Rod, on the other hand, tossed and turned most of the night. He had never spent so much time and had so much fun with a member of the opposite sex before. But he had had never met anyone like B. A. before, either. What were the odds of a girl moving to Reston with so many interests similar to his? This was a whole new ball game for him, and he had to do some serious thinking about it.

Chapter 3

Big Shirley

Two weeks had gone by for B. A. in her new school. She sat in the school cafeteria eating the same lunch that she took to school every day—a turkey sandwich, chips, an apple, and two cartons of milk. She had skipped lunch the first day, seeing what the school cooks had to offer. "This stuff will knock you stupid," was one of Tank's favorite sayings. When she asked what it meant, he told her that it was just short of getting knocked out. When a football player says something unintelligible after a big hit, the other guys in the huddle rib him about getting knocked stupid. Of course, according to Tank, some of them didn't have that far to go.

From her position in the middle of the room, she observed the students around her. The tough guys and the girls who hung around them always ate in the far corner by the windows. The rough girls took up a couple of tables in the opposite corner. Both groups took only about ten minutes to eat or slam a soda and then they all left about the same time. Some of them hustled across the street to have a smoke. Others just wanted to get out of the building for a while. Since the smokers were off school property, they were rarely hassled. B. A. thought it was strange that the students under eighteen were not allowed to buy cigarettes by law, but once they had them, it was okay to smoke in public. A phone call from the principal asking the town cop to cruise by would cause some real panic. Maybe the principal didn't give them any grief because he was a smoker too.

The self-proclaimed "cool" kids had their own regular tables, too. These were the girls with too much makeup and the guys who were trying to impress them. She considered them harmless. The ones she worried about were the guys and girls who were always out to have a good time. To them a good time came first, and nothing else mattered. These were not B. A.'s favorite people. They were rude and self-serving, and they were usually the first to admit it. To them it was the only way to be. It also appeared that they were growing in numbers, which was scary. She wondered how much they were influenced by today's professional athletes and musicians. What a bunch of followers! They were easily led by anyone who had something to sell them.

Their taste in music wasn't any better. If a song had nasty lyrics or real heavy bass, they thought it was awesome. It didn't take a lot of talent to put out that kind of noise. They would have been surprised to see the CDs in her truck—Savoy Brown, Deep Purple, Robin Trower, and of course her dad's band, Gambler's Folly. A lot of it went back decades. Her dad had always said, "The good stuff will stand the test of time, and the rest will just fade away."

The jocks hung together in small groups and were usually real loud. The rest of them, the ones who didn't fit into any special category, sat in the middle of the room where she was sitting. There were boyfriends and girlfriends, musicians, drama people, and of course, the video gamers. The top students were there, too. They usually looked through their textbooks or notes as they ate and talked. Most of these guys were just trying to be themselves and didn't worry much about how they looked or what kind of impression they made on their classmates. B. A. wondered how much they would all change in the next ten years.

The bell rang, and B. A. moved with the rest of the crowd out into the hallway. PE was her next class, and she usually looked forward to it, but today she heard they were playing dodgeball. B. A.'s locker was only a couple away from Chip's. She was friendly to B. A. but didn't go out of her way to talk to her. B. A. remembered what Rod had said about Chip's disappointment when she didn't go out for volleyball. She looked at Chip and chuckled to herself as they both dressed for class. They had played flag football for the first two weeks of school and B. A.'s assignment was to block for the quarterback. In two weeks she never even touched the ball once. It was raining today, so they were headed for the gym to play good old dodgeball.

Chip fell in beside the new girl as they walked up the steps to the brightly lit gym. It was B. A.'s first time inside the facility. The bleachers were pushed back so there was a lot of space for activities. Six basketball goals were cranked into their "up" position. A large flying eagle was painted on the side wall with a football, a basketball, a volleyball, and a baseball in its talons. Above the eagle, printed in bright red, was written: Reston Fighting Eagles. There was a dark, silent scoreboard at each end of the gym. One scoreboard was surrounded by banners telling of the accomplishments of past boys' athletic teams. The wall around the opposite scoreboard told of the girls' accomplishments. It looked uncluttered, as there were only a handful of banners, with the most recent date being 1990.

"Man, these girls do need some help," muttered B. A.

"Did you say something?" asked Chip, walking along beside her.

"I was just talking to myself," said B. A. with a smile. "This is a nice gym for such a small town."

"Yeah, some guy died and left the school a lot of money. They used some of it to build a new gym about fifteen years ago. I suppose you're from a big city school?"

"No, I'm from a town about this size."

"You ever play dodge ball with the guys before?" asked Chip.

"I don't think so," answered B. A. "We used to play a game called bombardment or killer ball. You had a line you couldn't go across, and you tried to hit the guys on the other team with a ball. If they caught it, you were out. If you hit them or knocked a ball out of their hands, they were out."

"That's the game. There is one problem. The guys are real maniacs. They're always trying to impress the girls, so they play real rough. And the last game is always guys against girls. It's usually a massacre. If you're afraid of getting hit, just go over and sit on the stage a few minutes into the game. Mr. Jacobs will think someone put you out. If you go too early, he'll make you get back into the game."

"Thanks," said B. A.

The room got real noisy as the boys poured through the opposite door. After roll call, there was about five minutes of halfhearted calisthenics. Chip watched B. A. closely as they went through the warm-up. She seemed to be coordinated. It was hard to tell what kind of body she had because her shirt was way too big for her. Come to think of it, all her clothes seemed to be big and baggy. She always wore a big T-shirt with a college or athletic company on it and jeans. At least she wasn't loaded down with makeup like a lot of the other girls. Chip approved of that. Maybe she wasn't an athlete, but she might be a decent friend. She made a mental note to get to know her better. The last exercise was fifteen push-ups. Chip was proud of her push-up skills. She did them boys' style and could usually do nine or ten. Most of the other girls did them with their knees on the floor. Chip got to ten and then collapsed on the floor. As she lay there panting, she looked over at B. A. and was surprised to see her breeze through all fifteen, boys' style. *Wow,* she thought. *She must be pretty strong. Her form was perfect. Who is this girl?*

The first two games were typical. There were fifteen on each side, guys and girls mixed. The girls were usually the first to be eliminated. Most of them didn't throw very well, and their catching skills were even worse. Some even threw off the wrong foot. The games ended with two or three guys from each side battling it out. The third game was a little more interesting. It was guys versus the girls. B. A., Chip, and Darby Quinn were left on their side and the other team had four guys left. One of the guys came flying across the floor and was about to unload on Darby when Chip hit him in the thigh with a well-placed throw. The guy was out of the game, but he took two more steps and let loose with a hard throw that caught Darby in the stomach. She actually tried to catch it, but it was moving too fast and almost knocked her down. Even though she wasn't out of the game, she went to the sidelines holding her stomach. B. A. didn't like cheap shots, so she scooped up another ball and nailed the cheater as he walked to the side. It hit him in the rear, which drew catcalls from the other guys sitting there. He spun around and gave B. A. a menacing stare. She didn't have time to return the look as balls were now flying all over the place.

A minute later, it was down to B. A. and one opponent. He was a fairly athletic-looking boy with a confident grin on his face. He obviously thought he would have little problem getting this new girl out. He had one ball while B. A. was holding two. She decided to try an old snowball-fighting trick. There was a good chance these Texas boys hadn't been in too many snowball fights. There was about twenty feet between them, so with an underhand motion she lobbed the ball in her left high up over his head. In a snowball fight, you would throw a snowball as high as you could over your opponent's head, and when he looked up, you would try to drill him with a second one. Even if he didn't look up, you might get lucky, and your first toss would come down on top of his head. All she expected him to do was glance up at the lobbed ball, giving her a chance to throw her second ball and knock the ball he was holding out of his hands. He surprised her by dropping his ball, thinking he was going to catch her soft toss. She rifled her second ball at him. The ball that came out of her hand was connected to one of the most respected arms in Arkansas high school softball. Underhand or overhand, there were many stories about the prowess of her throws. No one wanted to bat against her when she was on the mound, and competitors did not want to run against her when she was in right field. The ball bounced hard off the boy's chest just as he was reaching for the first ball. He was knocked back a couple of steps with an incredulous look on his face. Game over.

The girls in the gym leaped to their feet cheering and high-fiving each other. It was the first time the girls had ever beaten the guys at dodgeball or any other game. B. A. hadn't meant to throw the ball that hard. She was going to tell him that, but the bell rang, and everyone scurried toward their respective locker rooms.

Chip fell in beside B. A. on their way back to the girls' locker room. She stared at the new girl as they headed down the stairs.

"What?" asked B. A. looking down at the shorter girl. "Why are you looking at me like that?"

"That was a great throw. Why didn't you go out for volleyball?" asked Chip, getting right to the point.

"You'll see why when we start playing volleyball in class. I stink."

Chip was disappointed at this statement; with an arm like that, B. A. had to be good at something. She followed B. A. back to the lockers where she got another surprise. B. A. grabbed her clothes and a towel from her locker and headed for one of the small personal showers that were located throughout the locker room. She couldn't believe it. Girls, including her, usually didn't take a shower after gym class. Chip made a spur-of-the-moment decision. She grabbed her clothes and a towel from the coach's office and went to the shower next to B. A. The two girls exited the shower simultaneously. They were the only two left in their row as the other girls had quickly dressed and went back to the gym to sit on the stage until the bell rang. Chip watched B. A. as she brushed her hair. When B. A.'s sleeves fell back, Chip got a good look at her arms. They looked like she lifted weights or something. Chip made up her mind on the spot. There was something different about this new girl, and she was going to get to the bottom of it. As they headed for the door, the last two girls in the locker room besides them were standing in front of their lockers with spray bottles.

"Just spray some extra perfume on, sweeties," said Chip. "That way you won't smell so bad."

They were just about to give themselves a good drenching. They glared at her and quickly stuffed their perfume back into their lockers. Chip and B. A. both laughed.

As the girls came out of the gym, some of their boyfriends were waiting. One of the guys put his hand on his girl's shoulder.

"Don't touch her, Jimmy," hollered Chip. "She didn't shower. Yuck."

The girl turned and gave her a nasty stare as they receded down the hallway. Chip chuckled and looked around for B. A. She was headed down the hall with Jack Hansen, the boy she hit in the chest, right behind her. Chip hustled to catch up so she could be of help if needed.

"Hey, sweetheart—uh, I mean B. A., right?" asked Jack as he caught up with her.

"Yeah, that's right," said B. A. "Listen, I'm sorry I threw so hard at you. I didn't mean anything by it."

"Hey, no sweat. Anything goes in a good game of dodgeball. You sure surprised me, though. It's going to take a while for me to live that down. Next time I'll be ready for you. With an arm like that, you'd make a great pitcher. I know, 'cause I'm a pitcher myself."

"Really?" asked B. A.

"Yeah, I'm the number one pitcher here. Anyway, since you embarrassed me so bad in front of the guys, I figure you owe it to me to let me take you out for a pizza sometime. Say, right after Friday night's football game?"

"Sorry, I'm already going to the game with someone, and we're going out afterward."

"Is that so? What's his name?"

B. A. hadn't figured on getting the third degree, so she came up with the only name she knew: "Rod."

"Okay," said Jack as he started to jog toward his next class. "Maybe some other time."

"Wow," said Chip. "You just turned down the quarterback of the football team. Good job. He's a party boy, just looking for a good time. Not your type."

"I don't know. He seemed real nice. The quarterback, huh? Maybe I better chase after him and tell him I've changed my mind."

Chip looked at B. A. for a few seconds and then they both started to laugh. Maybe there was something to this new girl. Chip turned and ran down the hall to her next class.

"Hey," she hollered over her shoulder, "can I have a ride home?"

"Meet you in the back parking lot," hollered B. A. "I've got a black truck."

* ◆ *

Chip barely made it to class on time. She slouched down in her seat and got ready to hear another Shakespeare lecture from Mr. Wallace. Suddenly she sat upright in her seat. *Rod,* she thought. *I only know one guy in this town named Rod. She's seeing him? Man, does she work fast. Does she know he's a sophomore in college? Somebody's getting a phone call tonight, and he's got a lot of explaining to do.*

Mr. Wallace was looking expectantly at her as if he had just asked her a question.

"Well, class, since Ms. Fullerton is so eager to get started, let's get into it."

Chip immediately slouched back down and tuned him out.

* ◆ *

B. A. was sorry she had used Rod's name to get out of her predicament. Chip was his cousin, and she would no doubt tell him what she had said. And now, she couldn't go to the game with anyone but Rod, or she would look foolish for using his name. She knew he was really busy at school. In fact, she only saw him on Sunday afternoons when they went to play ball at UNT. Well, she would have to call him tonight because he never called her unless it had to do with the Sunday game.

* ◆ *

Rod closed his phone and smiled to himself. He didn't mind that B. A. had used his name to get out of a sticky situation. Actually, he was kind of flattered. After he calmed her down and told her it was fine with him, he asked her if she wanted to come over and work out with him a couple of nights a week. He explained that he had meant to ask her earlier, but his studies and his job had kept him away from home every evening for the past two weeks.

She had secretly been hoping he would invite her over ever since he had given her the tour of his garage. She readily accepted his invitation and agreed to show up the next night at eight.

Right after Rod had finished talking to B. A., he received another phone call. This one was from his pint-sized cousin. She fired several questions about B. A. at him. Chip wanted to know, among other things, how long they had been seeing each other and why he hadn't mentioned it to her. Rod explained that they weren't "seeing" each other and, if they were, he didn't have to check with her to get her approval.

Chip tried to extract every bit of information she could but didn't get much. Rod went from being amused to being annoyed. What a nosy little creature she was! Just before they hung up, he did say something he hoped he wouldn't regret later. Since Chip didn't mention their Sunday afternoon basketball games, Rod didn't bring it up either. But he did tell her that B. A. had a big secret. He was thinking of her basketball ability that no one at Reston High School knew about yet.

Chip took this last bit of information in an entirely different way, and she couldn't wait to talk to Luke about it. He fancied himself a supersleuth and believed he could dig up information on anyone or anything. Well, she had some information that he had failed to dig up. And it was in his area of expertise—sports. At least she now knew that there was something not quite normal about B. A. Her imagination was fast at work. After saying good-bye to her cousin, she called Luke, and the two talked late into the night, as they often did. But this time they didn't talk about sports.

* ◆ *

Two days later, B. A. and Chip were walking through the parking lot after school heading for B. A.'s truck when they came across two elementary kids wrestling on the pavement. Some of the high schoolers just stood around and watched. B. A. stepped in and quickly grabbed the bigger kid on top and lifted him off the smaller one.

"Cut it out," she hollered at him as he squirmed in her grasp. "Didn't your momma tell you not to pick on people smaller than you?" The older kids just laughed.

The little bully let loose with a string of profanities, while Chip helped the smaller boy up. Before either girl could respond, the high school principal stepped in and took the bigger boy by the arm. He had been watching through the window when the fight started and had gotten out there as quickly as he could.

"Thanks, girls," he said. "I'll take it from here. It's too bad some of these big strong high school men didn't break this up sooner."

The crowd quickly dispersed.

"I'm going to start hanging around you more often," said Chip as they got into the truck.

"Why is that?" asked B. A., laughing.

"Stuff just seems to happen around you. You're like an action magnet. Also, I noticed that you haven't made many new friends yet. I've been elected, in case you haven't figured it out, to steer you to the right sort of people. You know, so you don't fall in with the wrong crowd."

"Oh yeah," exclaimed B. A. "Which crowd should I stay away from?"

"Ha! Most of them," laughed Chip. "There are so many weirdos running around the halls, you wouldn't believe it. Between the snobbies, the druggies, the preps, and the flakies, it's hard to find just a plain old normal kid anymore. And good friends are in short supply. That's why I'm latching on to you before someone else tries to corrupt you. Say, you don't have any hidden secrets that you don't want me to know about, do you?"

"If I didn't want you to know about something, why would I tell you now? That wouldn't make sense. Anyway, the answer is no. I'm just trying to fit in and be one of the normal people. My mom got a better job at a Fort Worth hospital so we moved down here. The idea of relocating did bother me a little, but I'll get used to it here. My dad died a few years ago in a plane crash, so this is a new start for both my mom and me. I've got an older sister who's married. Doesn't sound very exciting, does it?"

"I don't know," said Chip in deep thought. "That's too bad about your dad. What was he like?"

"He was unbelievable. He was the best dad a girl could have—when he was home. He was a musician, so he traveled a lot. The band he was in wasn't the commercial type. They played more for the music than the money. They had sort of a cult following. They would travel a lot with another cult band, Black Oak Arkansas. My dad always said they were the last of a dying breed. He believed that modern music has little depth and has gotten way too commercial. Most groups are in it more for the money than anything else. It's getting so almost anybody with a drum machine, a computer, and a microphone can come up with something that people will buy. Mostly people our age. They're pretty clueless when it comes to music. That's only my opinion, of course, but I got it from a very reliable source."

"So he was in a country band?"

"Not hardly," said B. A., reaching down under her seat, pulling out a CD, and handing it to Chip. "He's the second one from the right."

"Wow! Gambler's Folly. You know, I've heard of them. I'm serious. I mean, I don't listen to them, but I do know who they are. It must have been cool to have a rock star for a dad."

"Yeah, it was pretty cool. We didn't travel with him very much because I was so little, and he wanted us to have as normal a life as possible. There's that word again, normal. Anyway, he was a great guy. We played ball together, wrestled, watched movies, and listened to music. There wasn't much he didn't know about music. He could really play that guitar. I'll show it to you sometime, if you want to see it. It's in my room."

B. A. eased her truck into Chip's driveway. Chip got out and leaned back through the window.

"I'd like to see that guitar sometime. Hey, thanks for the ride. Are you coming to the game tonight? We might just win one for once."

"I'll be there. I heard you were our star setter."

"It doesn't take much to be the star on any of the girls' teams at this school. It sure would be nice to be on the other end of a lopsided score for once. We won five basketball games last year. Can you believe that?"

"Well," said B. A. as she put the truck into reverse, "lopsided scores aren't much fun for either side. See you at the game."

Chip waved as the truck backed down the drive. She hoped she would get the chance to see that guitar real soon. It would be a good excuse to see what she could see inside B. A.'s house. B. A.'s dad being a famous musician couldn't be the big secret that Rod had mentioned. It had to be something else, something bigger and more mysterious. What did B. A. say about relocating being real tough? *Wait a minute.* She stopped as she was halfway through the back door. *Relocating. New start. Witness Relocation Program! Trying to fit in and leading a normal life. That was it. B. A., or her mom, must have witnessed a murder or something.* She hurried inside. She couldn't wait to pass her theory on to Luke. If she could come up with some proof, he would be very impressed with her detective abilities. Of course, she had to be careful not to blow B. A.'s cover. This could be a very interesting situation.

* ◆ *

B.A fell onto her bed after turning on her CD player real low. She usually cranked it when her mom wasn't home, but all she wanted now was soft background music so she could rest. She was sore all over. Her workout with Rod the night before had taken its toll on her. When she showed up, he was waiting for her with a suggested workout that he had typed up. His routine kept him in a different area, so there would be a minimum of weight changing to do. They spotted each other when needed and generally just enjoyed each other's company. He liked country, and she liked classic rock, so the knob on the radio was just about as worn out at the end of the lifting session as they were. She had obviously overdone it, trying to impress him. And now she was paying the price. It certainly was a strange feeling—not being sore, but trying to impress somebody like that. Showing off wasn't usually her style. Her reflection on her behavior didn't last long, as she was fast asleep in five minutes.

* ◆ *

B. A. and Chip stood in front of B. A.'s locker right after their last class. They were discussing the previous night's volleyball match. B. A. complimented Chip on her play. She had quick feet. They had to be quick since she was scrambling all over the place trying to catch up with errant passes. Her sets were excellent, but the hitters seem to be out of sync most of the night. The last point of the evening summed up the whole experience. The visitors from Grand Prairie were serving

with a 24 to 13 lead when Chip gave Tammi Olsen a perfect set. The 5'
11" junior jumped too soon and tried to spike it on her way down. As
a result, she just nicked the bottom of the ball and it came down and
hit her on top of the head. They were snickering about it when Chip
looked over B. A.'s shoulder.

"Uh oh, it looks like your action magnet is on full power today," said
Chip. "Remember that fight we broke up a couple of days ago? Well,
we are about to have repercussions. I think Big Shirley Fosse wants to
talk to you. The bigger kid that you pulled off the little guy the other
day was her little brother."

B. A. looked in the direction that Chip was indicating. A very large
girl was ambling down the hall with a small group in tow.

"Let me handle this," volunteered Chip. "In a duel of wits this girl
is totally unarmed."

"Let's hear what she has to say," said B. A. "Maybe she wants to
thank us for setting her little brother straight."

"Ha. And maybe she wants my autograph for last night's performance.
Hey, there's Mr. Fox, the counselor, in the doorway. If this escalades,
he'll come over and put a stop to it."

Shirley stopped in front of the two girls. There were about a dozen
students behind her now. High school students, like sharks sniffing
blood, can smell a confrontation from a long way off. B. A. could see
Mr. Fox watching as he stood leaning in the doorway of the cafeteria.

"Hey, are you the chick that roughed up my brother the other day?"
asked Shirley.

"I didn't rough him up," responded B. A. "I pulled him off a much
smaller boy. Your brother's got a nasty mouth for such a little kid."

"I know he didn't learn that kind of talk from a classy girl like you,
Shirley," added Chip.

B. A. was trying to think of a way to defuse the situation. She didn't
need Chip, who she knew was only trying to help, to rile Shirley any
more than she already was.

"Shut up, midget," barked Shirley. "I'm not talking to you. I'm giving your friend a choice. My brother got in trouble because of her. She gives me ten bucks and an apology for sticking her nose into other people's business, or she gets it."

"When you say she gets 'it,' do you mean like a prize or something?" asked Chip in a futile attempt to keep the situation from getting serious.

"No, stupid," said Shirley. "I mean we go outside and someone gets her butt whipped—maybe two someones." Shirley looked over her shoulder for approval, thinking her last statement was very clever.

Chip started to say something when B. A. held up her hand to shush her. She had an idea.

"If you feel so strongly about it, we don't have to go outside," said B. A. "We can settle it right now."

"Oh yeah, how's that?" asked Shirley, not sure what the new girl was talking about.

B. A. looked over big Shirley's shoulder and hollered, "Hey, Mr. Fox."

She walked around a bewildered Shirley and the rest of her followers. Chip groaned, thinking this was not the way to handle the situation. She was saving her good stuff to rip Shirley when the discussion got heated. Now it looked like her new friend was wimping out and running to a teacher. The rest of the crowd felt the same way. It was going to be hard on B. A. if this was the way she operated.

B. A. talked to Mr. Fox for a few moments, and he nodded. He pulled his keys out of his pocket and turned to open the cafeteria doors.

"Well, c'mon," said B. A., turning to the crowd, "let's get this over with."

Shirley stood in front of her group with a questioning look on her face. What was this newbie trying to pull? The crowd, sensing that something was going on, had now swelled to about thirty students.

Shirley and the rest of them headed toward the cafeteria. While the students shuffled through the door, Mr. Fox hustled over to one of the tables and rolled it out from the wall. He unlocked it and pushed it into the "down" position.

B. A. went over to a bewildered Chip and whispered, "Maybe we can settle this and have a little fun too. How much money do you have?"

"Uh, about five bucks, I think," said Chip, still not grasping the situation.

"Here's ten more," said B. A., pulling a bill out of her back pocket. "Bet on me, but do it quietly."

"What's going on?" asked Shirley with a little less confidence than she had had in the hallway.

"Mr. Fox has agreed to referee an arm-wrestling contest to settle this, if it's okay with you," said B. A. "I mean, you won't get as much pleasure whipping me this way as you would kicking my butt outside, but this way our clothes won't get all bloody."

"It's fine with me," said Shirley.

"Here's the deal," said B. A. so everyone could hear. "If I lose, I will stand up in the middle of this cafeteria tomorrow and tell everyone that Shirley rules, and I am dirt. If I win, Shirley has to keep her little brother from bullying or fighting anyone for the rest of the school year."

When B. A. mentioned that she might win, the crowd snickered. By now, Chip had walked to the back of the room and was talking quietly with a couple of guys.

"Deal," said Big Shirley, sitting down. "Let's go. This will be over quick."

The crowd gathered around as the two girls faced each other across the table. Mr. Fox sat on a chair at the end and gave them instructions. He would make sure no one had an advantage before he said, "Go," and they could only use their arms and shoulders. They couldn't lean with their whole bodies. The two combatants locked hands and stared at each other. Mr. Fox had both his hands on top of theirs, making sure they were perfectly straight. The crowd closed in and started to yell encouragement, mostly to Shirley.

Mr. Fox was just about to take his hands away when B. A. pulled her arm away and said, "Wait."

The room went silent. All eyes were on B. A. It looked like she was having second thoughts.

"What was I thinking?" she asked to no one in particular.

The spectators groaned. They'd had a feeling she wouldn't go through with it. What a pansy! Wait until Shirley got her outside.

"I think I need a better deal. I mean, if I win, what's to keep you from catching me outside and kicking my tail anyway? I want your word that you and your brother will not pick on anyone or fight for the rest of the school year."

"All right, all right," said an agitated Shirley. "Let's just do this. You're gonna lose anyway."

Mr. Fox lined them up again and said, "Go."

The crowd started screaming as the combatants went at it. At first, neither arm moved. Then Shirley slowly gained the advantage. Chip's heart started to sink. Shirley smelled victory. When her hand was halfway down, B. A. started to come back. The room got even louder. B. A.'s face was getting red as she slowly recovered and bent a groaning Shirley down to the table. The onlookers couldn't believe it. This girl was giving away at least fifty pounds to Shirley. When the back of the big girl's hand softly touched the table, Mr. Fox slapped his hand down and said, "Winner!"

Chip and a couple of other voices were the only ones cheering. She went back to the boys she was talking to earlier. They were starting to dig into their pockets, when Shirley hollered.

"Wait! I want a better deal too. You changed the rules once. I say it should be two out of three. Agreed, or are you backing out?"

Murmurs went through the room. "Shirley's gonna wear her down."

No way she can beat her twice. The first time was a fluke. Did you see the way she was straining? It looked like she was going to blow a gasket."

B. A. was rubbing her arm and looking around at all the faces. She met Chip's gaze. A look of understanding passed between them. Chip turned to the two guys and said something to them. Then she turned back to B. A. and nodded.

"Well, okay," said B. A. meekly, as she rubbed her arm.

They went through the same routine with Mr. Fox's hand steadying theirs.

"You're dead meat," leered Big Shirley. "I ain't holding back this time."

Mr. Fox let go, and Shirley put everything she had into it. B. A. held her for a few seconds and then she looked at the big bully, winked once, and slammed the back of her hand to the table. Shirley yelped like a little pup. She stood up with wide eyes on B. A. The crowd dispersed quickly. The show was over.

"I hope you'll keep your word," hollered B. A. as Shirley headed for the door minus her followers. Shirley just waved without looking back. This was a new experience for her, and she wasn't taking it very well.

"Thanks, Mr. Fox," said B. A. as the counselor locked the doors.

"No problem," he chuckled. "I rather enjoyed it."

He headed down the hallway jingling his keys and whistling.

* ◆ *

"Well," said B. A. to Chip as they headed out the door to the parking lot, "did you get our money?"

"Yes, I did," said Chip waving forty dollars in the air. "I bet all fifteen on the first round and ten more bucks on the second one. I had to give them two-to-one odds the second time. How did you do that? Was it some sort of trick? When you sat down, I didn't think you had a chance."

"Mr. Fox made sure it was just a test of arm strength. Shirley isn't as strong as she looks. She's just big. If she could have used her weight, I would have been in real trouble. It would be nice if she kept her word, but that's one thing I wouldn't bet on. Anyway, pizza is on me tonight. Should we call your boyfriend to see if he wants to join us? And by the way, an Escalade is a Cadillac SUV."

Chip looked as if she were deep in thought for about two seconds.

"Whatever. The pizza idea is great, but Luke is not my boyfriend. We just do a lot of stuff together, that's all. Speaking of boyfriends, do you have one yet?"

"Nah, I'm still waiting for that smart, good-looking, athletic, rich type to find me," said B. A.

"Sweetheart," said Chip with a real thick southern drawl, "Reston, Texas, is probably not the place to find a guy like that. You might have to lower your standards a little bit."

"Never," hollered B. A. "I refuse to lower my standards, whether it's pizza or men."

Chip just rolled her eyes and took out her phone to call Luke. He never turned down a free meal.

●◆●

Later that evening, an orange Topaz sat fifty yards down the street from B. A.'s house. The girl in the passenger seat was looking through a pair of binoculars when the light finally went out in B. A.'s room.

"Can we go home yet, Spy Queen?" asked Luke as he munched from a bag of Doritos. "I didn't know that a few slices of pizza came with an all-night stakeout duty."

"Do you really think she is sixteen like she says she is?" asked Chip, ignoring his complaint. "Maybe she's like one of those movie stars who plays a high school kid but is really in her twenties. Today's makeup can make you look any age or sex. Did you see *Mrs. Doubtfire*? No? I didn't think so. She might even be thirty-five or even forty. I haven't seen her do anything remotely goofy yet. You know, like teenagers do."

"Hey, I'm a teenager, and I never do anything goofy."

"I'm gonna let that pass. C'mon, work with me on this. This could be your greatest piece of detective work ever. Why don't you send back to her old school for her grades or something? If they refuse, then maybe we're on to something, like maybe she wasn't even in high school last year."

"Yeah, and what if they want to know why a high school student is asking for confidential material that he's not supposed to have? We don't want the FBI or any other government agency hassling us. Maybe I could ask for something that wasn't confidential, just to see what comes back. I'd have to say I was somebody else, and if I got caught, I could be in big trouble. I'll have to think about this. C'mon, this is a waste of time. Let's go home."

"All right," said Chip, somewhat annoyed at Luke's lack of enthusiasm. "Let's go, but I'm not giving up on this. There is something strange about this Smith girl, if that's even her real name. And I—I mean *we* are going to dig it up. You should have seen her handle Big Shirley Fosse. It was beautiful. And I was handling the finances."

"I dig better when I'm fully rested," said Luke as he put the car in gear.

The truth was, he liked sitting in the car with Chip even if they were doing something pointless like this. He had kissed her a couple of times, but it was to congratulate her for something and not to show her he really liked her. Maybe these late-night stakeouts would lead to bigger and better things. A guy could dream, couldn't he?

Chapter 4

The Real Deal

B. A. was starting to get comfortable in her new surroundings. She was six weeks into her junior year, and the Shirley incident was the only thing that had happened out of the "normal" range. Her mom was happy with her new job, which, in turn, made B. A. happy. She knew her mom was glad to leave Jones Ferry and all the memories behind. A lot of memories were good ones, but the unpleasant ones were tucked away in a special part of her mind and visited only when she was ready to relive them. In Jones Ferry too many things reminded her mom of her deceased husband. Martha would never forget him, but it was time to move on to a new chapter in her and B. A.'s life.

B. A. liked her relationship with Rod. They now lifted together every Tuesday and Thursday. She even helped him study for tests as they worked out. He would do a set of incline presses, and she would fire a question from his notes or from a study guide. He would reciprocate by helping her with her algebra. She had never liked the subject and always struggled with it. It was a very convenient relationship.

The second time they lifted together B. A. brought a strange-looking piece of rubber with her. It looked like a bicycle inner tube. She held one end with her left hand at shoulder height. It crossed her back diagonally where she would then hold it at hip level with her right hand. She pulled it hard in an underhand motion for ten reps and then switched sides. She walked around doing this constantly between sets of free-weight lifting. She also had a hard time keeping it where she wanted it, so she was always adjusting the band to get it in the proper position.

The next time she showed up, Rod walked her over to a two-by-four he had screwed into the wall about the same height as B. A.'s waist. He took her tube from her and attached it to a couple of hooks that were in the center of a row of eight. After she did ten reps with her right arm, he motioned for her to stop. Without saying a word, he now hooked the band over the hooks on each end. This gave the band a wider base, which in turn, made it tougher to pull. Now she understood why there were so many hooks. She could adjust the tension by placing the band so it had a narrow or wide base. She could really crank on that piece of rubber when she didn't have to hold it with the other hand.

He knew he had done well when he received a big hug for his efforts. This particular exercise was still a mystery to him. He had never seen anyone do it before. He didn't ask about it—he just assumed she would tell him when she felt like it. That was one of the things he liked about her. At times they didn't say much to each other. They just went about their work. He enjoyed conversing with her, but it was also just nice to be in the same room together doing something they both loved to do. The following Sunday he found out all about the piece of rubber and the exercise she was doing with it.

• ◆ •

Rod and B. A. were in good spirits as they got out of his car for the Sunday afternoon basketball game. Most of the guys were already there, shooting around. A radio was turned up loud so they could listen to the Cowboys' football game. It was eighty-one degrees, and a few soft clouds floated across the sky. B. A. and Rod joined the group and started talking trash right away. Dogging your opponents was almost as much fun as beating them.

"You gonna take your boots off when you play us today, Chuck?" asked Rod, winking at B. A.

"What are you talking about?" asked Chuck. "Are you jealous of my footwear? They aren't cheap. Maybe someday you'll be able to afford a pair—by the time you're forty."

"I'm talking about how you were barely able to get off the big ball to shoot the little ball. Did you see any light between his toes and the planet's surface last week, B. A.? I mean, there were elementary kids lined up for a chance at slapping one back in his face."

"No," added B. A. "I think they were lined up to get a look at those $180 shoes. You could feed a small village for a week with what you paid for those things."

"Y'all think you're real funny, don't you?" asked Chuck. "Did you practice that routine on your way here? You're gonna be begging for mercy when I get these babies warmed up."

"You better figure out how to start them first," said B. A. looking down at his shoes. "Isn't there a rope you pull or some kind of switch?"

"I liked her better the first couple of times you brought her, big guy," said Chuck. "She didn't say much then."

Everyone laughed. B. A. was accepted as part of the group because of her play and her attitude. They all seemed to be genuinely fond of her, and they were all extremely impressed with her skills. They weren't sure when they saw her for the first time. Even Rod had second thoughts when he found out that she intended to play and not watch. That was all ancient history now, and he had to admit that the games were a lot more fun since she'd started playing. The teams were evenly matched, so they kept them the same. When someone didn't show, a substitute was easily recruited from another court.

B. A. had settled in to a routine and was starting to enjoy her new surroundings. She didn't know why, but she had more fun doing things with guys. She hadn't made a lot of friends yet at school. Chip and Jenny Olsen were the only two she talked to on a regular basis. They usually ate lunch together, and the talk usually turned to the upcoming basketball season. They both filled B. A. in on what to expect.

Jenny was tall and slender, with medium-length brown hair. She had a dry sense of humor and was usually instigating something with Chip. At lunch she was always looking around apprehensively for someone or something as they ate and talked. After their second lunch together, Chip told B. A. that Jenny had a twin sister, the "infamous" Tammi from volleyball, who wouldn't approve if she saw Jenny eating with them.

Chip and Tammi Olsen were rivals, and Jenny was sort of caught in the middle. Tammi wanted to be known as the school's star female athlete, and she felt that Chip got a lot of underserved credit. When Luke wrote an article on a girls' sporting event, he tried to be unbiased, but it was hard for him to do when it came to Chip. Tammi thought she was being slighted when it came to Luke's reporting. She was a little stronger in basketball than volleyball, but certainly not a star. She was a pretty decent pitcher and hitter in softball, and that was a fact that she reminded people of constantly. Jenny, on the other hand, was actually better than her sister in volleyball and basketball, but she had severe issues with confidence. It was less hassle just to follow her sister's lead.

* ◆ *

It always seemed to B. A. that when things were too good to be true, something would happen to disrupt the status quo. The disruption started when Butch McCoy got out of his car followed by a 5' 11" redheaded girl with similar facial features. They were obviously related. Butch introduced his sister, Kay, to the group. He told them he brought her along because he knew they would be short one player today. The other reason was the fact that she had been bugging him for weeks to bring her. Victor Reyes rolled his eyes at Rod as they exchanged a knowing look. It was apparent that they were both thinking the same thing. Their suspicions were confirmed shortly into the game. Kay roughly pushed B. A. aside and held her hand up for the ball. Victor threw her the pass instinctively, expecting B. A. to call the foul, but she remained silent. Kay caught the pass and banked the ball in. Victor was about to say something when he saw Rod shaking his head as if to say, "Don't interfere. Let B. A. work it out for herself."

On more than one occasion, B. A. had good rebounding position only to be pushed in the back as she was about to leave her feet. B. A. didn't see the point in challenging the other girl and only scored one basket the first game while Kay made several.

Kay became more vocal and aggressive as the game wore on. The redheaded senior couldn't figure out that she was the only one playing "maul ball." The other guys played aggressively but they didn't push or grab their opponent. They also didn't foul intentionally if the opponent had a clear shot at an easy basket. Kay did all of the above.

B. A. couldn't figure it out. Butch seemed like a nice guy. Why would he bring his sister to the game just to rough her up? It didn't make sense. And now Butch had this strange look on his face. It looked like a combination of disappointment and embarrassment. Well, whatever the story was, she didn't feel like being a part of it any more. An opportunity came when she was elbowed to the ground on the other team's winning basket. She limped over to the sideline and sat down.

"Are you okay?" asked a concerned Rod as he sat down beside her.

"Yeah, but I think I turned my ankle," said B. A., unlacing and removing her left shoe. "I think I'll sit out the next game. It should be easy to get a sub with all the extra guys around."

"Butch's sister is a real hacking machine," observed Rod. "I was going to tell him to calm her down, but I didn't think you would like that so I kept quiet. It looks like Victor is talking to him now. He's probably telling him that her style is not our style."

"My ankle feels pretty bad. I don't think I should play anymore today. I'll just sit and watch."

Rod looked at her ankle and didn't see any noticeable swelling. He wasn't sure what he could do to fix the situation so he didn't push it. His team recruited a sub from one of the other courts, and the play continued.

Kay kept up her chatter and was extremely annoying. The guys went easy on her, since otherwise it would look like they were retaliating for her rough play towards B. A. They played three more games, with Rod's team taking two of them. Kay was hollering that they should play a fifth to see who would be winners for the day. Butch put a stop to her complaining as he ushered her into his car. The guys thought he was acting a little strange, and they voiced their opinions as they picked up their stuff.

Rod helped B. A. back to her truck and helped her climb into the passenger side. He didn't think she would want to operate the clutch with a bad ankle.

"I'm sorry I didn't step in and say something before you hurt your ankle," he said as they pulled out of the parking lot.

"I can take care of myself," she responded, looking out the window. "I've played rougher people than her. It was just a freak thing. I started to go down, and my foot just sort of rolled over. It'll be okay in a couple of days."

"I wonder why Butch brought his sister along?" asked Rod. "I heard she was all-conference where she goes to school in Arlington, but without all that rough stuff, she looked like an LBA player to me."

"LBA. What's that? Ladies Basketball Association?"

"No, Limited Basketball Ability," said Rod. "You see it more and more all over the place. Guys and girls don't have the skills to play really well, so they try to make up for it by fudging on the rules or pushing everyone around. If the officials let them, they will hold you on defense or push off on offense. They're just trying to make up for their deficiencies. A player with good fundamentals can usually find a way to beat them, though. You're definitely good enough to straighten somebody like Kay McCoy out. You're an awesome rebounder, and all those jump hooks and fade-aways you shoot are hard to defend. She doesn't have any of those skills. How come you didn't give it back to her or at least call some of the fouls? We would have backed you up. Heck, even Butch would have been on your side. Did you see the look on his face? I don't think his little sister will be back anytime soon."

"I know what you mean," said B. A., sensing the fire and competitiveness in Rod's voice. "I just didn't think it was worth it today. Maybe next time."

Rod was confused by her answer but decided to drop it. He drove for a couple of miles before saying anything. He finally looked over to ask her about stopping for a couple of sodas at their regular place, but he just kept on driving. She appeared to be sound asleep.

• ◆ •

B. A. was in her half-awake, half-asleep zone. She was dreaming that she was back in Arkansas at a summer three-on-three tournament. Tank and Riley had asked her to go to Jonesboro to watch Riley play. Darcy Turner, Riley's girlfriend at the time, was with them. B. A. was sitting courtside with Darcy watching Riley and his teammates, who were way up on their opponents. Tank had disappeared earlier saying something about seeing somebody he knew. Annie felt a tap on her shoulder. She turned to see Tank standing behind her with an odd look on his face.

"Uh, Annie, can I talk to you for a minute?"

"What's up?" asked Annie.

He put his big paw out to help her up. She took it, and they walked away from the noise so they could talk at a normal volume.

"I kinda offered your services over at the girls' courts," said Tank without looking directly at her.

Annie just stared at him with folded arms waiting for him to continue. He had the look of a little boy who got caught telling a fib.

"Look, it wasn't my fault. I was tricked into it. Smoke Radford is over there coaching his sister's team, and they are getting killed. It's not just the score. The other team is playing real dirty, and the court monitors are letting them get away with it. Anyway, I played in a couple of football all-star games with Smoke, and he's a real nice guy. He and Riley are probably two of the best quarterbacks in the whole state. Anyway, I sorta let it slip that I knew someone who could help his sister's team out. I told him you could beat those other chicks all by yourself. I know I shouldn't have done it without asking you first. But you should see those cocky girls. You could eat them up. I know you could."

"Nice try, Tank. Even if I said I'd play, I couldn't. You have to turn in your roster before the tournament begins. If you're not on the roster from the beginning, then you can't play. So please don't go volunteering my services again without asking. I know you meant well, but this isn't even basketball. The only thing different from this and football is the shape of the ball."

"Okay, I'm sorry. Let's just go over and watch. I want you to meet Smoke. He's a pretty cool guy, for a quarterback."

Annie and Tank walked over to the girls' court where the last game of the winner's bracket was being played. They only saw the last couple of points. It was just like Tank said, rough and dirty. Smoke's team lost to the Nasty Girls. The name was appropriate. Annie turned away as the winning team walked by. There were four of them—three starters and a sub. She recognized the sub.

"Where did you say that team was from?" she asked Tank.

"I didn't. But I think they're from Jonesboro, like Smoke's team."

"Well, there's one girl that isn't from Jonesboro. She's from Charles City. I'm not surprised they recruited her. She's pretty nasty in her own right."

Smoke walked over to the two from Jones Ferry, and Tank introduced him to Annie.

"Is this the girl with the cape?" he asked Tank. "From the way you described her, I thought she would be about seven feet tall."

"Tank's imagination is almost as big as he is," said Annie. "I wish I could help, but the rules say you can't add extra players after the games start."

"That's true in official tournaments," said Riley. "This one isn't sanctioned. It's an athletic fundraiser. If a team is down to only two players because of an injury or heat exhaustion, you can add another player. The only catch is the other team has to agree on the player. That's in case you try to bring in a ringer. Tank says you are only going to be a sophomore and played on your school's fresh-soph team last year, so I don't think they will object. What do you say? We sure could use you. We're down to three players, and we've got a girl with a bad foot. She really shouldn't be playing."

Annie couldn't believe that Tank had tricked her. He knew about that rule all along. He steered her over here knowing she might say something stupid like, "I wish I could help." She needed a graceful way to bow out without looking like a wimp and without making Tank look bad. So far she was coming up empty. Smoke turned and looked over his shoulder. The next game was about to start.

"Tell you what," said Smoke. "If we win this next game, which would be a long shot, we'll be winners of the losers' bracket. Then we would have to play the Nasty Girls again. Are you with us?"

Annie didn't know what to say. She watched Smoke's sister walk out on to the court. She looked dead on her feet. There appeared to be no way they could win another game.

"Okay," she said. She didn't know why she said it. Maybe it was because they looked so beat, and it would take a semi-miracle for them to win another game. Down deep she knew there was another reason. The girl from Charles City! She didn't even know what her name was, but she recognized her face. She didn't play against her in basketball, because the other girl played varsity, and Annie was a freshman playing on the fresh/soph squad. But watching her and her teammates from the sidelines was enough to get you going. Annie did remember her throwing her bat after Annie had struck her out for the third time a couple of months ago, in a varsity softball game. She probably didn't like a freshman getting the best of her.

"If it comes to it," hollered Tank, "Tell them her name is Barbara Smith."

"Aren't you the sly one," said Annie. "I can't believe I let you trick me into this. You owe me one, big time, even if I don't play."

"Seniors tricking sophomores goes back to the dawn of history," said Tank proudly.

Riley and Darcy walked up.

"Can you believe it?" said Riley. "We were ahead 14 to 11 when some little punk hits two long two-pointers in a row and beats us. What's going on here?"

"Annie's going to put on an exhibition if the High Flyers win," said Tank.

"They don't have much of a chance," said Annie. "We might as well get ready to go."

"Let's watch a few points," said Riley trying to figure out how Annie could play if she wasn't on the team's roster.

As the four watched, Tank explained about the rule saying that if you didn't have enough players to continue and the other team agreed, you could add someone to your roster. Both teams looked very sloppy. Annie had forgotten that the other team had been moving up through the loser's bracket and had played more games than Smoke's team. Shots from behind the two-point line seemed to be the strategy on both sides. It didn't take much energy to take one dribble and heave up a two-pointer. When Smoke's team went up 11 to 7, Annie started stretching. At 13 to 10 she told Tank to go buy her a tournament T-shirt if she gave him the signal. She was wearing her favorite Detroit Tigers jersey, and she didn't want to ruin it. Her dad had brought it back from a concert he did in Detroit. Tank stood in front of the T-shirt vendor waiting for the thumbs-up signal. The game looked to be over, but Annie still didn't give him the go-ahead signal. Smoke was talking to the court monitor and the captain of the Nasty Girls. The captain of the Nasty Girls had no problem if the High Flyers wanted to add an incoming sophomore to their roster. They felt they were obviously the best team there, and they didn't want to win by forfeit. Actually, the other team members tried to talk her into taking the forfeit, but she convinced them it wouldn't take long to crush the High Flyers one more time. Tank got his signal and purchased the shirt.

Riley, Tank, and Darcy stood around Annie in a tight circle facing out, as Annie changed shirts. She didn't have her basketball shoes, her basketball shorts, or her sports bra, but Annie was the type who kept her word when she gave it. What had Tank gotten her in to?

Smoke introduced Annie to his sister, Ashley, and to the other player, Brooke. The third member of the High Flyers was sitting in a chair with her leg up, rubbing her sore foot. The mobile DJ who was making the announcements and providing the entertainment announced that the high school girls' championship game was about to begin. Immediately a large crowd surrounded the court.

Annie was the freshest girl on the court, so she had the advantage, and she decided to use it immediately. She scored the first basket after beating her girl off the dribble. A minute later she had an open jumper and was hammered to the ground. She called the foul and got up a little shaken. She looked over at Riley and Tank. They both gave her the thumbs-up sign. She actually liked the contact that came with a somewhat normal basketball game. She was used to getting hacked by opponents. Her leaping ability and long arms made her a nontraditional forward. At 5' 8" she didn't look very impressive until she went through her assortment of moves. She scored most of her baskets from twelve feet and in, often against a much taller player guarding her. Her fade-aways and jump hooks with either hand were almost unstoppable, unless you double-teamed her. She liked aggressive play but not cheap shots. The court monitor could have stepped in and called a flagrant foul, but she didn't say a thing. The adrenaline started to flow.

The opponents concentrated on Annie and fouled her every time she took a shot. The Charles City girl must have told them about her 33-point performance that single-handedly destroyed their fresh-soph team last winter. Annie never called another foul and scored over three-fourths of her team's points. She also never failed to get a rebound that came to her side of the basket. It was a struggle, but the High Flyers won by three. She was glad it was over. One knee was scraped up, and she was sore all over. She also had a small cut on her elbow that Riley had to minister to. What a bunch of poor sports those Nasty Girls were! She walked over to her friends and took the water bottle that was handed to her. She was about to take a big gulp when she heard the announcer say there would be a ten-minute break before the championship game started. That's when it hit her. This was a double elimination tournament. They still had one more game to play. Each team now had one loss. There was no way they could last another game with those girls. Her teammates could barely move. Riley saw the surprised look on her face. He sent Tank to the first aid station for more supplies and Darcy for more water. He then took Annie by the arm and steered her away from the crowd.

"How are you feeling, champ?" asked Riley.

"Not like a champ, I can tell you that," she answered. "This isn't as much fun as I thought it would be. There's no way we can survive another game, let alone win it. I'd just as soon go home."

"I can't believe I'm hearing this! This is right up your alley."

"What, playing dirty and cheating?'

"Listen, sport," said Riley taking her by the shoulders. "I probably shouldn't tell you this, but who does everyone say is the best basketball player to play at Jones Ferry for the past twenty years or so?"

"You," said Annie with her eyes cast downward.

"Yeah, well who do you think my coach says has the opportunity to be the best ballplayer to ever put on a JF uniform? I'll give you a hint, it's not someone with hairy legs and a deep voice. It's you. He says you're a textbook rebounder and a phenomenal scorer. And he says you see the big picture better than any high school player he has ever seen. He told me all that after watching you play only a couple of games as a freshman. He says you are the real deal, whatever that means. I don't think you realize how good you really are, or could be. You're not cocky enough. I don't mean on the outside, but on the inside, in your mind. You need to feel like you can do anything out on the court. You know, like when you were pitching."

"I understand what you are saying, sort of. But why are you telling me all this now, at a stupid three-on-three brawl?"

"Because it's time for you to turn it up a notch—right here, and right now. There was a reason you agreed to play, and it wasn't because Tank tricked you. He's not smart enough to do that. Don't tell him I said that. It's time to make the jump from real good to great. You've got it in you. You're tougher than these girls, and I think you agreed to play to get a shot at them—to test yourself. Listen, it's not how much you can dish out that makes you tough, it's how much you can take and not let it throw you off your game."

"What do you want me to do?" asked Annie with tearful eyes. Riley was finally getting to her.

"You see those little girls over there?" asked Riley pointing to a handful of elementary girls sitting courtside. "You need to go out there and show them that your style of play is the best style. Don't let them think that even for a minute that dirty play and bad attitudes is the way to go. They're going to imitate the style of the team that wins this game. Kids are always like that. You can bet on it. So here's what you need to do…"

* ◆ *

The High Flyers had the ball first. Ashley threw the ball in to Annie, who took two quick dribbles toward the right baseline. She leaned into the defender as soon as she was half a step by her, which made it hard to establish good guarding position. Annie was an expert at leaning into anyone who was guarding her. She hit the brakes and jumped back, attempting a fade-away shot. Her defender almost caught up to her. Annie felt her elbow get hit and then she was knocked to the ground as the Nasty Girl ran into her. The shot fell short, but a fired-up Annie Smith bounced up off the ground, got her own rebound and banked it back in. The rest of the players relaxed, thinking the court monitor would call a foul that was so obvious. Just like Annie, she wasn't going to call any fouls either. Like Riley said, it was not how much you could dish out; it was how much you could take and still maintain your game. And Annie had plenty of game to throw at them. With her team leading 11 to 10, she tossed in a soft jump hook from the right baseline. At 12 to 10, she duplicated the shot from the other side, with her left hand. The crowd whistled their approval. The High Flyers were two points away from victory and Annie had scored all their points. Her teammates didn't seem to mind as they voiced their support. The Nasty Girls took a time-out.

"Who is that girl?" asked the team captain as they stood in a circle. "She can't be a high school sophomore, like they said. I think we should protest this game. It looks like they brought in a college ringer."

"You're the one who agreed to let her play, stupid," said one of her teammates.

"And she *is* going to be a sophomore," added the Charles City girl. "She's a real good softball player too. Haven't you ever heard of "Fast Annie Smith," the pitcher from the Franklin co-op team? Well, that's her in the flesh. You've got to give her credit. That chick can play."

"If she thought this game was rough before, she ain't seen nothing yet," said the captain. "The next time she gets the ball, we double-team her and hammer her hard. This game isn't over. One player isn't going to do this to us. This is embarrassing."

The Nasty Girls came out and scored, making the score 13 to 11. Then they stole a pass intended for Annie and scored again. They were high-fiving and celebrating as if they had already won. On the next play, Annie was double-teamed, so Ashley took a shot and missed. The Nasty Girls tied it up with a quick basket. Annie looked over at Riley, who gave her a clenched fist and hollered something she couldn't hear. The crowd was going crazy. The Charles City girl was guarding her with a firm arm in front of her, holding her back. Annie pushed the arm down and went to meet the ball. She caught the pass and dribbled hard toward the basket with her left hand. Six feet short of the hoop she stooped sharply and went into a crouch. She hesitated for a second, pump faked, and then jumped with all her strength. The hesitation gave a second defender enough time to leave her girl so she could double-team Annie. The second girl had a running start and was just as high up as Annie. Annie knew she couldn't get her shot off, so when she reached the top of her leap, she held on to the ball. Just before her feet hit the ground on the way down, she bounced the ball behind her back to a startled Ashley Radford. Ashley was standing wide open with her toes just behind the two-point line. She caught the pass and let it fly—a bit too hard. The ball cleared the back of the rim, hit the board, and came back through the basket. It was an unintentional bank shot, but it still counted for two. High Flyers win! The Nasty Girls were totally shocked. Annie looked at the handful of cheering elementary girls and winked at them. She wasn't much for celebrations. The crowd spilled onto the court and congratulated the High Flyers.

"Say your good-byes," hollered Tank as he grabbed Annie by the arm. "We gotta go. I've got chores to do."

Annie thanked the High Flyers for letting her play and was hustled off by her three friends. She didn't stay for the winning team's picture, which was just fine with her. As they were getting into Tank's car, a little girl came running up behind them.

"Hey wait," shouted the girl.

"Hey yourself," said Annie turning to face the fifth-grader. "What's your name?"

"Penny."

"Well, Penny, my friends are sort of in a hurry. What can I do for you?"

Penny shuffled her feet and looked down at the ground.

"Could I, you know. Could I have an autograph?"

"Hey, Tank," hollered Riley from the backseat. "The kid wants an autograph. You're the biggest human being she's ever seen."

"Funny," said Tank, looking for something Annie could sign. He found a piece of paper and a pen and handed them out the window to Annie.

Annie knew just what to sign—"Penny, play hard and play fair, A. Smith." She handed it to the girl and jumped into the front seat with Tank. A few miles up the road, Tank started looking around frantically.

"Oh no," he hollered. "That sheet of paper that Annie signed was a list of stuff I was supposed to pick up on my way home. My mom is going to be ticked."

"Way to go, Annie," laughed Riley. "Your first autograph and it's on a shopping list. That should be very valuable someday. This girl is on her way to legendary status."

Riley's prophecy turned out to be more accurate than even he would realize.

• ◆ •

B. A. looked over to say something to Tank and saw Rod smiling at her. She couldn't believe that they were already home and sitting in her driveway. A feeling came across her that she hadn't had in a while. It was a mixture of anxiety and frustration. There was only one way to get rid of it, and playing basketball or lifting weights wouldn't do.

"Would you consider doing me a big favor?" she asked Rod in a timid voice.

"Sure," said Rod even before he knew what the favor was.

"Are you busy right now?"

"Now is good. What am I getting in to? It's not against the law is it? I'm still on probation. Hard jail time would set my college education back some."

He was obviously trying to cheer her up, given the events at the game. She just shook her head and rolled her eyes. She liked his sense of humor. It was on the dry side, but there was usually a lot of thought behind it.

"It will only take about half an hour," she explained. "You go home. I need to get some stuff, and I'll be right over."

"Okay," said Rod, wondering why she was acting so mysterious. He walked out to the street where his car was parked and headed home.

• ◆ •

Rod was straightening the garage up when he heard B. A.'s truck pull up. He finished up the sweeping and was headed for the door when she came hustling through with a big smile on her face. This was a definite change from her demeanor earlier in the day. He decided he liked the bubbly side of her personality more than the frustrated, quiet side. She went over to the rubber band that was attached to the wall and began to pull on it. He sat on a bench and watched her.

"What's this all about?" asked Rod. "And what is that exercise for? You do it all the time, and I can't figure out why. It doesn't have anything to do with basketball unless you're going to throw the ball underhand."

"Come on outside, and I'll show you," said B. A.

They walked out to the area between Rod's garage and the neighbor's garage. The area was only about twenty feet wide. You could barely see the house through all the shade trees in the back yard. Directly across the alley in the other direction was another three-car garage that blocked the view of the house in front of it. The only way you could see what anyone was doing between the garages was to be standing in the alley right behind them. It was perfect for B. A.'s needs. Rod looked at her and shrugged his shoulders. She pointed toward an upturned five-gallon bucket sitting on the ground. On the bucket were a catcher's mitt, a mask, and a red bandanna. In front of the bucket was a home plate. Rod kicked at it and started to pick it up.

"Leave it there," she said. "It's right where it's supposed to be."

"Hey, this is a real plate. Where did you get it?"

"It was given to me."

"Okay, what's the bit?" asked Rod picking up the mitt and trying it on. "Do you want me to help you become a pitcher? I gotta tell you, I don't know much about pitching a softball. I don't think I've ever even played softball."

"I just want to play catch for a while if it's all right with you. Then, if my ankle feels okay, I'll pitch you a few."

"Sure," said Rod. "Let me get the radio."

"No country, please, and not too loud. I don't want anyone to sneak up on us."

Rod found a classic rock station that was currently playing a J. Geils song. He thought this whole situation rather odd. He and B. A. talked a lot about sports, but softball rarely came up. He knew that she played and that she was an outfielder, but that was all. He had played first base on the high school baseball team. He couldn't remember the last time he played catch with someone. They threw the ball back and forth for about five minutes. He marveled at her throwing motion. It was fluid and she had a perfect wrist snap. She also looked at him over her left shoulder as she threw, like someone who knew what she was doing. If you don't turn your upper body and look over your shoulder before going into the throwing motion, it looks weak and inefficient. People who threw without turning were often said to "throw like a girl." Well, B. A. certainly didn't throw that way. Her last two throws had a lot of velocity. Harder than he thought a girl could throw.

B. A. stopped and looked at the plate in front of him and then kicked at something in the grass as though she were lining it up. The grass was high enough so he didn't see it at first. He finally recognized it. It was a pitching rubber. When she was done adjusting it, she motioned for him to sit on the bucket.

"I didn't know if you could crouch on your bad knee, so I brought the bucket. Put the mask on too, please."

"I don't need the mask. What's the bandanna for?"

"You don't need it yet. Mask please."

Rod put the mask on. She threw the first four pitches overhand. She didn't know why she always did this. It was a habit she had gotten into when she first started pitching to her dad. Maybe she wanted to show him she was capable of pitching overhand as well as underhand. Anyway, it was now a tradition that she stuck with. Each successive pitch was thrown harder than the one before. Rod was impressed. She could pitch for the guys' team. Then she switched and started to throw underhand. Nothing fancy, just smooth fastballs, about three-quarter speed. After ten pitches, the big guy called for "time" and put the bandanna inside the mitt for more cushion. B. A. counted her pitches and was only going to throw about thirty. She hadn't thrown for a while and didn't want to overdo it. Her timing and control were excellent. As always, she got an adrenaline rush after the first few fastballs. She loved everything about pitching. It also brought back memories of spending quality time with her dad. At thirty, she decided ten more wouldn't hurt. The last ten approached game velocity. Rod was in awe behind the plate. After the first few pitches he didn't say much. Each pitch deserved his utmost concentration. After number forty she waved that she was done. Rod came up holding the mask in one hand.

"Who are you, and how much did that bionic arm cost? When my pesky cousin finds out about this, she's going to be psyched."

"I'd just as soon keep this between you and me," said B. A. "I'm not sure I want to pitch anywhere else just yet. I just like to throw every once in a while. You don't mind catching for me do you?"

"No, I don't mind. I'll catch anytime you want. Why do you want to keep this a secret? You're a whole lot faster than any softball pitcher I've ever seen. I couldn't believe the way you spotted your pitches. You threw one down the middle and the next four moved about two inches farther outside than the one before it. How fast were you throwing, anyway?"

"Somewhere in the mid sixties, I guess."

"Is that the fastest you've ever thrown?"

"No, I had a little more in me, but I just wanted to tease you and not show you the good stuff right away."

"I can't believe you want to keep this quiet. You would be the talk of the whole Dallas–Fort Worth area—maybe the whole state. I love the way you made a couple of them rise. I never saw a baseball do that."

"That's exactly why I want to keep quiet about it. I just want to be an average high school kid. There's nothing wrong with that, is there?"

"Look, B. A.," said Rod, draping his arm across her shoulders. "Average is something you will never be. Some people aren't meant to be average. Look at me. I've stood out ever since I was in sixth grade because of my size. I'll always stand out in a crowd unless I'm standing next to a bunch of NBA players. I had to learn to live with it. Tall and handsome is what I'll always be, and short and cute is what you will always be. We might as well resign ourselves to that fact."

"I'm not that short," she said elbowing him in the ribs. "C'mon, handsome, I'll buy you a soda for the compliment and for being so nice to me."

"I can't imagine anyone not being nice to you."

"Well, son," she said with an exaggerated Southern drawl. "That's because you haven't been around. You're just a small-town Texas boy who doesn't know the ways of the real world yet."

Rod knew she was just kidding, and he enjoyed it. Still, there was something about what she said that he would bring up at a later date—when he knew her better.

* ◆ *

They sat on Rod's front porch swing, drinking sodas and watching the sun set to their left. Rod liked sitting close to her. He wondered where this was leading.

"There is one more favor I'd like to ask," said B. A., leaning on his shoulder. "When we're together, just you and me. You know, just hanging out and doing stuff."

"Okay."

"Would you call me Annie?"

"Why Annie?"

"Because it's my name," she said, trying to make herself more comfortable on his muscular shoulder.

* ◆ *

Later that night, as B. A. was getting ready for bed, she received a phone call. Butch McCoy was on the other end, and he was very apologetic. He explained that he never approved of the way his sister played, and that she needed to be taught a lesson. That was the reason he brought her to the Sunday afternoon game, so she could see how B. A. played the game. He thought the idea was a good one until the game started and the whole thing backfired. Butch told B. A. that he lectured his sister all the way home. Anyway, he was sorry that she was treated so roughly and hoped that she wasn't mad at him. He also said that his sister wouldn't be coming back until she changed her attitude.

After assuring Butch that she was all right and wasn't mad at him, B. A. closed her phone. She wasn't sure this was what she had had in mind when she pictured her new "normal" life. She didn't waste too much time reflecting on it. She was asleep moments after her head hit the pillow.

Chapter 5

Future Stars

C hip sat at the kitchen table watching her mom make supper. She was explaining her witness relocation theory in detail. Mrs. Fullerton didn't look anything like Chip. She had black hair that was usually put up out of the way. She was only five feet tall with a stocky frame. Her most discernible feature was her constant smile. She always seemed to be happy and tended to look at the bright side of things. Chip looked more like her dad but acted more like her mom. It was as if they had each given her their best qualities at birth. As usual, Chip was talking at a speed that would leave the average listener in the dust. When she was in this mode, only her mom could understand her, but even she often had trouble too.

"Slow down, child," said her mom. "You're starting to babble. I thought you had outgrown that."

"But mom, I really think we're on to something big here. Besides, I need something to keep me interested until basketball season starts. Our volleyball season is already in the tank. It's just not any fun. It would be a lot better if that snotty Tammi Olsen and her disciples came down with some kind of rare disease—eventually curable, of course."

Her mom looked at her with raised eyebrows.

"Why do you always have a problem with her? You two have been feuding since sixth grade. Is she really that bad?"

"Mom, she walks around school like she is some kind of sports celebrity. The only thing she can do is pitch. She's just fair in the other two sports. Her twin, Jenny, is a lot better in volleyball and basketball. It's too bad Jenny doesn't stand up to her bossy sister. When I signal the play in volleyball, you know, what fingers I'm showing behind my back? That's how I tell them who I am going to set. Well, it gets confusing because Tammi thinks I should be setting her most of the time, so she will holler out numbers and do all sorts of weird stuff to try to get her way. The coach has talked to her about it, but she won't change. I think the coach should just bench her until she shapes up. That's what I would do. Can you believe it?"

"Are you sure there isn't just a little jealousy in that reasoning?"

"Me? Jealous of her! No way. Mom, you know my attitude has always been pretty good. I mean, I don't complain, except to you, but that's just normal mother/daughter talk, right? Parents have to listen when their kids vent. It's in their contract. In practice and in games I keep my mouth shut, most of the time, and I do my job. Man, I wish this B. A. would turn out to be a good basketball and softball player. I need someone on my side for once besides Jenny. Did I tell you how hard B. A. can throw a ball?"

"More than once," said Mrs. Fullerton, looking out the window. "Here comes Luke. I better set another plate. That boy's always hungry. But we have to wait until your dad gets home. You know how he likes us all to eat together."

"Luke's coming over to plan our next step to uncover the B. A. mystery—if that's her real name. I hope we don't come up with something weird or illegal. I really like her."

Luke knocked on the back door and entered when Chip waved him in.

"Hi, Mrs. F.," he said, trying to sniff out supper's main dish. "That sure smells good."

"We won't be eating for another fifteen minutes, Luke," said Mrs. Fullerton. "Think you can wait that long?"

"Sure. I had a little snack on the way over."

"Will you forget your stomach for once," said an anxious Chip. "We've got work to do. I know you haven't dug up anything lately, so here's what I have. She goes somewhere with Rod every Sunday at about two o'clock. When I asked him about it, he said if B. A. wanted me to know she would tell me. That sounds like something a parent would say, huh, Mom?"

Mrs. Fullerton just snickered and nodded her head.

"I suppose this is hilarious to you, but this is serious stuff. She could be into something real diabetical."

"I think you mean, diabolical," said Luke.

"Whatever, Mom knew what I meant."

The two sleuths put their heads together and talked in low whispers until Mr. Fullerton arrived. The talk around the supper table continued to be about the new girl and what her situation was. The Fullerton parents were quite amused about how serious the two teens were about their far-fetched theories. Neither of them had even seen the girl in question, but they figured she must be something special to draw so much attention.

Chip's dad added fuel to the fire by throwing out some weird ideas of his own.

"Just for conversation's sake," he volunteered. "What if she's an FBI undercover agent sent here to investigate high school kids that are trying to overthrow the U.S. government?"

"I doubt that, Dad," said Chip, somewhat seriously. "We've got it too good here. Why would we want to upset a system that lets us play video games until three a.m., then show up at school and sleep in class?"

"I hope there aren't too many parents and teachers who let their kids get away with that," said Mrs. Fullerton.

"More than you know, Mom," said Chip as she and Luke headed for the living room to do their homework and continue their brainstorming. They decided that after their homework was done they would drive by the Smith house just to see if there were any new developments. Their timing couldn't have been better. They were fifty yards from B. A.'s house when two men with hair down past their shoulders got out of a van and went up to the front door. B. A. came to the door and let them in.

"Smokes, did you see that?" asked Luke. "Who were those guys? Undercover agents or even worse, mafia guys."

"They weren't from Reston, I can tell you that," whispered Chip. "Pull over. Let's see how long they stay. Maybe B. A. is in trouble, and we should call the cops. No, let's just sit tight and see if she tries to signal a passerby. Then we can call the cops and save the day."

Normally, when Luke heard this sort of reasoning, he would offer up a logical argument, but he just sat there looking at the house, with all sorts of scenarios running through his head.

The light came on in B. A.'s room. The two detectives looked for clues in the shadows but couldn't make out what was going on inside. They sat and waited for something that would give them a clue to the events that were unfolding. Mrs. Smith pulled into the drive around 10:15 and went in through the back door. The two supersleuths didn't have an opinion on this new development. They didn't see one of the men come back out to the van to get something, and they didn't see B. A.'s mom come home. The truth is—they were both fast asleep.

Chip opened her eyes when she heard tapping on the passenger side window. Someone was shining a flashlight into her eyes. She looked over at Luke, who was just opening his eyes.

"Luke, wake up. You fell asleep. The government guys are trying to get in."

The flashlight moved around the front of the car and shone through the driver's window. "It's just Officer Rubio," said Luke. "And I think we're in big trouble. Look at the time. It's after midnight."

After explaining to the officer that they were doing an assignment for school and just fell asleep, they promised to go straight home. They drove up the block past the van that was still parked in front of the house. Officer Rubio didn't believe them for a minute. No way those two were doing a school project. However, it was rather strange that they were just sitting in a residential area and not at one of the usual make-out locations. He had immediately checked out the prime spots after receiving a phone call from Chip's dad. When he came up empty, he was starting to get worried, until he spotted Luke's unmistakable vehicle sitting by the curb.

• ◈ •

"What happened to you last night after you got home?" asked Chip during algebra the next day. "I got hollered at and grounded for a week. Sometimes my parents have no sense of humor. I explained it to them, but they weren't very understanding."

"Nothing happened to me," answered Luke. "Everyone was asleep when I got home."

"That's not fair," whispered Chip. "You big goof. Why did you fall asleep? It's your fault I got in trouble."

Luke seemed to be ignoring her as he stared into his algebra book.

"I'm talking to you, sleepy boy. Aren't you listening?"

"I'm listening, Ms. Fullerton," said the teacher standing behind Chip. "Why don't you head up to the board and solve the next problem for us?"

"Oh man," said Chip, "busted again." She scowled at Luke and headed toward the board.

•◆•

B. A. was watching TV and trying to study when she heard a van pull up in front of the house. She looked through the window and was surprised to see two long-haired freaky types walking toward the house. When they got closer she recognized one of them and threw the front door open.

"Desert Jack Murphy, what are you doing in Texas?" she exclaimed.

"Hot dog, look how big you are, Annie girl," said Desert Jack as he jumped through the door and gave Annie a big hug. "Hey, this is Bing Sweeney, the new bass player for the band. He wanted to meet the daughter of the great Jimmy Smith. Is your mom home?"

"No, but she will be in a couple of hours."

She led the two musicians into the kitchen. They sat around the kitchen table talking about old times as they waited for Martha to get home from work. The rest of the band was going to meet them in Austin for a gig the following night. B. A. asked how Billy Burton was doing. Billy had been her dad's best friend. He and her dad were the founding members of Gambler's Folley. Billy had taken it real hard when her father died. He moved over to play lead guitar, and Bing was brought in to play bass. Billy was also the lead singer, although all the guys in the band sang at one time or another. One thing Billy wouldn't, or couldn't, do since Jimmy's death was sing "The Gambler's Run." It was the band's theme song and the number that really brought down the house. Jack told B. A. that the rest of the band members wouldn't even mention the song around Billy because he would get all misty-eyed and had trouble keeping it together. The song was always a mystery to B. A. and when she had asked her dad about it, he would always tell her that he would explain it to her someday. That someday never came. She almost asked Jack about it right then, but she decided it wasn't the right time. Someday she would get to the bottom of the history of that particular song. The strange thing about it was it was still growing at the time of her father's untimely death. It was still getting longer, with new verses being added. The original length was about five minutes long, but the last time they played it, it was a little over twelve minutes. It was a mystery to her.

B. A. knew why the guys had come. They wanted to look into the contents of a box she had hidden in her closet. She had written to Jack about it when she found out she was moving to Texas and had invited him to come down so they could go through it together. She went to her room and brought it back to the kitchen. It was full of songs that Jimmy Smith had written or was in the process of writing. Some were for his band and some were written with other musicians in mind. In the margin of two half-written numbers was a note that read, "Show this to Robin." Her dad looked up to Robin Trower and told her more than once that he wished he could play guitar half as well as Robin. After half an hour of sifting and sorting through all the sheets and notes, Jack went out to the van and brought back his guitar. B. A. went to her room and brought her bass back for Bing. For the next two hours, they played what was written and did some improvising on Jimmy's music. B. A. loved it. Bing even showed her a couple of ways to improve her own bass playing. It was like when she was little, and the guys would come over and just jam for hours. Jack and Bing picked out four songs that they really liked. They were taking a break when Martha Smith walked through the back door.

"Oh no," she hollered. "Long-haired rockers, right here in my kitchen, corrupting my daughter."

Jack jumped up and gave her a big bear hug. Around midnight B. A. hugged her mom, the new band member, and the old one, and went off to bed. On her way down the hall, she heard her mom ask Jack whether he was still thinking about marrying the girl he had been seeing a couple of years ago. His response was something B. A. had heard the other band members say, including her dad.

"I didn't have a gambler's chance of ever marrying her," answered Jack.

Martha sat and reminisced with the guys for another two hours. She offered to put them up for the night. They politely refused, figuring they'd drive about halfway to Austin before stopping. Besides, two a.m. wasn't all that late for musicians.

As she lay in bed, B. A. thought about what Jack had just said. The band members, including her dad, were always saying stuff like, "only the gambler knows," or "you need the luck of the gambler to pull that off. " It was as if this gambler they referred to was a real person and not just a character in a song. Her last thoughts, before she drifted off to sleep, were about getting to the bottom of the whole gambler thing— the sayings and the song. Little did she know that two of her classmates were just down the block dreaming of solving their own mystery.

● ◆ ●

Basketball season was only a few weeks away, and B. A. was anxious to start practicing. She was running a lot, and she was in excellent shape. She ran some long distance, but most of the time she ran sprints, as you would in a game. Her Sunday afternoon games with Rod and the guys helped her to work on her skills. She felt she was ready to see how she fit in with her new teammates. On one of her frequent after-school runs, she saw some junior high girls playing three-on-three at a court in the middle of town. She stopped to watch for a few minutes. Their fundamentals were awful, and they seemed to have no idea of what they should be doing. There was a collision between the dribbler and the girl guarding her, so they asked her who the foul was on. This was her chance to set them straight on some basic fundamentals.

She walked onto the court and called for the ball. She asked them if she could show them a few things, and they readily said, "Yes." She showed them how to dribble the ball—a crossover without palming the ball—and how to dribble low in traffic—an efficient behind-the-back dribble that wasn't just for looks. Then they asked her to demonstrate some shots for them. She started with a simple layup from both sides. Then she did running bank shots from about five feet, right and left-handed, followed by hook shots, also with both hands. She ended up with some fade-away jumpers from twelve to fifteen feet from the basket. B. A. had only missed two of her demonstration shots. She could tell that the little girls were impressed, which was exactly what she was trying to do. If they liked what they saw, they would try to copy her. She explained to them that heaving the ball up from the three-point line was not a good way to put points on the board, unless you have shot hundreds of threes and were good at it. Then they asked her to shoot some threes. The future stars looked disappointed when she made only one out of five.

"I've never shot many threes in a game," she explained. "I'm a forward, and I play closer to the basket. Maybe I can get Chip Fullerton to come over and show you her form on the long ones. She's an excellent shooter from out."

One of the girls, who identified herself as Cassie, asked B. A. why she didn't play guard. She said her sister was a forward, and she was a lot taller than B. A. The older girl explained that there was a lot more to playing close to the basket than just standing there holding the ball over your head like some tall girls do. She knew right away that her answer didn't come out quite right and it sounded as though she were making light of tall players. She didn't elaborate, as she didn't want to confuse her audience. Anyway, she said she would stop by again if they wanted her to, and she would show them some more stuff they should be working on. Their response was unanimous. They definitely wanted her to come back and coach them.

Cassie was all excited when she got home and couldn't wait to tell her big sister about how this high school girl had showed them how to play basketball the right way. Actually, she told both her big sisters, Tammi and Jenny. Jenny seemed interested in what Cassie had to say, while Tammi didn't like it at all. She usually didn't pay much attention to Cassie, but she didn't like some stranger showing her the wrong stuff. All tall girls do is just hold the ball above their heads! She was going to have a talk with B. A. and set her straight before things got out of hand.

• ◈ •

B. A. was excited. Basketball practice had finally started. The first week was drills and conditioning, and she loved every minute of it. Even though Coach Todd said some strange things, B. A. decided not to pass judgment on her right away. She was happy just to be playing.

Coach Suzanne Todd was about thirty years old. She was slender five feet eleven inches tall, with long black hair. She liked to bring up her high school and college playing days a lot. Chip had warned B. A. about this. Todd seemed to dwell on the past, like a lot of older athletes do. Their high school and college days were probably the most fun they ever had, and sometimes it was hard to let it go. On the fourth day of practice, the coach stopped a shooting drill to show a couple of players how she wanted them to shoot. B. A. couldn't believe it. The technique she was demonstrating was all wrong. Shooting from chest height inside fifteen feet was an invitation to have the ball slapped back in your face. B. A. figured it out real quick. It wasn't that Coach Todd played an older style of ball—she just wasn't that skilled. The competition that she played against in her playing days probably wasn't very good, which made her and her teammates look a lot better than they actually were. And she didn't even realize it! This could turn out to be a long season.

• ◈ •

B. A. sat alone in the bleachers after Friday's practice and looked at a sheet of paper that Chip had given her. Chip told her to make sure no one else saw the contents of the paper. She also said that Luke agreed with her assessments, so they had to be accurate.

**CONFIDENTIAL. FOR YOUR EYES ONLY.
DESTROY AFTER READING.**

Chip Fullerton—5'4" junior guard—good hands, good dribbler, great outside shooter—strictly a perimeter player who doesn't want to get her hair messed up driving to the hoop, very cute with a dyamanic personality

Kris Ritter—5'4" senior guard—quick, average shooter, no moves, good team player, quiet—plays second base on softball team

Tammi Olsen—5'11" junior forward/center—thinks she is God's gift to basketball and all other sports on this planet and all planets yet to be discovered—weak shot, doesn't jump well, fair hands—can bank it in from two feet (which is probably why she thinks she is soooo good)

Jenny Olsen—5'11" junior forward—awkward shooting motion, can create shots, jumps better than Tammi, willing to work hard, influenced by her toady sister too much, otherwise a nice girl

Missy Springer—5'11" senior center—weak hands, slow, wants to be popular, hangs around Tammi

Juanita Esperanza—5'6" junior guard—doesn't have much—will speak up when provoked

Amanda Brewer—5'5" senior guard—space cadet—otherwise nice

Darby Quinn—5'8" senior forward, Tammi's loyal subject

Monica Sharp (Mony)—5'2" junior guard—nasty mouth, plays dirty, Tammi's friend

Carmen Espinosa—6'2" junior center—no catch, no shot, just big

Rachael Moon—5'9" junior forward—hard-nosed hustler, very quiet

Xiu Lu—5' 6" junior guard—hard worker, has potential if Todd or Harbison would work with her—real shy

B. A. Smith—5'7" junior ????

B. A. smiled at some of Chip's comments. She wasn't sure what "dyamanic" was, but she was sure Chip would explain it if asked. The assessments probably were fairly accurate. She folded the paper up and put it into her bag. She was about to leave when the evening janitor walked into the gym. Old "Pops" was one of those guys whose age you couldn't figure out. He was a slender black man with salt-and-pepper hair, somewhere between fifty and seventy. Most of the students, except for some of the rowdies, liked him. Pops didn't put up with any nonsense, and he called them out if he caught them doing something stupid. He had an upbeat personality and loved to talk trash with anyone who would listen. It was the good kind of trash, where he didn't get too personal—just enough to get a rise out of you. He was quick-witted and usually came out on top when trading barbs with the students or even the high school staff. Rumor had it that Pops was retired from the army or the Marines. He had a tattoo on his shoulder that the students would get a glimpse of on occasion.

"Hey, Smitty girl," said Pops when he saw her getting up from the bleachers. "What are you still doing here?"

B. A. was surprised that he knew her name.

"Just resting after practice, Pops. I'm heading home, unless you want to take me on in a game of 'horse'."

"I'm on for the horse game," said Pops, picking up a ball that the team manager had failed to put away, "but first I want to see you get by me one time."

He tossed the ball to B. A. and assumed a defensive stance at the free throw line.

"I don't know. What if I hurt you? I mean when I slam it on you, you might be standing under the hoop and I might land on you and break a bone or something. Then I'd get into big trouble—not to mention the law suit that would follow."

"You're a cocky young thing, aren't you? I think you're afraid that these old bones can shut you down anytime they want. Come on, little missy. A soda says you can't score on old rickety bones Pops."

B. A. took the ball to the top of the key.

"Now you're talking my language, Pops. One time for a soda."

Pops checked the ball and waited for her at the free-throw line. It looked like he was daring her to shoot from out. B. A. dribbled twice with her left hand to close the gap, then did a quick crossover to her right and drove down the right side of the free-throw lane. Pops was only a half step behind. B. A. figured that he would be a lot quicker than he looked, so she faked the shot. Not an exaggerated fake like a lot of players do, but just a quick head and ball movement. Pops flew by. She did a little step-through and banked it in.

Pops retrieved the ball as it bounced on the floor and tossed it to her.

"You're pretty quick for a girl. And you've got a nice rhythm with the ball. What would you have done if I hadn't gone for the fake?"

"I can usually get my jump hook off against the guys, so that was my backup plan."

Pops gave an approving nod.

"Yeah, you're pretty fast, B. A. Smith. Hey, I like that—'Fast B. A. Smith'. How's that for a nickname?"

B. A. stood with the ball pinned to her hip. She had a peculiar expression on her face as she tried to figure out what Pops was getting at.

"Where are you from, Pops?" she asked.

"Born and raised right here in Texas. Got a lot of relatives, though. I like to visit them when I get the chance."

"Any of these relatives live in Arkansas?" she asked.

"As a matter of fact they do," he responded. "Jonesboro, to be exact. Ever been there?"

"Yeah, I've been there. Didn't like it much. Too crowded for a country girl."

"Well, I think you will like it here in Reston, Smitty. Just be yourself, and everything will work out fine. Give people a chance. A lot of times they're not as bad as they first seem. It looks like you're hanging with the right crowd. Fullerton is a talkative little thing, but she has a good heart and a lot of talent. She's been waiting for you, or someone like you, for a long time. You two should complement each other on the court."

"Thanks for the advice," said B. A. as she headed for the door. "And I think I'll buy you a soda anyway."

"That would be nice," said Pops with a sly grin. The game of "horse" was forgotten.

When Pops showed up for work on Monday, there was a twenty-ounce soda on his work cart with a big ribbon on it.

⁂

B. A. barely made it through practice on Monday. She wasn't feeling very well. She had a sloppy practice and went directly home to bed. Tuesday was even worse. Twenty minutes into practice she told her coaches she was sick and sat in the bleachers. She knew she should have gone home, but Coach Todd was going through the offense, and she didn't want to miss any of it. There was going to be a scrimmage the next day with Arlington High School.

The scrimmage didn't go too well the following day. Chip was the only bright spot. Her quickness and her accurate shooting from the perimeter was the only offense that Reston could muster. Time and time again she would try to run the offense. Most of the time it just broke down, so Chip would improvise just to get them a decent shot. They did put some points on the board, which kept them from being totally humiliated. B. A. never got to see the inside of Arlington's gym. She was home in bed with the flu.

Chip called B. A. when she got home and told her all about it. She also told her about the big argument she got into with Tammi on the bus trip home. Tammi had called her a "ball hog" and that didn't sit too well with the little point guard.

"What did Coach Todd say?" asked B. A. in a weak, raspy voice.

"She told us to shut up and work together as a team," answered Chip. "Real insightful, huh? Do you know anything about voodoo? I've been thinking about making a little doll that looks like Tammi. I wouldn't stick pins in it or anything. That would be cruel and would possibly carry a jail sentence. It might improve her attitude though. I was thinking about putting it in the fridge or setting it in the sun all day, just to see if it had any effect on her. Or, how about this, putting Vaseline on its little hands? No, that wouldn't work because she catches like she's already got slippery hands. Ha. Are you even listening?"

"I'm listening," whispered B. A. "The problem is, though, what if Jenny started getting chills or too hot? She's a carbon copy of her sister, if you don't consider the differences in their attitudes."

"I never thought of that. We'll have to find out if Tammi has any birthmarks or scars that her sister doesn't have. Then we could put them on the doll so the voodoo gods won't be confused. Good idea?"

B. A. chuckled and said good-bye. Chip certainly came up with some strange ideas. She was always entertaining, that was for sure. B. A.

would have been surprised at Chip's next phone call. She called Luke to get an update on his efforts to learn more about B. A.'s past. Luke said he might be on to something, and it might be risky. Saying you were someone else to get information could get you into big trouble.

• ◆ •

A few days later, B. A. was almost fully recovered. It was a beautiful Saturday afternoon, and she was half-walking and half-jogging through town when she passed the little park with the basketball court. Sure enough, the girls she had met the week before were shooting hoops. She stood alongside the court and watched, not saying anything.

"Hey, B. A.," hollered Cassie Olsen. "Will you show us some more of that cool stuff that you showed us last time? I don't think we're doing any of it right."

B. A. called for the ball and did a short version of the dribbling and shooting fundamentals that she had showed them the first time she was there. Then she talked to them about rebounding position and how to hold your ground.

"Just being between your opponent and the basket is only the first step," she explained. "If you're not in a crouched position, it's easy for your opponent to push you off to the side or under the basket. Think of it like pushing a stump or a tree. It's obviously tougher to move a stump because it's closer to the ground. And if you crouch way down, you are not only harder to move out of the way, but you are in a position to put everything in to your jump. And don't put your hands up into the air. They should remain at your sides with your elbows out, until you start your leap. Then you need to throw them up into the air as you jump. It will give you added momentum. Plus, if the ball doesn't come directly to you, and you have to move to get it, you want your arms by your side and not up in the air. It's kinda hard to run around with your hands up in the air, right?"

The girls tried hard to emulate B. A.'s rebounding form. A couple of them weren't bad, but most of them needed a lot of work. At least it was a start. The girls thanked B. A. and told her to come back any time. They said they couldn't wait to see her play on the high school team. Their last comments bothered her. If she continued to play in the backcourt, which was where Coach Todd had her playing, she wouldn't get much of an opportunity to play and do what she did best.

Later that evening, B. A. received the strangest call. It was from Tammi Olsen. Her message was simple—"Stay away from my sister. She doesn't need you putting all sorts of strange ideas in her head."

B. A. couldn't understand why Tammi was so worked up. She had made up her mind to help Jenny become a better player. And Jenny was willing to listen and learn. If Tammi didn't like it, she would just have to live with it. It was obvious that they would probably tangle sometime during the season, so it might as well be sooner than later. It was also obvious that B. A. didn't know that Cassie's last name was Olsen.

Chapter 6

Number One Fan

B. A. pulled up in front of Chip's house and laid on the horn. She had "Stone Blue" by Foghat cued up on her CD player. Since Chip knew very little about music, B. A. had taken it upon herself to educate her. B. A. would play a song and then they would discuss it a while. After that, they would vote to see if it would fit into their "classic rock songs of all time" list. Sometimes the discussions would get pretty intense, but both of them enjoyed it. Chip finally admitted that she was a pawn in the commercialism game that the pop radio stations played. If a station played a song a lot and kept telling everyone the song was a hit, a lot of young people would eventually believe it. When you heard the same song a year later, you couldn't figure out why you liked it in the first place. That's why teens usually want to hear the "new" stuff all the time. The "hit" stations peddled a lot of nonsense that they tried to pass along as good music. And now that Chip was on to them, she was fast becoming a real "rock dog" like B. A.

Classic songs had to meet several criteria before they could be nominated for the list. They had to be of substantial length, have memorable lyrics, and great musicianship. The debates came about when a song was lacking in one or more of the categories but made up for it by being special in the others. Exceptions had to be made for some songs. B. A. had successfully lobbied for *Like a Rolling Stone* by Bob Dylan. She claimed that the lyrics alone put the song in their classic category. Chip finally gave in, but only if B. A. would consider a similar song where the instruments took a back seat to the singing. She really liked "Maggie May," by Rod Stewart. She had an ulterior motive for that song, as her middle name was May. She didn't share this information with B. A., who was surprised that Chip had even heard of the song, let alone liked it.

B. A. was about to hit the horn again when Chip came flying out the front door. Her uniform was over her shoulder, and her gym bag was open, with clothes starting to fall out. On top of that, her shirttail was out, and her hair was a mess.

Good gosh, thought B. A. *This girl is a disaster. She must have been taking a nap or something. Look at that hair. It's like one of those Halloween fright wigs. Two-to-one she drops something before she gets to the truck.*

Her sports bra was just about to hit the ground when Chip saw it and reached down to scoop it up. She grabbed the bra, but she caught her foot on something and down she went. The gym bag cushioned her fall as her uniform flew off her shoulder onto the wet grass. She popped up immediately, stuffing her undergarments back into the bag. The she discovered her uniform lying in the grass. It was now partially soaked, with a little mud on it for effect. B. A. leaned over and opened the passenger door.

"Are you all right?" asked B. A. holding back a snicker.

"I'm okay," she said. "I was taking a nap, and when I heard you honking, I thought we were late. But it looks like we have about forty minutes until the bus leaves."

"I thought we'd stop by the store and get something to drink and a snack," said B. A. "From the looks of you, you could use something. What kind of hairdo do you call that—early cave girl?"

"Real funny," retorted the little guard. "I told you, I was napping and psyching up for the game and didn't have time to put on my makeup, like you."

Both girls laughed at this statement because neither one wore makeup. They agreed that red lips, rosy cheeks, and blue or green eye shadow made you look like a circus clown. Chip dug a hairbrush out of her bag as B. A. put the truck into gear and started down the street.

By the time they arrived at the convenience store, two blocks from school, two things had happened. They decided that "Stone Blue" belonged on their classic rock list and Chip looked like a girl who actually owned a hairbrush. B. A. maneuvered her pickup into a side parking space, and the girls got out. As they rounded the corner of the building, B. A. looked through the window and saw a face from the past. Standing at the counter was Dr. Snyder from Jones Ferry. She gasped, stepped back, and flattened herself against the building, pulling Chip with her.

"What?" hollered Chip in an excited tone. "What did you see in there? Another murder?"

"No," said a pale B. A. "I was just surprised to see that man here in Reston. Let's get out of here. Rats, I need to think. Quick, get in the truck. You drive."

B. A. got in on the passenger side and scrunched down real low.

"This is freaky," said her friend. "I'm not very good with clutches, but I'll give it a shot."

The little guard ground the gears and killed the truck twice before they were back on the road headed out of town. For good measure, she squealed the tires as they left the parking lot.

"You were right about clutches," said B. A. as she sat up. "Do you think he saw us? What is he doing here? Oh man, this is awful. Slow down. You're gonna get a ticket."

Chip had roughly gone through the gears and was doing forty-five in a thirty mph zone.

"I thought he was after you," exclaimed Chip.

"No, he's not after me," said B. A., staring out the passenger window. "He's my old boyfriend, and he's here to find our baby that I gave away."

"What!" hollered Chip as she dropped the right front tire off the road. "A baby? He looked old enough to be your father. Wow, this is weirder than we thought. Luke is not going to believe this."

"Watch the road, goofy. He's a doctor and a good friend of the family. He kinda took a liking to me after my father died."

"So he tried to move in on your mom and you had to come here to get away from him?"

"It's nothing like that. You've got a monster imagination. Dr. Snyder is a happily married man. He's a real sweet guy and a rabid sports fan. And what's this about Luke and being weirder than you thought?"

"Nothing, I was just referring to one of his crazy ideas. You know what he's like. Sometimes it's hard for me to keep him in line. Okay, this doctor is a great guy and a real family man, but we have to figure out why he's here and what he's up to. This is like the mystery books I used to read when I was a kid. You know, where the stranger comes to town and lurks around and then you find out he's from the lottery commission and wants to give someone a check for ten million dollars."

"Earth to Chip," said B. A. as she felt the driver's forehead. "I know why he's here. That's the problem. This could get real embarrassing. Stop the truck, I need to think."

Chip pulled over on to the shoulder of the country road they were on.

B. A. reached behind the driver's seat and felt around on the floor. She came across some schoolbooks, a hairbrush, and something she couldn't readily identify. She reached farther and came across her glove with a ball inside it. Her hand jerked away from it as if it were hot. *I'm sure that will be a complicated issue too*, she thought. *Why can't things be simple? Black-and-white with no rough edges. But if everything was simple, there wouldn't be people like Chip. I really like her. Up to now, most of my friends have been guys. We became good friends so fast. It was as if she were waiting for me to move here. I guess I can open up to her a little. Basketball wasn't supposed to be a big secret, like softball. It was supposed to be simple and fun. I was willing to play any role on the team, but I'm just not a guard. Right now basketball isn't simple or fun. I guess it's time to change a few things, and I'll need some help doing it.*

She found what she was looking for—a warm bottle of Gatorade. She opened it up and took a sip. Chip was staring at her with an expectant look on her face. B. A. gave her a warm smile and got out of the truck. She went to the back, dropped the tailgate and sat down.

"C'mon back, Chip. We have to talk."

Chip bounded out of the truck full of excitement.

"I knew it! Luke said I was nuts. Wait until he finds out I was right. He thinks he's so smart. He calls himself a supersleuth. His jaw is going to drop when he finds out the truth."

"What's this about the truth?" asked B. A. as Chip hopped up on the tailgate and sat down.

"First of all, I just want to tell you that only Luke and I know. And we haven't talked to anybody about you or your mom."

"I give up. What about my mom and me?"

"Well, it's just that we know all about the witness protection program you are in. If it wasn't a murder, what did you see? Was it a kidnapping or something? You can trust us. We won't blow your cover."

"Let me feel that forehead again," said B. A. as she put her hand above Chip's eyes. "Listen, we're not in any kind of protection program. It's nothing like that at all. How much time do we have?"

"About ten minutes before we have to head back."

"Okay, here's the deal," said B. A., handing Chip the bottle. "Dr. Snyder is here to see me play basketball. I played pretty good last year, and he never missed a game. He was the team doctor for the girls' sports teams. The only thing I can figure out is that he has probably been communicating with Doc Rupert and knows that the team we are about to play is real good. He doesn't know anyone in Reston, so the town doctor would be a logical choice. Our team was pretty exciting last year, and our fans went absolutely crazy at games. It was like a circus at times, but we never made fun of or disrespected the other team. I don't believe in that and just hate it when other teams or coaches do it. And they do it a lot. Sometimes it's obvious, and at other times it's very subtle, but how they do it doesn't really matter. It's like they don't even know what sports are all about. I'm sorry. I was starting to ramble. It's one of my pet peeves. Go ahead. I know you are dying to ask me some questions."

"Okay," said Chip with a confused look on her face. "It's not that I don't believe you, but I need to get a few things straight. How many points did you average per game?"

"About eighteen."

"That's good, but not front-page material. I'm averaging about sixteen, and nobody's asked me for my autograph yet."

"Well, sometimes I scored a lot and sometimes just a few, depending on who we were playing. If the team didn't need me to score, I would rebound and pass off a lot. You know, to the girls who usually didn't score that much. A lot of times I would just take myself out of the game and give someone else a chance to play. The press had a heyday with that, saying I thought I was too good and all that nonsense. They can think whatever they want. I'm done with them."

"I've never heard of anyone doing that. B. A., I'm sure you had some great games, but varsity is a lot different than fresh/soph ball."

"I played varsity last year."

"Wow! No way! I mean, I believe you, but I'm trying to get this straight in my mind. You say you were a varsity player as a sophomore, and you had some awesome games. Okay, I've got to be honest with you, hon, what you've shown us this year doesn't look like all-star quality."

"And you'll never see it as long as I play guard in Coach Todd's offense."

"Were the girls in Arkansas about the same size as Texas girls?"

"Yes, silly. Texas doesn't grow them any bigger. I can't figure out why our coach won't give me a shot at forward. I told her the first day of practice that I played the three or even the four position."

"It's time to head back," said Chip, still not totally convinced. "By the way, what was the most you scored in one game last year?"

"Fifty-two," said B. A. as she headed toward the driver's side of the truck. She whipped the truck around and headed back into town. "Dr. Snyder is going to be crushed. He comes all the way down here, and I score my usual two points. Don't get me wrong, I don't think scoring a lot is all there is to basketball. But he gets such a kick out of it, and he's such a nice man. I'll just have to explain to him that things change. It's just not like it used to be. He'll understand—I hope."

Chip was quietly thinking. If what her new friend was saying was true—and she wasn't doubting her, she was just skeptical—if it was true, it would make for a great season. Fifty-two points in a game was the most she'd ever heard of any high school girl scoring. She did get a lot more shots when B. A. came in and played guard opposite her, which was very rare. B. A. was a better passer and dribbler than Kris, but at times she seemed confused about where to go on the offense. And so far she hadn't gotten to play all that much. Todd wasn't big on subbing, whether they were ahead or behind. Actually, most of the team complained about the offense they were supposed to run. It just didn't seem to fit the personnel. B. A. was a real good jumper, and she seemed to see the floor well. In their last game she chased down a loose ball that was headed for the sideline and whipped it two-handed backward overhead right through Tammi's hands. Tammi was only two feet from the basket, and it would have been a sure score, even for her. Two-footers were well within Tammi's range. Was that pass a fluke or did she know right where Tammi was, without seeing her? And Coach Todd hollered at B. A. instead of Tammi. Her outside shot was just fair, but if you played close to the basket, you wouldn't need to shoot from out. And she was strong enough to play power forward. She proved that when she took care of Big Shirley. In fact, she was about the strongest girl Chip had ever seen, even though she didn't look like it. One thing was true. Coach Todd was playing B. A. about three minutes a game and in the wrong position. A change was in order if the team was going to get any better.

The girls arrived at school with five minutes to spare. They hustled inside to get the rest of their gear. There were severe penalties for being late.

* ◆ *

Chip closed her locker and looked at B. A. She started to speak but held back when she saw Luke coming down the hall. He was reading something on a clipboard and not paying attention to his surroundings. This gave her an idea.

"Hey, Luke," said Chip as he passed by them still reading.

Luke didn't respond and kept right on walking. Chip looked at B. A. and rolled her eyes. She ran around in front of him and grabbed him by the front of his jacket with both hands and pinned him up against the lockers.

"I said, 'Hey Luke.' Why didn't you answer me?"

"Hey, cut out the rough stuff, squirt," said a flustered Luke. "I was concentrating on something. What's so important that you have to mug me in the hallway and right in front of another woman?"

"Stop overreacting," said Chip, softening her tone. "We're in a crisis situation, and we might need your help if you're up to it. The supersleuth's reputation is on the line, if you know what I mean."

"A crisis?" asked Luke, still pinned to the lockers. "Does this have anything to do with our stakeout?"

"No. You were way off on that one. This is more immediate. B. A. has a friend who came to watch the game, and she has to play all or most of the game at the three or four position. Got it?"

It was obvious that Luke adored Chip. Why else would a six-foot-two, 190-pound guy let a little thing like Chip boss him around? She was usually pretty rough with him in public, but he was so easygoing, it didn't seem to bother him.

"Hands off," said Luke taking her hands in his and removing them. "Maybe I can think of something."

Chip let him go and stepped back a few steps. B. A. was watching the whole exchange with amusement. Chip was entertaining all by herself, but when these two got together, they were a riot. She got the feeling they were closer than they let on.

"So, B. A. has to play forward so this mysterious stranger can watch, huh? No, don't answer that. Hey, it's getting late. Let me think about this on the drive over to Ferguson. Ya'll better get on the bus or you'll get into trouble."

As the two teammates hurried down the hall, Luke hollered after them.

"You've got one thing going for you. Coach Todd is sick. She's got the scoots or something and probably won't make the trip."

Luke turned and ran down the hall in the opposite direction. When he got to the publications room, he tested the door to make sure he had locked it. It was open. It's kind of hard to lock the door when your keys were lying on the desk. He snatched his keys up and was back at the door before it had time to close. The air wafting in from the hallway ruffled a few papers on a nearby table. He stepped over to straighten them up when something caught his eye. There was a sheet of paper in the incoming fax tray. *No time for that*, he thought. He had to get to Ferguson High School. As the sports reporter and editor for the *Reston Talon,* he had to cover the fresh/soph game too. He jogged down the hall and out to his car.

The self-proclaimed supersleuth was just about to put his Topaz into gear when he got the feeling that he had forgotten something. His tape recorder! He always taped his comments on a small minirecorder and then typed them up later on his laptop. He raced back to the publications room and grabbed his tape recorder off the same desk his keys were on. As an afterthought, he took the fax from the basket and stuck it in his back pocket. He'd read it later. Right now he was running late, and he had a problem to solve for his date to the Sprinter Dance coming up in early February. He decided that it would be Chip's treat, as his reward for solving this new crisis.

• ◆ •

The Reston varsity bus turned west on the highway toward Ferguson. B. A. and Chip were sitting in the back seat listening to their MP3 players. B. A. was staring out the window, and Chip was staring at B. A. Chip tapped her friend on the shoulder, and B. A. took off her headphones.

"What are you thinking about?" asked Chip.

"About what I'm going to say to Doc Snyder. It looks like he came a long way for nothing. Things rarely turn out the way you expect them to. I certainly wasn't prepared for this."

"Can I ask you a couple more questions?"

B. A. smiled. "Isn't that a question in itself?"

"Yeah, I guess it is. Anyway, why did this doctor friend of yours pick this particular game to come and see you play? I mean, we're one and three for the season, and the one win was pretty lucky. Although the last-second shot I made wasn't luck. I'm not bragging, mind you, but I knew it was in the moment I let it go. The luck part was getting fouled like that."

"Dumb luck, wouldn't you say?" asked B. A. "I'm sorry, that wasn't very nice. The girl who fouled you had marginal skills. She's probably a real nice person. I'm just a little frustrated right now."

"Well, it was stupid to foul someone on a last-second shot to tie the game. What did you mean when you said she had marginal skills?"

"First, she took a big step forward to shoot. A lot of girls start out doing that, and it's not fundamentally sound. You can get a shot off if the defense is only two feet away, because you don't take that big step. A shooter that takes that step has to be open by at least six feet, because the defense is going to be stepping at her, and that will cover about two feet. And when the shooter steps at the defense it will also cover about two feet. So, a stepper needs six feet to get that two-foot cushion needed to get her shot off. Let's watch Ferguson during warm-ups to see how many take that big step."

"Why do girls take that step if it's so dumb?"

"I didn't say it was dumb. It's just not fundamentally sound. Let me ask you this. When you were in six or seventh grade, what did your fans, especially parents, holler at you all the time?"

"Most of the time they hollered, 'Shoot.' And now I know why. From the stands where they were sitting, we looked like we were wide open and they couldn't understand why we weren't shooting. But if we didn't have at least six feet, we didn't feel like we could get our shot off."

"Right," added B. A. "And because most girls shoot flat-footed, they were getting their shot blocked or deflected. From a defender who didn't even jump. So they were 'gun shy.' It's too bad that moms, dads, and coaches don't know more about the game. Then they could help little girls with their shooting before bad habits form. I'm sure someone along the way told them to take a step toward the basket when shooting, because it gives you more power. That's true, but once you get older, the power will come. The guy who told them to step when shooting was probably the same guy who told girls to hit themselves in the back with the bat, when taking a practice swing in softball. It doesn't make sense, even if you're trying to exaggerate something. Exaggeration isn't a bad way to teach a skill. It should make sense, though."

"Hey, is that what you were doing the other day with those little kids? I saw you playing with them."

"Yes, but I'm afraid I didn't make a very good impression on them.

After I showed them the proper way to shoot, they wanted me to demonstrate shooting three-pointers. You know what I'm like outside fifteen feet. I should have had you with me. They weren't ready for the kind of shots I'm used to shooting. I told them you would stop by sometime and show them how to shoot the long ones. Once they see someone their size putting up threes, they'll be impressed."

"Funny. Let me know the next time you go. I'd be glad to demonstrate the form that strikes terror into opposing teams. You sure know a lot of stuff about basketball. You should be coaching instead of the Toddster."

"Naw, you head cases would drive me nuts. You know what would help us, though? We should scrimmage the freshmen guys. Guys pass the ball harder and crisper than girls do. They also tend to throw the ball where you're supposed to be, not to where you are standing at the time. Girls tend to do too much standing and waiting for someone to pass the ball to them, when they should be moving and anticipating what's going to happen. Scrimmaging the guys would help in a lot of ways."

"Speaking of guys. I heard you and Rod were pretty close, if you know what I mean."

"I rarely know what you mean, and where did you get that info from?" asked B. A. a little louder than she intended.

Most of the bus turned around when B. A. turned up her volume— even the ones with headphones on.

"Turn around," hollered Chip. "We're talking back here and don't need any eavesdroppers."

Tammi hollered back, "Why don't you two quit gossiping and focus on the game?"

B. A. whispered to Chip, as some of the girls were still looking at them.

"Rod and I are just good friends. What about you and Luke?"

"We're just good friends, too. Once in a while we work on a project together. He totally blew the last one. Hey, we're here. Ferguson Central

High School, where the mighty Lady Tigers haven't lost a home game in two years. And it's the home of 'Crazy Jane' Miller. You never answered my first question. Why do you think your friend came down to watch this particular game?"

"If I had to guess, he probably wanted to see me go head-to-head with Jane Miller," answered B. A. as she started down the aisle.

"You against 'Crazy Jane'? She's six feet tall and first team all-conference. She's also one of the dirtiest players I've ever seen. She's always grabbing and pushing. But that's not the worst of it. I've never seen anyone so animated on the floor. All that jumping around and fist pumping makes you sick. And you know what else she does? She hollers, 'Shot,' real loud in the face of the girl she's guarding whenever she shoots. It's pretty much an insane experience, but I'm lucky 'cause she doesn't guard me. I don't think I'd like her even on her best day."

Chip followed her friend off the bus. The sun had just set, and it was a beautiful evening in northern Texas. She looked at B. A.'s back as they went through the side door and into their locker room. *Girl,* she thought, *if you went head-to-head with Jane Miller, somebody would get eaten alive.* Chip didn't know how right she was.

◦ ◆ ◦

Luke was cruising down the highway about five minutes behind the Reston bus. He had stopped to pick up his assistant sportswriter, one Clarice Trimble, freshman. Clarice was a perky little red-haired, dimple-laden, wide-eyed, pain in the neck to the junior sports editor. She spent the first five minutes punching the buttons on his radio to, as she put it, 'score some good tunes.' She even changed the settings on a couple of stations.

"Clarice," hollered Luke. "Get your freshman fingers off my radio. You don't go messin' with a guy's equipment without permission."

"Sorry, chief," replied Clarice, sitting back in her seat. "I just thought we needed some cool traveling music for our first road trip together. Would you consider this our first date?"

"No, it's not a date, and don't call me chief. Why do you want to be a sports reporter, anyway?"

"I don't know. Probably because I really like sports, but I'm not very good at them. Kinda like you, huh? Having three older brothers that were athletes probably didn't hurt, either."

"One small difference, Red. I actually know a lot about sports, and you don't."

"Try me."

"Okay. How about a little sports history? What year did Lou Gehrig hit sixty homers?"

"Nice try, trickster. Gehrig never hit sixty dingers, but Ruth did in 1927."

"Who won the first Super Bowl, flame-head?"

"You don't have to get nasty. A lot of people think red hair is sexy. I know you're just trying to throw me off my game with insults, but it won't work. The Packers won the first two Super Bowls."

"You're right, I was trying to fluster you. Sorry. However, freshmen are too young to be considered sexy. Here's your final, so don't blow this one. What famous coach said, 'No player ever dominated the game of professional basketball from the forward position'?"

"That's easy. The late Red Auerbach. He was talking about Larry Bird before his rookie year. He recanted his statement a few years later."

"Not bad for a know-nothing freshman. You might make a sportswriter yet, if you don't get too cocky."

"I've got one for you, chief."

"Go ahead."

"Whose temperature gauge is maxed out, and whose punkin'-colored car is about to spew all over the highway?"

Luke looked down at his temperature gauge and hit the brakes.

Steam was starting to roll out from under the hood of his orange Topaz. He guided his prize possession to the shoulder and shut it off.

"Don't worry," he said, looking over at his assistant. "This has happened before, so I'm prepared. I've got a couple of gallons of water in the trunk. All we have to do is wait about fifteen minutes until it cools down enough to pop the radiator cap."

"That sounds like an excuse to get some naive freshman into the backseat," said Clarice with a hopeful expression.

"Oh, brother," responded Luke. "Listen, we'll just sit here and wait for the engine to cool down. You can listen to whatever radio station you want to. And stay over on your side. Got it?"

"Got it, chief."

Luke looked out the window while Clarice turned her attention to the radio. With this delay, they might miss part of the fresh/soph game, but they wouldn't miss the main event. He wanted to pay close attention to Miller, Ferguson's big star. She was going to be the main topic of his next editorial. He wouldn't use her name, but it would be hard not to figure out who his example was. He felt that poor sportsmanship was rampant among athletes at all levels of sport, and it was time he had his say on this sorry state of affairs. Dancing, gesturing, and taunting had no place in sports to a purist like Luke Slowinski. Maybe if these hot-shot athletes had his love of sports, along with his talent (or lack of it), they would respect the game and their opponents more. Even though he couldn't play the game, he could be part of it by reporting it in a forthright manner. And if his editorial had any impact, he might be able to make an impression on somebody. If it was good enough, it might be mentioned in *Sports Illustrated.*

*   ◆   *

Dr. Joe Snyder sat looking out the window of Doc Rupert's SUV. The countryside was flat, with very few trees. He decided he liked northeast

Arkansas better. There was something to be said about the warmer temperatures in Texas, though. It was almost seventy, and it was mid-December. What he didn't like was what he was hearing from the driver, his new acquaintance, Doctor Tony Rupert. He had called Tony before the season started and asked him to send any information he could on the girls' games. The similarities between the two men were incredible. Both were about sixty years old, medium height and weight, with brown hair that was trying to turn gray. They even were dressed alike, in blue jeans and white, short-sleeved shirts. They could have easily passed as brothers.

"Look, Joe," said Doc Rupert. "I'm sure this girl was a genuine star where you come from, but it's different for her down here. She's a new kid trying to fit in, and that's not easy. Kids are tough on each other, and maybe she's having trouble making new friends. That can carry over into sporting activities. It's obvious you are very fond of her, and I'm afraid tonight is going to be a bit of a disappointment. I realize that the press clippings and box scores that I've been sending you aren't what you expected."

"Tony, you misunderstood me when I described this girl's athletic talent on the phone. Annie is a legend where I come from. She has done so many magnificent things in her short career. Words simply cannot describe her. I saw her score twenty points in one quarter last year. And it wasn't a blowout like when that Leslie girl scored one hundred points in a half out in California. I mean, the only way you can score that many points is to have your team press an overmatched opponent and then throw you the ball, so you can keep dropping it in. Annie would never do anything like that. She's the epitome of sportsmanship. When the other team is overmatched, she stops shooting altogether and even takes herself out so her teammates get more playing time. She is totally selfless. Have you ever heard of a player doing that?"

"No, I can't say that I have ever heard of that. What did you call her?" asked Doc Rupert.

"Annie. Annie Smith. Why?"

"I hope we're talking about the same kid. The girl I'm talking about is about 5'8" with blondish hair and gray eyes. She is built like an athlete, though. I did her physical, and she seemed to be in excellent shape. She introduced herself as B. A."

"This is strange," said Joe, running his hand through his hair. "Her full name is Barbara Angela Smith. I wonder why she is going by her initials? You can't tell me you have never heard of 'Fast Annie Smith'? A name she detests, by the way."

"No, I don't recollect any 'Fast Annies.' Is she a track star too?"

"She was only clocked as one of the fastest high school pitchers ever, as a freshman!"

"No kidding?" asked Doc Rupert looking over at his passenger. "This is intriguing. Did she ever lose a game?"

"As a freshman on the varsity team she started the season throwing three consecutive no-hitters. She got all kind of write-ups in the state and even some national papers. That was a lot of pressure for a fourteen year-old, but she handled it well. There was a big disagreement with the coach, though. He told the papers that he was going to pitch Annie every game, even doubleheaders. She continued to pitch for a while and was fabulous but then had some injury problems. I kept a close eye on her. She ended up the season playing right field."

"How did she do in her sophomore year?"

"Well, her arm was still bothering her, so she played right field the whole season. She hit around .500 and was the team's Co-MVP. Ironically, with the girl who wouldn't have gotten to pitch if the coach had had his way."

"How could she throw the ball in from right field if her arm was still bothering her? If softball is the same as baseball, your strongest arm is usually in right."

"I told the public it was an inflammation of the teres major. Just between you and me, it was her decision not to throw the ball underhand, and I backed her up. Let's just say it was more of a psychological injury and not a physical one. Did I tell you that the girl who took over most of the pitching duties received a partial softball scholarship?"

"This story is getting more interesting. I had no idea that we had such a superstar in our midst."

"That's part of the problem. She doesn't want to be a superstar. I mean, she does, but she doesn't want all the nonsense that goes with it."

Doc Snyder knew that Annie could pitch without any pain. It was an understanding between them that he would not dispute her claim of pain in her arm. He had absolutely no compunction when it came to Annie's "sore arm." She was mature beyond her years, and if she said it was sore, then he was not going to question her. He knew she had her reasons, and he respected them. A second opinion on her arm was not even pursued.

"This is starting to sound like a real mystery," continued Doc Rupert. "Why do you think she is going by her initials instead of what everybody called her back in Arkansas?"

"I don't know. I'll ask her when I see her. Like I said, she hated all the publicity when she was pitching. The press pestered the heck out of her, and her teammates were pretty rough on her in softball and basketball. They were quite jealous. Maybe she is just laying low and trying to function in a world where she's not the center of attention. Somehow I find that hard to believe with Ann—I mean B. A. Let's keep everything I told you between us until we find out what's going on."

"That's fine with me, Joe," said Doc Rupert. "I just hope you are not too disappointed if tonight doesn't turn out the way you want it to. I've seen these girls play, and they aren't very good. Fullerton is fun to watch because she's such a character, and she does have a lot of talent. But the rest of them haven't shown very much. Things change, you know."

Five minutes later they turned into the Ferguson parking lot.

"Wow!" exclaimed Doc Rupert. "Look at all these cars. This must be a special night or something. I hope your legend gets her chance, because the timing looks perfect."

• ◆ •

B. A., Chip, and the rest of the varsity stood at the north end of the gym waiting for the fresh/soph team to file by. They were soundly beaten by thirty-five points and were grumbling about the officials. Ferguson was notorious for having "homers" for officials. Their coach looked for every advantage he could get. B. A. looked around the corner and saw Doc Snyder sitting in the front row with Doc Rupert. *The Ferguson team doc must have reserved them the seats,* she thought. It reminded her of old times. Doc Snyder always sat directly opposite their bench in the first row so he could get onto the floor immediately if his services were needed. Now there were two docs there.

Tammi led the team out onto the floor. She was the team's co-captain along with Missy. Chip was the obvious choice for the junior captain, but Tammi's little group swung the vote to her. Since Missy was a senior, B. A. thought she should lead the team. It was just like Tammi to take center stage whenever possible. The plan was to shoot a few layups and then go over and talk to Doc Snyder. Maybe they would go get a pizza after the game like they used to. After a Jones Ferry victory, Doc Snyder always offered to buy pizza for the team. Maybe he would forget about pizza after they were demolished by Jane Miller and company.

B. A. told Chip not to look at the two docs until she gave her the signal. They had shot a couple of layups when a loud, annoying song came over the gym speakers. The noise was deafening. Good, guitar-oriented rock was meant to be played loud, but not this stuff. Out of the girls' locker room came the Ferguson Lady Tigers. 'Crazy Jane' was in the lead with a ball under her left arm and her right fist in the air. As the girls came through the locker room door, each one banged the door against the wall. You could even hear it over the music.

"I forgot to tell you about that," hollered Chip into B. A.'s ear, as they were standing in the layup line. "It's some kind of stupid ritual. I'd like to bang their heads into that door. Last year they beat our varsity by forty points here. They pressed the entire game."

"That's not too cool," said B. A. She took a pass and dribbled toward the basket. She went up as if she was going to shoot a right-handed layup but kept gliding through the air, reached under the basket, and shot a nifty little reverse with her left hand. Chip had never seen her do that before. When they broke into their three-man weave, B. A. acted as though she had seen Doc Snyder for the first time and walked over to him. She shook his hand and gave him a big hug.

"What are you doing here?" she asked, trying to hold back the moisture that was collecting in her eyes.

"I came to see how you were doing. You know Doc Rupert, don't you?"

"Hi, Doc," hollered B. A., extending her hand. "How long have you known the best doctor in Arkansas?"

"Just for a little while," said Doc Rupert shaking her hand.

Dr. Snyder leaned close to B. A. so he didn't have to shout at her. Between the music and the crowd, it was almost impossible to hear each other.

"Annie, what's going on down here? Are you hurt or something?"

"No," said B. A., wiping the tears from her eyes with the back of her hands. "Let's just say things aren't going as well as I had hoped they would. I'm kinda out of position here."

"If you want, I'll talk to your coach," said Doc Snyder.

"No, no, don't do that. I don't think that would help at all. She's not even here tonight. I think she's sick."

"Well, whatever happens this year, you're still the best high school player I've ever seen. It looks like their star needs to be taught a little something about humility."

They both looked across the floor to see Miller whooping it up and high-fiving the fans in the front row. Apparently she thought she had to be a cheerleader as well as a player.

"Yeah, she looks like a real go-getter," said B. A. "Listen, Doc, I go by my initials here. Everyone calls me B. A. Oh, I almost forgot. I want you to meet a friend of mine."

B. A. waved Chip over and introduced her to Doc Snyder. They only exchanged pleasantries, as the noise was deafening. As they turned to join the rest of the team, Doc Snyder hollered something about getting back together in Reston for pizza. The girls nodded and went back to finish their warm-up. There were five minutes left on the game clock.

B. A. took a few shots and then went out by center court to stretch and watch the Miller girl. She wanted to see what was so special about her and the Lady Tigers. She was surprised that Coach Todd didn't have any videos of Ferguson. Todd probably thought they didn't have a chance, so why bother. Miller was definitely a right-handed player. In fact, she never made one move to her left during the rest of the pregame. She didn't appear to jump very high, either. She also dribbled the ball real high, like a lot of guys did. B. A. knew this came from watching too much TV. Good dribblers didn't dribble much higher than midthigh when in traffic. Poor dribblers not only bounced the ball too high, they palmed it on a lot of their crossover moves. The problem was, a lot of players did this, so it had to be real extreme for the refs to call it. It's too bad they didn't call it, because it would have forced young players to dribble properly. B. A. was an excellent dribbler. The ball rarely got higher than her knees in traffic, and she was deceptively quick.

The horn blew, and B. A. headed for the Reston bench. She had come to the conclusion that guarding Miller, even with her height disadvantage, wouldn't be too tough. Shutting her down wouldn't be possible, but she was sure that she could keep her from taking over the game.

The two teams came back out on to the floor for the National Anthem. B. A. couldn't believe how many people were crammed into the gym for a regular season girls' game. It hit her as soon as the song started. A flood of emotion immediately engulfed her. The "Star-

Spangled Banner" was always inspiring to her, but this time her knees started to shake, and her eyes started to leak. Tears ran down her cheeks. Chip looked over at her with a concerned glance. *This is not right,* thought B. A. as she stared at the flag. *There must be thousands of girls across the country who are frustrated just like me. But there's not much they can do about their situation. I can do something about the predicament I'm in if they would only give me a chance. I've got to straighten this out. Not just for me, but for all those who have to live with the luck of the draw and who can't do a thing about it.*

B. A. knew there were a lot of players who loved sports but didn't get much of a chance to play. Girls whose coaches refuse to play them, except for the last couple of minutes—even when their seldom-present parents finally showed up to watch. How many coaches announced to their players at the beginning of the season that if a game had special significance to please let them know? She remembered a junior high game back home where a reserve player's dad showed up for the first time. It was the first game he had ever attended. He was divorced from her mom and was a long-distance trucker. He had to make a special side trip just to see his daughter play. When B. A. found out about the dad, she informed her coach. Then she went out and orchestrated a big lead so the reserves could get in a lot of playing time. But the coach had her own agenda. Apparently she wanted to win by a large margin, and she told the team to press at the start of the third quarter, even though they were up 34 to 14. B. A. had a few words with the girls on the floor and then turned her ankle on the next play. Right after that, three of the other four starters either sprained an ankle or jammed a finger and had to come out of the game. The nonstarters all got a lot of playing time and did a respectable job. After the game, the little-used reserve brought her dad over and introduced him to B. A. It gave her a nice feeling. A feeling she vowed to have more often.

B. A. was drawn out of her daze by an arm around her shoulder.

"C'mon, little one," said Chip. "I'll show you where to go."

B. A. was surprised to see that they were the only ones left out on the floor. Everyone else had gone back to their respective benches. The two of them jogged back to the bench and received a questioning look from Coach Harbison and the rest of the team. After the visitors were introduced, B. A. took a seat at the very end of the bench. She thought about sitting next to Coach Harbison and offering some suggestions, but she knew she didn't have the credibility with the coach to do that. Coach Harbison meant well and would be the first to admit that basketball was not one of her strengths. The girls figured out that she was the assistant because she was a second-year teacher, and no one else wanted the job.

B. A. felt a little embarrassed about not coming off the floor with the others. She stared at the floor and tried to make herself very small. This was not a good day.

The home team was introduced with a lot of hoopla and fanfare. The announcer explained that this would be victory number 200 for the coach. That explained why the place was packed to the rafters. While they were being introduced, Chip was talking to Coach Harbison, and they were both looking in B. A.'s direction. This embarrassed her even further. She knew that her friend was lobbying for her, but the look on the coach's face showed that she was skeptical.

The teams took the floor, and Miller was high-fiving everyone as if they had just won the state championship.

What a phony, thought B. A. _I'd like just one quarter with her. This is just a game, right? Most of the time, yes. Most of the time it's just a game. But right now it doesn't seem like it. Right now it's not a game. Not to me, it's not! Somebody should do something about all these injustices. That's silly. You can't rectify all the bad things that happen to people just by scoring a few baskets. But it sure would be a start._

B. A. leaned back and looked across the floor—right into Rod's eyes. He was sitting about ten rows up with some of his college buddies. What else could go wrong? This was the first game he had been able to come to. She recognized some of the guys they played with on Sunday afternoons. Rod saw her looking, and held up his right hand in a fist. She waved back meekly and averted her eyes.

After only six minutes into the game, Ferguson was up by ten points.

"Rats," said B. A. leaning forward with her chin on the palms of her hands and her elbows on her knees.

"What did you say?" asked Rachel Moon, who was sitting next to her.

"I said, 'Rats,' Rachel. Haven't you heard anyone say that before?"

"Just you," said Rachel, shaking her head.

B. A. had to look up at Rachel from her bent-over position and saw someone raising a commotion up in the stands. It was Luke working his way through the crowd, and he appeared to be heading for the Reston bench.

Chapter 7

Doc's Reward

Luke and Clarice made it to the game at the start of the fresh/soph fourth quarter. They had to stop twice more because the "punkin'," as Clarice had dubbed it, was still overheating. The second time it began to overheat they were close enough to a gas station to coast in. It was Clarice who suggested they buy some radiator stop-leak. Luke felt a little embarrassed that a freshman girl had come up with a possible solution that he should have thought of. Not that he was any good with cars, but he should have come up with something that simple. While they were waiting for the engine to cool down, he went in and bought them each a soda.

"Here," he said handing her a soda through the window. "That was a good idea you had about the stop-leak. I'll add it along with some more water as soon as it's safe to pop the radiator cap."

"Thanks for the drink," said Clarice. "Is this diet? Never mind, it doesn't matter. You don't like me much, do you? Is it because of my red hair?"

"I do like you. It's just sometimes you get on my nerves with all the questions. You fire two more off before I even get the first one answered. I know you mean well, and you'll probably make a good sports reporter someday. You're just a little too hyper for me, that's all."

"Chip Fullerton is hyper, and you like her, don't you? Are you two going together or something? I see you and her together a lot."

"See, there you go," said Luke, starting to get annoyed all over again. "You ask two or three questions at a time. And before I can answer the first one you are already busy thinking of more questions. Let's just have a normal conversation, okay?"

Clarice had a snappy comeback but thought better of it. She turned and looked out her window and sipped on her soda. After a few minutes, Luke got out and added the stop-leak and enough water to fill the radiator. He hustled back to the driver's side and fired up the engine, hoping that his car problems were solved.

"The directions say to drive as soon as you put that stuff in," he said to Clarice, who was still looking out the window. "I hope this does the trick. We've already missed most of the first game."

Luke steered the "punkin'" back onto the highway and headed for Ferguson. He knew Clarice was mad at him, so he had to figure out a way to get her talking again. He looked over at her, and all he saw was the back of her head. He started to say something clever, but instead of words, a big burp came out.

"Uh, excuse me," he said, somewhat embarrassed.

Clarice snickered and took a long slurp of her drink. A few seconds later, she let out a belch with much more depth and quality than Luke's. He looked at her in disbelief. She turned and gave him a mischievous smile. Luke took this as a personal challenge. He was famous for his bullfrog belches, and no little redhead was going to beat him at one of his specialties. After a few more modest attempts from both sides, he went for his "A" material. He started with a small one and crescendoed it into a thing of beauty. Clarice looked at him with one eyebrow raised. He thought he had her. That was his best shot, and a mighty fine effort it was. She sat for about thirty seconds with a strange look on her face. She looked at him with disdain, and then artfully belched out his first name, "Luke," followed by a beautiful, well-enunciated, "S-L-O-W-I-N-S-K-I." It was three syllables of belching perfection.

Luke reached over and ruffled her hair. "Kid, you've got potential," he said in admiration. With that, he turned into the Ferguson parking lot. They hustled inside and squeezed into a small area about ten rows up right at midcourt. As they settled into their seats, Luke stood up and flashed his press pass to the Reston fans sitting behind him. His official-looking "credentials" were made on the school computer in the publications room. He always did this to get them going. The catcalls started immediately.

"Sit down, ya weenie." "You're taking up space that real fans could be using." "Pseudojournalist." "Tabloid vulture." *That last one was especially creative,* he thought.

"You sure know how to make an entrance," observed Clarice.

"I like to get them riled up, and this press pass gets them every time," he said. "I'll make one for you if you want one. I saved the template."

He hated to admit it, but he was actually starting to like her. Maybe not "like" her, but she was becoming easier to tolerate. No, he liked her. Her hair looked soft and pretty, sitting this close. Maybe he was just a little prejudiced against redheads. There was no time to dwell on it. He turned his attention back to the court, where the fourth quarter was getting underway. By the looks of the score, there wasn't much of a story here. The Reston fresh/soph was getting waxed. As usual, the Ferguson girls were playing real rough. Not only did they foul an obvious poor shooter behind the three-point line, they actually knocked her to the floor. Luke leaned forward to see if the Ferguson coach had anything to say to his player after she made such a stupid move. The coach was talking to one of his starters and didn't appear to be paying any attention to the game. *Typical,* thought Luke. *Didn't his second and third team players deserve the benefit of his knowledge and experience too? It seemed like all too often the players with the least amount of skill got the least amount of the coach's attention? Did the coach think that once his starters were off the floor, his coaching duties were done for the evening?* This might be a good topic for a future article. He took out his tape recorder and made a verbal note on the subject.

The first game ended with Ferguson victorious by thirty-five. Ferguson was by far the more aggressive of the two teams, but the fouls were rung up three to one in their favor. Go figure. Between games, Luke and Clarice went to the scorer's table to look at the scorebook. He made a few notes and then showed her what a good reporter could glean from just looking at the stats. After a restroom break, they were back in their seats, discussing the upcoming varsity game. They both agreed that it wouldn't be much of a contest. Miller would push everyone around, and neither Missy nor Tammi would be able to stop her. The only thing that would make this game even close would be the proverbial 500-pound gorilla. And the last time he looked, the Reston team didn't have any 500-pound gorillas. He should have looked a little harder, because the proverbial gorilla was standing at the end of the bleachers next to his best friend.

The opening play of the game was a bad omen for the twenty or thirty Reston rooters in attendance. Miller tipped the ball to her forward, and she turned and threw a nice bounce pass to a cutting guard. The result was a layup with only three seconds gone on the clock. The home crowd erupted with whistles and noisemakers. The cowbell was especially irritating. Some of them even started to holler at the Reston players on the floor. The game was only thirty seconds old when Luke began to squirm in his seat. The hard bleachers were always rough on his back, and it was so crowded that he couldn't stretch his feet out or move in to a more comfortable position. And there was a lump in his back left pocket that was digging into his rear. He leaned forward and extracted it with difficulty. It was the folded up fax that he had put there earlier as he left the publications room. He carefully unfolded it and began to read:

Dear Coach Slowinski;

I'm sure by now you have figured out what a gem you have in Ms. Smith. Our community was sorry to see her leave. I guess our loss is your gain. Her stats for last season, as you requested, are as follows:

Scoring---487 total points (18.7 avg.) Rebounds---11.4 Assists---4.3 Steals---2.9

She was first team all-conference, as well as third team all-state. This was the first time in our conference history that a sophomore was voted in as a unanimous first team selection. However, if you haven't found out by now, her character is much more impressive than her stats. She was probably the most team-oriented player I have ever seen. If her coach wasn't quick enough to take her out of a game, she would take herself out. She could have easily doubled her scoring average (no exaggeration here, as she is a scoring machine when she wants to be), but she wasn't the least bit concerned about her scoring stats. The first three categories above were all school records, as well as her fifty-two-point effort against our biggest conference rival. Good luck to you this season and to the finest forward to ever play at Jones Ferry High School.

Emil Thomson
Head Boys Basketball Coach
Jones Ferry High School

Luke reread the fax. *Oh man,* he thought. *I forgot all about helping those two with their problem. Stupid car! Stupid redhead! No, I can't blame her. She's okay. A little dippy, but not that bad. Chip is gonna be real mad if I don't do something about this. How could I miss the signs pointing to B. A.'s talent? An experienced sports reporter would have picked up on something. There's got to be a way to make this right. But how?*

Clarice was talking to some friends over her right shoulder when Luke tapped her on her left one with the paper.

"What's this, chief?" asked Clarice.

"I guess you could call it a letter of introduction," said Luke, still trying to figure out a course of action.

"A letter of introduction," she said, taking the paper and unfolding it. "For who?"

Luke looked down to see B. A. sitting on the end of the bench with her chin in her hands.

"For the all-star gorilla sitting on the far end of the bench."

Clarice read the fax and looked at him with a raised eyebrow. It was the second time she had given him that look. He wished he could do that with his eyebrows, but he had no talent for interesting faces.

"I know what you're thinking," he said. "I've pulled a few pranks in my time which makes me a skeptical person when it comes to anything out of the ordinary. Let's go over our facts, so we don't make fools out of ourselves. The first week of practice was mostly drills and conditioning, right? I watched one whole practice, and Smith looked to be in real good shape. Everyone else was huffing and puffing, and she just cruised through the drills." Clarice nodded without interrupting. "Then, during the second week, they worked on the offense. And Smith was sick. She had the flu or something. She even missed a day of school. And that was the day the team scrimmaged Arlington."

"So you're saying," asked Clarice, trying to be helpful, "that this could be legit and not some student at Jones Ferry pretending to be someone he isn't? Is it possible this girl is that good, and Todd doesn't even know it? Is that what you're saying, 'Coach' Slowinski?"

"Right," said Luke, not taking the bait about pretending to be someone he wasn't. "She played about two minutes in the first game because she was just getting over the flu. The next two games she played about four to five minutes each. And in a position she's not used to playing, with players she has never played with before. She's not a shooting guard, so she just passed the ball and hung back to be the safety valve against a fast break. See where it says she's a forward? She's used to playing in close to the basket. Come to think of it, I remember her shooting a hook shot in one of those games, and Todd got all over her. Said something about not wanting anyone taking silly 'circus' shots. And here's the clincher. If you were this great team player in every sense of the word, would you come in as the new kid and try to take over the show and impress everybody, or would you try to fit in as best you could and make as few enemies as possible? Girls can be awfully hard on each other. And let's be honest, Coach Todd was a good high school player and a fair college player, but that doesn't automatically make her a good coach. So, to answer your question—yes. She probably is as good as the fax says, and Todd doesn't know it."

"So what do we do?"

"I'm going to do two things. Coach Harbison needs to see this right away and, if anything comes of it, we're going to write an awesome story for next week's edition. I've got an idea that I need to pass by you. We'll talk about it on the way home."

With that, Luke stood up and began to make his way down the bleachers toward the Reston bench. It was slow going, as he had to tap people on the shoulder to get them to move over so he could have a place to step. The boys at the top were watching and started in on him again.

"Sit down, ya big goof." "Whatsa matter, can't you hold it?" "Get him a uniform, Coach. He's ready to play." "Show your press pass, Slowinski. Maybe she'll let you coach the rest of the game."

The sports editor of the *Reston Talon* didn't have time to trade barbs with the comedians behind him. He had a higher purpose in mind.

He worked his way down to the bench and squeezed in beside Coach Harbison and the scorer's table.

"How's it going, Coach?" asked Luke.

"Awful," replied Todd's assistant. "We're getting killed, and I don't think there's a thing we can do about it. I knew we wouldn't have much of a chance against them, and now they're making such a spectacle of it. You would think they're winning the state championship, the way they're carrying on after every basket. Sportsmanship must not be part of the vocabulary here at Ferguson. I feel bad for the girls. Hey, are you allowed to sit here?"

"I don't think there's any rule against it. Let's just say I'm your assistant for the day. Anyway, I think I can help."

Luke handed her the fax from Coach Thomson. While she was reading, he looked up at the scoreboard. It read: HOME 20 VISITORS 8. Chip had hit two threes for most of Reston's points. The other two were a put back by Tammi, which came after a Kris Ritter air ball. The team was averaging 34 points per game so far, so this was typical of their offense. There was a lot of motion, with very little opportunity for creative thinking. Everyone had their spot to go to, and that's just what they did, running around from spot to spot, hoping one of the defenders would make a mistake or fall down. Usually it took only about two minutes for the defense to figure out what they were doing. Todd's offense didn't generate quality shots from the people who should be taking most of them. Ferguson was playing man-to-man defense and pushing and grabbing a lot. On the road they were tough, but at home they were downright brutal.

Coach Harbison gave the paper back to Luke.

"Nice try, Luke. This is a bad time to try to scam me. You better go back to your seat."

One of the Ferguson players was shooting a free throw, so Chip was standing back at half-court watching Luke and the coach. She held up her hands as if to ask, "What's going on?"

"I'll go, Coach, but if this is legit, what have you got to lose? You've got a new kid who hasn't played much this year. Look at her. You can't argue that she looks and moves like an athlete. She's quick, she can jump, and she's in great shape. I don't need to remind you about what she did to Big Shirley. Wouldn't the person this letter is talking about look something like her and maybe act like her, too? She's just trying to fit in without making any waves or enemies."

"She's not very tall for a forward in this conference," said Coach Harbison, weighing the facts. "The twins are 5'11". But then again, Charles Barkley didn't look like he could play forward in the NBA at 6'4", did he?"

She looked indecisively down to the end of the bench.

"All right. Let's give her a shot. It can't get any worse."

The coach hollered and waved B. A. to come sit by her. B. A. was watching Miller closely and thinking how she would guard her. She was also going over the events that led to her current situation. Her attitude could have been a whole lot better. It's not that she had given up, but she did act at times like her heart wasn't in it. In the past, she had always been the star, looking out for her teammates and trying to set a good example. She remembered hearing how great players are measured. When truly great players walk onto the floor, they make everyone else on the team get better. They have the ability to raise everyone else's game. That's what she always strived for. Even if she didn't play much this year, she could help Chip and Jenny. And what about the sixth-graders at the park? They seemed to want to learn the game the right way. Her concentration was broken by what sounded like her name being called. Coach Harbison and everyone else on the team were looking at her. She got up and went to sit by the coach.

"B. A.," said the coach. "I'm going to ask you some questions, and I want honest answers, okay?"

"Okay," said B. A., not knowing what the coach was getting at.

"Are you a lot better than what we've seen so far this season?"

"Yes," answered B. A., not making eye contact with the coach. She wasn't looking at her coach. She was staring intently at "Crazy Jane," watching her every move.

"Were you first team all-conference and an all-state player at the school you came from?"

"Yes," answered B. A., almost as if she was in a trance.

"Are you better than Miller?" asked Luke.

"Yes."

Luke leaned closer and asked, "Are you better than any player we have played against this year?"

B. A. looked at Luke. Her usual smiling eyes were very serious. "Yes," she whispered. She knew she wasn't normally like this, tooting her own horn, but enough was enough. She was conscious of the adrenaline that was surging through her body. This was not the way basketball was meant to be played. This was a circus. All she wanted to do was run, jump, pass, and shoot the way she used to. Miller's taunting, the crowd's lack of sportsmanship—it was all just so wrong! Somebody or somebody's needed to be taught a lesson. Maybe it was time for class to start, and maybe she should step up and start teaching.

B. A. reported in and waited for the next dead ball. With three seconds left in the quarter, the ball was knocked out of bounds by Ferguson on the far side of the court. It was Reston's ball, just back of half court. The official waved at her, and B. A. ran onto the court and pointed to Jenny Olsen. This brought a sneer from her sister, but Jenny just smiled and slapped B. A.'s hand on her way to the bench. Two girls got up from the Ferguson bench and were reporting in, so B. A. had time to formulate a plan.

B. A. went over to Chip, who was standing by the official with the ball. She quietly told her to go to the baseline and call for the ball. As Chip started toward her basket, she heard B. A. say something about falling stars but she couldn't quite make it out. Chip took her position on the baseline about five feet from the basket on the same side as B. A.

and began jumping and waving as if she were open. Ferguson was in their 1-3-1 half-court press with Miller on the baseline. B. A. was now standing right in front of the two docs. The official handed B. A. the ball and instead of tossing it in to Kris Ritter, who was open in the backcourt, she turned and threw it as hard as she could right at "Crazy Jane." Jane had stepped in front of Chip, not really expecting the pass to come her way. This was exactly what B. A. had hoped Miller would do. She was lined up perfect.

When the ball got to Miller, it was about two feet above her head. She had three options: (1) let it go, (2) catch it, or (3) attempt to catch it. B. A. was hoping for the third option. She had been watching Miller through the warm-up and most of the first quarter and had come to the conclusion that Miller had a huge ego in addition to weak hands. There was no way she would just let the ball go out-of-bounds. It would have been the smart move, because her team would get the ball at the point where B. A. threw it in. Miller's hands went up more as a reaction than an attempt to catch the fast-moving ball. The ball was thrown at a speed that was not meant to be caught. Miller didn't slow it down much, but she did deflect it on an upward path toward B. A.'s intended target. Right behind Chip, hanging on the gym wall, was an old-time "foul board." It was one of those blackboards that were used years ago to denote how many fouls there were on each team member. Modern high-tech scoreboards had long since done away with the old foul boards. Ferguson had adapted this particular board to show the team and individual records over the past ten years. Miller's name was up there more than once.

The crowd caught a collective breath when the ball came rocketing down the court. Heads on B. A.'s side of the court snapped to the left trying to follow the ball. It all happened in an instant, and if you weren't watching, you missed it. However, it would have been hard to miss what happened next. The deflected ball crashed right into the middle of the record board, and a few of the numbers and letters that were stuck in the slots came flying off. Everything that happened after that was a bonus. One of the wires that held the board up came loose, and the whole thing swung to the side. This was too much weight for the other wire, so the entire board gave way and came crashing down. Chip scampered off to the side when she saw the first wire break. The crowd, which had been deathly silent as the events unfolded, came to life with a monstrous roar. Most of the fans stood up to get a better look. Jane Miller just stood there with her mouth open. Chip came running up to her teammate with a big grin on her face.

"Tell me you did that on purpose," shouted Chip over the noise.

"I never expected the whole thing to come crashing down," hollered B. A. "I was just hoping for a few letters. Let's go get a drink."

Chip turned to go to the bench where her water bottle was, but her friend grabbed her arm and steered her toward the drinking fountain at the other end of the floor. They had a good five minutes before the janitor and a couple of volunteers could clear the wreckage out of the way. As they walked by the two docs sitting courtside, B. A. gave them a wink. Doc Snyder returned it. He looked up at the clock to see two seconds remaining in the quarter. He looked over at Doc Rupert and nodded without saying anything. He was glad he had come. Annie was going to be okay, and maybe he had just a little something to do with it.

Up in the stands, Rod and his buddies were whooping it up. Rod got the impression that Annie didn't like the Miller girl and that was confirmed by what had just happened. *What a little bearcat she is when she's riled,* he thought. *What did Victor call her the first day they had played together—Tigrita, little tiger? I hope she doesn't ever get mad at me. I would have had trouble catching that pass.*

As the girls got a drink from the fountain in the corner of the gym, B. A. told the little guard what to do on the out-of-bounds play that was coming up. They headed over to the bench and their waiting teammates.

"Come on girls, we've got three quarters left to play," said Coach

Harbison. "Try to stay focused." B. A. knew what she meant and decided right there that she liked Coach Harbison a lot. She didn't pretend to know a lot about basketball, but she was genuinely enthusiastic about the game. The official's whistle told them they were ready to resume play, and the Reston girls went back on to the floor. Coach Harbison grabbed B. A. by the arm and held her back.

"Look, Smith, I never played sports in high school, but I loved to watch. There were times I wished guys or girls like Miller would be taught a lesson, but most of the time they got away with that attitude stuff because their team usually won, and a lot fans and parents will look the other way regarding bad behavior as long as they are winning. So, if you've got it in you, go out there and show them what a real player can do."

B. A. came back onto the floor with a smile on her face. Even her coach was fired up. Jeez, it was only one pass. She wondered what Luke had told her to elicit that kind of faith. This was going to be a lot of fun. She took her spot on the baseline, just outside the lane, and waited for the official to hand her the ball. Her teammates were stacked up in single file right in front of her. As they came out on the floor, Chip had given them their instructions. The official and the ball were to B. A.'s right. B. A. held up her fist and said, "Ohio." All their out-of-bounds plays were numbered, so there was no such play as "Ohio," until now. Chip and Missy chuckled, so they had gotten the joke. Tammi, standing directly in front of B. A., just stared at her chewing her gum. B. A. slapped the ball, and all four of them stepped into the lane and called for the ball. Chip appeared to lose her balance and put her hand down to keep from falling. The girl guarding Chip looked back over her shoulder at the ball when Chip appeared to go down. That was a big mistake. When she looked back, Chip was gone. She was up and sprinting hard for the right corner. B. A. faked into the mess in the lane and then threw a soft behind-the-back pass with her right hand. The pass looked as if it was intended for no one and was about to go out-of-bounds when a fast-moving Chip reached it. She caught it and, with one smooth motion, turned and dropped in the neatest three-pointer you ever saw. The horn sounded while the ball was in the air. The scoreboard flashed: HOME 22 VISITOR 11.

When a team is up by eleven points after only one quarter, and when the same team is going for their coach's 200th win, you would expect to hear some noise from the fans. The crowd was buzzing about what had just happened, but there was no cheering. The events at the end of the first quarter gave them reason to worry. When the two teams came back for the second quarter, Miller brushed by Chip and growled at her.

"You little dweeb. We're going to crush you and your little hot dog friend. No mercy now."

Chip took the inbounds pass uncontested and threw a hard pass to B. A. on the left wing. B. A. dribbled hard toward the lane with her left hand and when she looked as if she were going to go around the forward guarding her, she hit the brakes and tossed in a fade-away jumper. Miller, who was waiting for her under the basket, stood there staring at her. She had never seen a high school girl jump that far back and shoot. Angrily, she grabbed the ball and stepped over the end line to throw it in. She was right in the middle of her throwing motion when B. A., who was heading up the floor, turned and stepped right in front of Miller's teammate. The Ferguson center tried to hold back the pass, but it was too late, and it slipped out of her hands and bounced weakly toward B. A., who then scooped it up and laid it back through the hoop. The ball was already through the hoop and in the net when "Crazy Jane" crashed into B. A., knocking her to the floor. It was an obvious, intentional foul, but the official didn't call it that way. At the least, Reston should have gotten the ball back, as the shot was well away. The official didn't call it that way, either. He did call the foul, but signaled to the official scorer for one shot. Chip came running in to help her teammate up and was about to holler something at the perpetrator when B. A. shook her off with a grin.

"Let it go," she said as she walked to the free-throw line.

The free throw was good. The scoreboard read: HOME 22 VISITORS 14. Only twelve seconds had ticked off in the second quarter. The Ferguson coach called time-out. He was screaming at his players before they even got to the bench.

Doc Snyder put his arm around Doc Rupert's shoulders.

"Let's see, Tony. She's been in the game for about fifteen seconds, right? And already she has scored five points, has one assist, has one steal, has the opposing coach foaming at the mouth, and has broken the record board of the opposition. At this rate, it looks like she needs about one full quarter to destroy the whole gym. Wouldn't you agree?"

Doc Rupert was staring at the new girl in the Reston huddle. Whoever this kid was, she was going to make the rest of the season real exciting.

"I've got one thing to say," he said without turning his head. "The postgame pizza that you said was a tradition back home—I'm buying."

He turned and looked at the visiting doctor, and they high-fived each other.

Over on the Reston bench, the girls looked at Coach Harbison, who was sitting and leaning back on her elbows.

"I've got nothing to say, girls. You were just over here a few seconds ago. Just go out and have some fun. Be careful, it's going to get even more physical, if I know these girls. Look out for each other. I don't want anyone getting hurt. Smith, you just do your thing and don't rough up Miller too much. She looks like the temperamental type to me." They all laughed and stood around nervously looking at each other. It was strange how a couple of good plays made them feel more like a team. Only two of them had been involved, but success breeds confidence, and most of the team was starting to get the good feeling that success brings. There were exceptions, of course. Tammi was clearly sulking, and Mony didn't appear to be very happy, either.

B. A. and Chip took over the Reston offense for the rest of the game. With a minute to go in the half, the visitors were down by only two points. The crowd was back in full force, sensing that this was not going to be an easy victory and maybe not a victory at all. This was because of the new girl who was playing forward for Reston. They didn't remember her from last year, on the varsity or fresh/soph team. She seemed to be everywhere doing everything. Anyone who wasn't a believer was instantly converted on the last play of the half. Miller took a shot with about eight seconds to go, and it caromed off the board on B. A.'s side. She snatched it out of the air and after clearing herself with one quick dribble, let go with a wicked pass to Chip at midcourt. Chip figured out early that taking an outlet pass from her new teammate at the top-of-the-key extended was a little too close, unless you wanted your head taken off. She caught it like a wide receiver and immediately dribbled to center court. There was no time to waste on this particular maneuver because right behind the pass came B. A. at a full sprint. If you didn't want to get run over, you filled the center lane as quick as you could. Kris Ritter had filled the left lane, and Reston had a classic three-on-two fast break going.

Chip stopped at the free-throw line and threw a nice bounce pass to Kris on her left. Kris caught the pass in stride and attempted a layup. She was fouled by the Ferguson defender, but it wasn't called, and the ball rolled off the rim. B. A. was running hard and very wide when Kris put up the shot. When she got to the baseline, she cut to her left and ran parallel with it toward the basket. The shot came off the rim on B. A.'s side and was about to be grabbed by a Ferguson guard. B. A. was directly under the board when she jumped and reached out with her left hand. The ball had just touched her opponent's fingertips when B. A. tipped it back toward the basket. The horn blew as the ball went through the hoop. She never heard the announcer say, "Reston basket by Smith," because she kept on going right out the door toward the visitor's locker room. The crowd was silent for about two seconds and then the

Reston rooters, all thirty of them, erupted. "Crazy Jane" was standing at half-court with her mouth open. Her gum fell out at her feet. She picked it up and angrily hurled it into the stands, where it stuck in the hair of a loyal Ferguson fan. The score was tied, and the home-team fans were in a state of shock.

* ◆ *

Ferguson changed their defensive tactics for the second half. They double-teamed B. A. every time she got the ball. This did not surprise her at all. She was used to getting doubled up. At first she tried passing off to the open girl, and when they had trouble getting shots, she took it right at her two defenders. She went to the free-throw line five times in the second half and made nine of ten free throws. When Jane Miller fouled out with three minutes to go in the game and her team down by five, the home-team crowd knew it was over. The final was: Reston 76 Ferguson 67. Seventy-six points was the most that a Reston girls' team had scored in ten years. B. A. totaled thirty-three points and Chip had twenty-six.

* ◆ *

"Did you see their forward eat up Janey?" asked a Ferguson fan as they filed out of the gym. "She must have had about thirty points in only three quarters. I wonder why they waited so long to put her in. The game sure changed when she showed up."

"Yes," said another. "And we put two defenders on her for the second half. Didn't seem to make much of a difference. Man, was she ever smooth."

"Probably the best performance by a girl that I ever saw. And those hook shots. Haven't seen shots like those in years. I hope some of the boys were paying attention."

Chip was very impressed with B. A. Not just the way she played, but the way she conducted herself on the floor. She didn't run around high-fiving people or fist bumping all the time, the way a lot of high school athletes do. Chip never did like all that stuff, especially when you messed up and someone would come over and slap or fist you. She never could figure out the rationale behind it, but she went along so she wouldn't look like a sorehead. B. A. just smiled at her a lot during the game and didn't say much. The way she looked at the other team was strange, though. It was as if she was looking right through them. She seemed to be concentrating on her teammates and not on the other team. They didn't seem to bother her in the least, especially Miller. She did help one of them up when she went to the floor after a loose ball. Chip thought that was pretty cool and obviously something that Tammi or Mony would never do. Another bright spot was the way Jenny played. It was by far her best game. She had ten points and a whole bunch of rebounds. The whole experience gave Chip a nice feeling on the bus ride home. She looked over at B. A., who appeared to be sleeping with her headphones on. She whispered a "Thank you" to her. This girl was going to make one of her wishes come true. She was finally going to be on a good team.

Chip sat back, put her ear buds in, and closed her eyes. She was already dreaming of future victories.

B. A. opened one eye and looked at the little guard. "You're welcome," she whispered.

Chapter 8

Team Player

C hip sat at the kitchen table Monday evening watching her mom prepare dinner. Chip was limited strictly to cleanup when it came to the kitchen duties. She had tried cooking on a few occasions, but it didn't work out so well. Her impatience always seemed to get the best of her. After one oven fire, a sparking microwave, and several boil-overs on the stove, she was banished from the cooking appliances for the safety of the household.

"When do I get to cook again, Mom?" she asked as she glanced through the local paper.

"I told you, the second Tuesday of each week is your day to cook," answered Mrs. Fullerton.

"All right! Hey, wait a minute. Real funny. How was I supposed to know that aluminum foil wasn't supposed to go in the microwave? The warning just said 'no metals.' That foil stuff is real soft, and metal is supposed to be hard and heavy. What do you have to be, some kind of chemical engineer just to run the stupid thing?"

"I thought you were getting an A in chemistry?"

"I am."

"Well, pay attention when the teacher goes over the section on flexible metals."

"Mom, you're becoming a real comedienne. I can't believe we didn't make the sports headlines with our win on Saturday. Did I tell you how B. A. kicked Jane Miller's tail? She was awesome. B. A. was four inches shorter, and she kept scoring on her and out-rebounding her. She can really jump and she's got these real long arms. It was a thing of beauty."

"She must be something," said Mrs. Fullerton as she started to mash the potatoes. "Why don't you ask her over for dinner sometime? Your dad and I would like to meet her."

"That's a good idea. There is still something strange about her that I can't figure out. I mean, she's real nice and a great basketball player, but she doesn't act like a high school kid."

"What about the witness protection theory?" asked Mrs. Fullerton as she put the potatoes on the table.

"I guess we were way off on that one. I can't believe I let Luke talk me into that."

"It seems to me that you are usually the one doing the talking, and he goes along with you. He really likes you, you know."

"We're just friends, Mom. Our love of sports is a common bond. We go to dances and other school activities together because we don't have regular dates, that's all."

"In my day, if you hung around with each other as much as you two do and went to social events together, it was considered 'going steady'."

"Mom, you're from an ancient generation. Kids don't 'go steady' anymore. They hang out or kick back with each other."

"Well, speaking of hanging out," said Mrs. Fullerton, looking out the kitchen window, "here comes your steady dinner date."

•—◆—•

The talk around the dinner table was mostly about sports and other school activities. Mr. Fullerton was in agreement about inviting the new all-star player to dinner. After dinner Luke and Chip washed the dishes together and then sat down at the table to study. Mrs. Fullerton could see them from her desk in the living room. She marveled at how well they got along. They never seemed to quarrel or pretend to be mad at each other the way a lot of adolescents do. Her daughter was usually fidgety and couldn't sit still for very long. But when Luke was with her, she sat still and paid attention to her schoolwork. They complemented each other with their academics too. Luke was strong in English, math, and history, while Chip was the health and science authority. She also noticed that they sat next to each other and not on opposite sides of the table.

"Just friends," she said to herself, smiling.

"Did you say something, mom?" asked Chip from the kitchen. Her mother smiled and shook her head.

"Check this out," said Luke as he pulled a typed sheet from a folder and handed it to her.

Chip took the paper and read it.

COACH TODD USES SECRET WEAPON
TO DEFEAT FERGUSON
by Luke Slowinski

The packed house at Ferguson High School was in a state of shock last Saturday evening when they left the familiar confines of their own gym. The home-team fans were expecting to be celebrating Coach Bob Williams's 200th win as the Ferguson mentor, but their wishes were denied. There was a lot of discussion as the fans thronged from the gym. The topic of those discussions was not their usual star, Jane Miller. Miller fouled out in the fourth quarter as she tried to guard B. A. Smith, who got the best of her in every category.

Smith's play at forward—that's right, forward—along with Chip Fullerton's accurate shooting and play-making from the backcourt spelled doom for the Lady Tigers. Coach Todd was unable to attend the game because of an illness, but her assistant, Coach Harbison, did a great job following the surprise game plan. With just seconds to go in the first quarter, and the score 22 to 8 in favor of Ferguson, Harbison could wait no longer. She sent Smith in at one of the forward spots for the first time this year. That's when the fireworks began. On the ensuing play, Miller deflected a pass from Smith to Fullerton, and the ball hit the home team's individual and team record board. The board came loose and crashed to the floor. After the cleanup, the quarter ended with Fullerton taking a behind-the-back pass from Smith and hitting a three-pointer at the buzzer.

The two Reston stars continued their stellar play in the remaining three quarters. Smith displayed an array of shots seldom seen in this area. Her fade-away jumpers and hook shots were very effective against the conference leaders. She even had two tip-ins. When the defense closed in on Smith, Fullerton took over from long range. Jenny Olsen was another bright spot, with her strong play on defense and on the boards. Kris Ritter's defense has improved, and Carmen Espinosa logged some quality minutes.

The Lady Eagles had three players in double figures. Smith had 33, while Fullerton and J. Olsen added 26 and 10 respectively. The final was Reston 76 and Ferguson 67. The 76 points scored by Reston may well be a school record. Hats off to the players and to the coaches for pulling off a great upset. The girls will again be on the road Friday night against Morningside.

If the Ferguson game is any indication of what is to come, the rest of the season may prove to be very exciting.

"How come you gave Todd some of the credit for B. A.'s play?" asked Chip after she had finished reading.

"It's supposed to be satirical in a sneaky sort of way," responded Luke. "That's how writers sometimes get their point across without coming out and actually saying it."

"I know what satire is," said Chip, handing back the article. "You better not make B. A. mad with your literary masterpieces. I don't think she will like this very much. I also hope this won't complicate an already delicate situation. At practice today, the Toddster told B. A. to fall in with the guards during drills. It looked like she and Coach Harbison were having a heated discussion a few minutes later. Harbison seemed really intense. I saw Tammi and Mony snickering. I think Tammi feels her position and playing time are safe with Todd in her corner. If B. A. doesn't get to play her natural position soon, I will be forced to take drastic measures."

"What kind of drastic measures?"

"You'll see."

"Don't involve me, please. You last idea wasn't so hot. I can't believe I took your witness relocation theory seriously. I could have gotten into real trouble faxing Jones Ferry High School and saying I was a Reston coach."

"Listen, future Paulsen Prize winner," she said, putting her hand on his affectionately. "You and I both know that our witness protection theory had merit, especially with the limited facts that we had to work with. By the way, the two long-haired guys that we saw on our stakeout— they were musicians from her late dad's band. They're like, famous."

"How did you find that out?"

"I just told her she looked real tired the next day," replied Chip. "She said she was up later than usual because two members of the band stopped by. I guess I forgot to mention it to you. Pretty slick, huh?"

"Not bad for an amateur," said Luke, putting away his article and the rest of his schoolwork. "I have to go. Promise me you won't do anything weird as far as Coach Todd is concerned. I want to think about this for a while."

"No promises, dude. Todd better come around to the Fullerton way of thinking real soon. We've wasted almost a third of the season already, and time is of the essence."

Luke shook his head and headed for the back door. He hollered his thanks to Mrs. Fullerton for dinner and headed home. He hadn't corrected Chip when she said "Paulsen" instead of Pulitzer Prize. When you like someone a lot, you're willing to overlook little things like that.

Chip went in and watched television with her mom for a while, but her mind was elsewhere. She was going to have a talk with Coach Todd the next day before practice and, she hoped, get things straightened out. With her mom's permission, she grabbed the remote and surfed through the channels until a ball game came on. It was the University of North Texas and some team she didn't recognize. She watched for a couple of minutes and then stood up, disgusted.

"Mom, do you think kids are getting dumber?" she asked.

"That sounds like a loaded question," answered her mom. "Why do you ask that?"

"Well, with all our modern advantages in communications and stuff, you'd think we would be a lot smarter. I mean, there's a lot more interesting things to do with computers, the Internet, Facebook, and stuff like that. When you were a kid, a long time ago, uh, I mean, not so long ago, you didn't have any of the stuff we've got today, right? Listening to the kids talk at school is very frustrating. They use bad language to try to impress each other, and they talk about such shallow things. Most of the time they talk about themselves. It's like they think they're royalty or something."

"That's why adults need to have a lot of patience with you young ones. Most parents hope that all that 'shallow stuff,' as you call it, is just a short-term fad and that you will grow out of it and become responsible members of the community."

"I guess all that stupidity just gets to me sometimes," continued Chip as she watched the game. "I know I'm no rocket scientist, but I sometimes look like a genius compared to some of the kids at school. Look at all those stupid tattoos on those guys. Now, to be different, you should *not* get a tat. What a bunch of sheep!"

"I'm glad to hear you say that about the tattoo," said Mrs. Fullerton. "And I do agree with you. Young people seem to be preoccupied with shocking the adult community. The thing is, adults are too busy with day-to-day matters to pay attention to the very people who are trying to get their attention. But if we were paying more attention, then maybe young people wouldn't try so hard to be so different. Both sides need to take more time to see the other's position."

"Look at that," hollered Chip, pointing at the game on television. "That's just what I'm talking about. The blue team with the real tall guy is trying to break the press. He caught that pass a couple of feet short of half-court. A second later, an obvious guard ran right by him with his defender chasing. All the big guy had to do was hand the ball off to his teammate and the press would have been broken. But no, he holds it above his head and the defender knocks it out of his hands. He's lucky it went out-of-bounds. That's just bad basketball. If you're going to give the ball in the backcourt to a tall person, he better know what to do with it. And here's the kicker, Mom. That big dude has got to be there on a basketball scholarship. So, it's like he's getting paid to play ball for the school, and he can't do a simple thing like hand the ball off to a teammate."

"What's your point, sweetheart?" asked Mrs. Fullerton.

Chip usually had a lot to say on a variety of subjects, but this was an entirely new topic.

"My point is, these guys play ball all the time and a lot of them are just not smart ballplayers. I don't understand it. The girls on our team, except for a couple of us, don't really care that much about basketball, so you shouldn't expect too much from them. But a scholarship player, like that guy, should know better, that's all."

"Wow, where did all this hostility come from?"

"It's not hostility, Mom. It's just frustration. We've got a real chance to be good for once, and that stupid Toddster won't let B. A. play forward, where she belongs."

"You know I don't like that disrespectful talk."

"I'm sorry. But it just makes me mad."

"What does your friend B. A. say about it?"

"She's not the type to say much. She's actually pretty quiet, but she knows more about basketball than the coach. Jenny and I are going to stay after practice so B. A. can show us some of the stuff she knows. I've already learned a lot from her. Luke was wondering if she was really seventeen years old. She knows so much. Almost too much for a high school girl—if you know what I mean. Hey, what if she's one of those crazy moms who's pretending to be a teenager so she can come back and relive her high school years one more time? You know, like that thirty-something lady did a few years ago. The one who enrolled in school saying she was a transfer student, just so she could make the cheerleading squad."

Mrs. Fullerton put down her book.

"So you think B. A. might be really old, like in her twenties? And she moved to Texas with another lady claiming to be her mom, so she can help you win the conference championship? That seems like a lot of trouble to me. Is that what you are proposing?"

"It does sound a little far-fetched when you put it that way," said Chip with a concerned look. "Luke's probably way off on that one, too."

Mrs. Fullerton went back to her book as Chip left the room muttering to himself.

"You know, a background check would clear up a lot of questions," she said without looking up.

Chip froze in midstride. She turned to look at her mom and saw a mischievous grin behind the book.

"Real funny, Mom. There are a lot of unanswered questions here, and you're making light of the situation. I'll get to the bottom of this, and you'll be very impressed when I do."

She headed to her room to phone her fellow detective. They, as usual, had a lot to talk about.

◦ ◆ ◦

B. A. sat alone on the gym floor before practice Tuesday afternoon and laced up her basketball shoes. She was feeling lower than she could remember. Saturday's celebration at Vitale's Pizza was just like old times. Having Dr. Snyder there was very special. She couldn't believe that he would fly down to Texas just to watch her play. She was glad she hadn't disappointed him. But yesterday Coach Todd started practice the same way she always did and hardly even mentioned the Ferguson game. Beating them was a big upset. It was too bad that only about thirty Reston fans were there. She was hoping the coach would say something to her about playing closer to the basket but nothing was mentioned. She even saw Coach Harbison having what looked like a serious discussion with Coach Todd. She appreciated Coach Harbison going to bat for her. What else would it take to change Todd's mind? What she was really thinking was, *What else would it take, without making most of the team resent me? This is similar to last year, but with different characters. On the bright side, my two best friends are people I can rely on for support. Just like Tank and Riley back in Jones Ferry. I should e-mail them tonight and tell them about the last game and Doc Snyder's surprise visit.*

B. A. had gone from feeling on top to rock bottom in just a couple of days. She went through the drills at a lackluster pace. This was different for her because for the first time during basketball season, she just didn't feel like playing. If last Saturday's performance wasn't good enough, then why bother? In the past, basketball had been a series of highs with just a few lows. Now that seemed to be reversed, and the lows had taken over, with the Ferguson game being the exception. Chip's constant chatter and poking fun at everyone didn't even cheer her up. So this was what it was like at the bottom. She didn't like it very much and wasn't sure there was anything she could do about it. She was glad when practice finally ended. One of Riley Buelow's famous pep talks would sound good right about now.

◦ ◈ ◦

B. A. leaned back against the headboard of her bed. She remembered the talk that Riley gave her at the Stanwood game last year. His pep talks, or whatever they were, always had a profound effect on her. It was a strange game. The Stanwood Lady Pirates were up by eight points at the half and her coach was as mad as she had ever seen him. She had hardly touched the ball during the first half and sensed that something was different with her teammates. In the previous game with Finley, she had scored thirty-two points and had pulled the game out of the fire with her last-minute free throws. Now it was like the guards and the rest of the team were freezing her out. She had only two baskets at the half and one of them was off an offensive rebound. It was apparent that her teammates didn't like her getting so much ink in the papers. Who cared who scored the most points as long as the team played well? Winning was a bonus, but a well-played game was always the goal. Her teammates obviously had decided on a new agenda. At halftime her coach asked her to remain on the bench. He was visibly upset. She liked Coach Huston well enough, but didn't connect with him the way she did with Coach Thomson, the boys' coach. She was informed later about what went on in the locker room.

"You know how I hate to lose to Stanwood," Coach Huston exclaimed to the team as they sat on the locker room benches. "I don't expect you to feel the same way I do, but I was hoping you would be a little fired up just the same."

The girls just sat with their heads down. They expected to get hollered at for their sloppy first-half play and the big freeze-out, but so far the coach seemed relatively calm. They sneaked knowing looks at each other.

"I need to come up with a whole new set of super plays if we're going to have any chance of winning. I told Smith to stay out there on the bench. She's only a sophomore and isn't experienced enough to be able to make the changes that I'm going to ask you to make."

More than one questioning expression passed between the girls. The coach started writing furiously on his basketball clipboard. It was one of those boards that already had a court drawn on it. He drew up a quick play with multiple screens. After ten seconds of explanation, he erased it and drew up an entirely different play. The team was looking at each other as though he were insane. What was this all about? He wasn't even giving them enough time to look at his drawings, let alone figure them out. The third set of X's and O's was fast appearing on his board when a senior guard spoke up.

"Uh, Coach, are you sure this is the way to go? I mean, I didn't even get a good look at that last play, and we're supposed to go out there in five minutes and do it?"

"You can handle this," said Coach Huston looking up from his board. "You girls are smart and real team players, right? Because this is going to take a real team effort."

No one answered. They just stared at his clipboard as it rested on his knee. He looked at their blank faces, wondering what was going through their minds. He finally tossed the clipboard on the bench and stood up. Pacing back and forth, he appeared to be in deep thought.

"You're right, this won't work," he said.

A moment later, he stopped pacing and snapped his fingers.

"I've got it! What do you think about doing something really different? I say we get the ball to our best player and see what she can do. Yes, that's the ticket. It would be incredibly selfish, and a downright shame, to have the best player in this whole area, maybe the whole state, and not give her a chance to perform. Man, I hate losing to Stanwood."

With that, he picked up his clipboard and walked out the door.

The girls sat in the locker room for another two minutes before they came back to the court. The coach wondered if he had gotten through to any of them. He thought his act was pretty good. They told him that coaching girls would be a challenge, but this was one thing he wasn't prepared for. He hoped that he had handled it right. It appeared his talk was all for naught, as Annie turned her ankle on the first play of the second half.

Annie sat on the end of the bench with her left leg up. Her shoe and sock were off, as she waited for Stanwood's trainer to come back with some tape to wrap her ankle.

Riley Buelow was sitting in the next row up.

"How's it feel, champ? It doesn't look that bad. It isn't even swollen."

"No, it's okay," answered Annie. "The trainer says it should be taped to protect it from further damage. I wish he would hurry. My foot is getting cold."

"That's not all that's getting cold around here," said Riley leaning in so no one else could hear. "Have you done everything that you came here to do? Because if you have, you don't need the tape job."

Annie had a hurt look on her face.

"What are you talking about?" she demanded.

"I'm talking about you," said Riley with a little more intensity than he intended. "These Stanwood fans are here to see how their team does against the player that everyone is talking about. You've already had several thirty-point games and two games with twenty rebounds. Since Stanwood isn't in our conference, we'll only play them once this year. So this is their only chance to see you. Do you think these stands are three-quarters full, on a weeknight, to watch the locals? Rather disappointing, don't you think?"

"You can't have a great game every time," said Annie in her own defense. She wanted to add, "especially when you rarely touch the ball," but she bit her tongue on that one.

"Maybe not," replied Riley softening his tone. "But you can put out a great effort. Give them something to talk about when the old boys meet for breakfast tomorrow. You've got more heart than the rest of the team put together. You just need to believe in yourself. Think about it. Why do you love playing so much? The crowd? Your teammates? Maybe a little. I think you like to be challenged. Put in a position where it looks like you can't do it. Then, you go deep down and find a way to succeed. Notice, I didn't say win. You win or lose in your mind and heart, not on the scoreboard. Anyway, it looks like you only have one quarter to do it now."

Annie looked up at the clock with tear-filled eyes. They always leaked when Riley talked to her like that. She knew he was just trying to psyche her. Why did he have to be so good at it? There were two minutes left in the third quarter, and Stanwood was up by twelve. The hometown players and fans were enjoying it immensely. What was she supposed to do? Her teammates wouldn't pass her the ball, her defender was holding her all the time, and the officiating was awful. A big part of her game was getting the opponent out of position and then drawing the foul. How could she have a great effort when the refs wouldn't call anything? She knew these were all excuses. Most players had to put up with all that nonsense, so why should she be any different? The trainer finally showed up with the tape and began to wrap her ankle.

With only a few seconds left in the quarter, Annie was lacing her shoe back up. That's when she heard a fan holler.

"Whatsa matter, superstar? Your team losing, so you fake an injury?"

There was a lull in the crowd noise, which enabled everyone on the bench side of the gym to hear the loudmouth's comment. Annie didn't look up, as she felt a rush of adrenaline. She stood up and tested her ankle. Coach Huston was looking at her from the other end of the bench, and she nodded. Riley crooked his index at her, wanting her to come closer.

"Just for kicks," he said as she leaned in. "Let's see how far you can take this team all by yourself. Don't pass up any shots. I know, that's not good team basketball, but you need to show everybody in the gym, especially yourself, what you are capable of. You don't have to feel bad about playing one-on-five. They certainly had no problem playing four-on-five for the first half. What do you say? It could be fun."

Annie smiled for the first time that night. "Okay. What have I got to lose, right? Let's have some fun."

The write-up that Annie got the next day in the local paper proclaimed her the best player in northern Arkansas and maybe the whole state. Her twenty points in the fourth quarter were a school record. Two of Stanwood's starters fouled out trying to guard her. The Jones Ferry strategy was simple. On the coach's orders, the first time down the floor the point guard held up her right hand clenched in a fist. She hollered out, "Thirty-three," which was Annie's number. The right side of the floor was cleared for Annie to go one-on-one with her defender. Basket, plus a free throw. The next time down, the guard held up her left hand and called Annie's number. Annie was on her own from the left side. Basket. The third time down, her teammates went to both sidelines and gave her the middle. Basket and a time out for Stanwood.

They came out and double-teamed her, but the results were the same. The home team finally went into a zone with two minutes to go, leading by three. Annie hit a leaning baseline jumper and was fouled in the process. Her free throw tied the game. Stanwood held for the last shot and missed it with nine seconds to go. After a time out, Jones Ferry came back out onto the floor with a play set up for Annie to shoot. She drove hard down the right side of the lane and was about to attempt what looked like a running hook shot to win the game. With two defenders on her and a third closing in from behind, she went into her hook shot motion, but instead of shooting the ball, she let it roll off her fingertips to a teammate standing flatfooted on the baseline. The fake was so effective that it got both defenders off their feet. The Jones Ferry center that the pass was intended for almost fumbled the ball out-of-bounds. She recovered and made a ten-foot shot as the clock ran out. That was the only basket for Jones Ferry that Annie didn't score in the quarter. Stanwood was held to eight.

As Annie ran off the floor, she saw Riley still sitting in the second row. He had his arms crossed against his chest and a satisfied look on his face. They made eye contact, and he winked at her. She always liked his wink and adopted the gesture occasionally. The wink and her smile were the only facial expressions she showed when she was competing. She had read somewhere that when Roger Maris, the famous Yankee slugger, hit a home run, he would always run the bases with his head down, so it wouldn't look like he was trying to show up the opposing pitcher. She thought that was a pretty cool thing to do. It showed sportsmanship at the highest level. Roger must have been a very classy guy. The situation was certainly different today. Classy was certainly not the adjective you would use to describe most of today's athletes. As she opened her eyes and looked around at her present surroundings, she wondered how Riley was doing at Northern Arkansas State.

* ◆ *

Jenny, Chip, and B. A. sat on the first row of the bleachers and waited for the rest of the team to clear out. Practice was over and B. A.'s two protégées were anxious to learn some of the moves and techniques that she had mentioned earlier. B. A. had offered to teach her two teammates some new moves if they were interested. They were more than interested—they were actually excited when she asked them whether they wanted to stay after practice. She figured this would be the best way to help the team and her two new friends. One thing they hadn't counted on was that the balls were always locked up after practice.

"How are we going to do this without a ball?" asked Chip, looking around.

B. A. was about to answer when she saw the familiar figure of Pops, the night janitor, come through the far door. He always swept the gym floor between the girls' and boys' practice sessions. Chip ran over to him and explained their predicament. A minute later, they had a ball.

"Let's make the most of this," said B. A. "We only have about a half hour before the boys start to wander in, and we don't want them to see us. If Coach Todd found out we're doing this, she wouldn't like it."

B. A. walked to the free-throw line, and her two students followed her.

"Let's talk about technique first," she said. "The better players have most of the basic fundamentals mastered. And I don't mean they can just do them. I mean they can do them flawlessly. Once you have the basics down, you can start adding something to them. It's like climbing a ladder. You can't just jump to the top rungs. You have to go up them one at a time. What you see in basketball today is just the opposite. Guys and girls are trying to do the fancy stuff without mastering the simple things first. Here's an example. Chip, please go stand under the basket."

Chip ran down and stood under the net. B. A. threw her a soft two-handed chest pass and motioned for her to throw it back. B. A. threw the next one a little harder, and Chip reciprocated. Four passes later, B. A. snapped a pass that Chip had trouble catching. She had to step to the side and catch it like a wide receiver in football.

"Wow," said Jenny. "You can really zip that sucker. The ball really snaps out of your hands. But if these are good fundamentals, how come you don't do them all the time? I mean, you usually pass the ball like the rest of us. Actually, better than the rest of us, but never like that."

"Right," said B. A. "Except to Chip. And I bet she can tell you why."

Jenny looked to Chip, who was concentrating hard on her answer.

"I know," exclaimed the little guard. "Because I'm the only one who has the hands to catch passes that fast. Right?"

"You've got it," said B. A. "It wouldn't be smart to throw passes your teammates can't catch, just to show everyone how hard you can pass it."

"The only time you want to throw a pass that someone can't catch, is when you are throwing it at a tall, loud-mouthed, obnoxious opponent. Right, B. A.?"

"Something like that," said B. A. "Let's get back to proper technique."

B. A. drilled her two pupils on passing and pass receiving for the next fifteen minutes. Then she showed them each a move that would help them get more open shots. With Chip, she worked on dribbling backward once and shooting. Chip had never seen this move before. B. A. stood in front of her at the top of the key, bouncing the ball. When Chip came out to defend her, B. A. blew right by her and laid the ball in. She had the quickest first step Chip had ever seen. B. A. came back to the top of the key and stood there with the ball. Chip backed off a full step and was now down in a solid defensive position. She didn't want to get burned again. B. A. took a hard dribble as if she were going to drive again. When Chip gave ground, she took one dribble backward and had a wide-open shot. She took it and missed.

"See how this works?" asked B. A. "When you thought I was going to drive again, you retreated enough for me to do a step-back dribble, which gave me enough room to get my shot off. You can also do the same thing without dribbling. Just take a jab step with the ball down by your hip, like you're going to start a dribble. When your defender starts to back up, just step back with one quick dribble and shoot. The real trick is selling the drive. You must make the defender think you are going to drive, which means you must have beaten them off the dribble earlier in the game, at least once. And, if you can, beat them bad. Put the fear in them that you are going to do it again. After you have used this to get off a few good shots, the next step is to fake the drive, step back, wait for them to recover, and then drive by them when they are coming at you. It's like a game of cat and mouse, and you are the cat. A good, quick shooter like you can use this several times a game to get open shots."

B. A. then put Chip out in front, Jenny on the baseline, and herself on the wing. She told them to pretend they were playing against a zone defense. They passed the ball back and forth to get the imaginary defense moving. B. A. threw a couple of passes holding the ball above her head with two hands. She explained to them, as they were passing, that a lot of girls passed this way because they could get more speed on the ball. Although guys also used this pass a lot. The girls weren't quite sure where B. A. was taking this lesson, when she surprised them both by taking a small step toward Jenny and pretending to throw another high, hard pass to her. B. A. did everything but release the ball. After faking the pass, she looked quickly at the basket and shot without bringing the ball down. She got the shot off real quick because the ball was already above her head in shooting position. This time she made it.

"A taller girl like you, Jenny, can get a lot of shots by perfecting this move. You actually shoot from a passing position. You just need to get the defense anticipating your next pass, which makes them rotate too quickly. For a tall person, they don't even have to rotate, they just have to start leaning, and you have your opening. This will also work against a 'man' defense, depending on how they are playing you. Anyway, the key is to practice this shot until you are comfortable with it. Don't bring your feet together and don't bring the ball down. Just shoot while you're holding it above your head in passing position. Once you get it down, it will feel more natural."

Jenny tried the shot several times. She wasn't very successful at first but finally made two in a row. That put a big smile on her face.

"Hey," came a shout from the other end of the gym. "I can hear boys in the locker room."

They threw the ball to Pops and scurried out of the building.

•◆•

The following day was not a good one for the transfer student from Arkansas. After first hour, the main topic of conversation was Luke's article. The paper was available at the start of the school day, and since very few fans had made the trip to Ferguson, they had a lot of questions for the Lady Eagles. Chip was glad to tell anyone who would listen about B. A.'s accomplishments. Tammi Olsen was telling everyone that it was a fluke and that B. A. had made a lot of lucky shots. Coach Todd was an elementary teacher, so she didn't see the paper until her lunch hour. She was not pleased with Luke's attempt at satire.

Suzanne Todd fit the mold of a lot of high school coaches. She played ball in junior college for two years and thought she knew a lot about the game. She had very few individual moves, which was the reason she didn't try to teach any to the girls she was coaching. Player development wasn't her forte. For her, it was all about the X's and O's. Coach Todd didn't realize that you rarely beat good teams by running plays. You beat them by making plays. Especially during the second half of the season, when you are playing teams that have videos of your early games or teams that you have already played earlier.

Coach Todd had considered giving B. A. a shot at the forward position earlier in the season, especially when B. A. mentioned that forward was her natural position. But there were two problems with that. One was that her offense called for two tall forwards, and she wasn't going to change her offense. Actually, it was the only offensive scheme that she knew, so she wasn't going to vary from it. Two was the problem of who B. A. was going to replace in the lineup. Tammi would be the logical choice because she was the weaker forward. But most of the girls seemed to look up to her, and Todd didn't think it would be a good idea to remove a two-year fresh-soph starter for a transfer student. She viewed Tammi as her leader on the floor. Tammi had even mentioned to her that she thought B. A. would fit in better as a guard because of her height. Not only was Coach Todd running the wrong offense, with at least one player in the wrong spot, she was also confused about who her leader on the floor was. Hollering at your teammates didn't make you a leader. Chip was a little more subtle and more effective when it came to guiding the team. She was the natural leader, and Todd didn't even realize it.

One thing was for sure—she wasn't going to change everything because of one lucky game. Even when her assistant had insisted that B. A. was a forward and should start in that position. What did Coach Harbison know about basketball? She had never even played the sport. Article or no article, she wasn't going to be pressured into doing anything she didn't want to do. It was her team. Besides, Smith had looked awful the last two practices. It must have been a fluke performance last Saturday. She had a feeling that all the commotion over Slowinski's write-up would die down, and things would get back to normal. Maybe she should say something to Smith about it. She hadn't really talked to her much. Actually, she hadn't said a word to her on a personal basis the whole season. Smith seemed to be well-adjusted, for a transfer student, so from a coaching standpoint, she might as well leave it alone. The new girl would just have to adapt to the guard position if she wanted to get any playing time. And that was that.

◆

Thursday's practice was the same for B. A. She hustled through the drills, but her heart wasn't in it when it came time to scrimmage. She knew she was getting a bad attitude about the whole situation and hoped it wasn't too obvious to her teammates. Playing guard on the

Reston "B" team wasn't her idea of a successful season. None of her close-in shots that she had worked so hard to perfect were effective from the top of the key. And with Todd's offense, this was where she spent most of her time. She did get off a couple of great passes, though. One went right through Carmen Espinosa's hands as she stood wide open under the basket, and the other was a neat little backhand toss that Darby Quinn completely botched. Darby was a Tammi booster, so she had a big smile on her face when Coach Todd hollered at B. A. for trying to get too fancy.

B. A. perked up for the postpractice session with Chip and Jenny. As before, she showed each of them one thing that would improve their respective games. Chip got a lesson on how to shoot over a screen. B. A.'s method was totally new to her. B. A. had her actually jumping on the screener at times. The step-back dribble also worked well with a teammate screening for you. Chip was a natural and soaked up everything B. A. showed her. She darted back and forth around Jenny, who was screening for her, at the top of the key. Shot after shot swished through the net as B. A. rebounded for her. She was an incredible shooter. The ball came off her hand with a beautiful rotation, and her arc was perfect.

Jenny was schooled in one of B. A.'s favorite areas—rebounding. She showed Jenny how to stay low and how to use quick feet to stay in position. Most rebounders didn't stay low with their knees bent. B. A. explained how a good rebounder should be able to box out her opponent solidly enough so the ball could hit the floor half the time, and it was still hers. The freak bounces were the tough ones. The balls that bounced hard off the rim or real high called for good timing and leaping skills. Jenny worked hard and made some progress, but she still had a long way to go. As B. A. was putting Jenny through the paces, two sets of eyes watched from the corner of the gym behind the edge of the bleachers. One set belonged to Pops, who usually found something to do so he could stay in the area while the girls worked on their skills.

He also served as their watchdog, so no one would walk in on them. The other set belonged to the boys' varsity coach, Bob Devers, who had silently walked up behind Pops.

"It looks like Smith knows what she is talking about," said the coach quietly. "Why isn't Coach Todd playing her more in her rightful position?"

"Don't know," answered Pops, without taking his eyes off the girls at the other end of the floor.

"Think it would help if I had a talk with her?" asked Coach Devers.

"Naw," said Pops. "Smitty should be able to handle it herself. I don't think she would want anyone messing in her business. She's pretty independent."

"Okay, but it looks like a waste of good talent. Anyway, I've got my own problems."

Coach Devers turned and went into the boys' locker room, and Pops started to sweep the gym floor. This was their cue to leave.

"Thanks, Pops," hollered Chip as she rolled the ball to him. "We owe you a soda."

"Make it a big one," said Pops as he scooped up the ball with one hand. "Hey, Smitty, got a minute?"

B. A. was about to go through the door when Pops hollered at her. She told her two friends to go ahead, and she would catch up. She walked across the gym floor where the good-natured janitor waited for her.

"How's it going?" asked the janitor as he leaned on his broom.

As she stood in front of him, she noticed for the first time that he had a tattoo on his right arm. His shirtsleeve covered about half of it, but she could still make out the word "Ranger." He saw her looking and quickly pulled his sleeve down.

"Oh, you know," said B. A. answering his question. "There are good days and bad days."

"More bad than good lately, huh?"

"It's not a lot of fun right now," admitted B. A.

"Man, I wish I could have seen you tangle with that Miller girl from Ferguson. She's a mean one."

"Now, that was fun," said B. A., wondering where Pops was going with this conversation.

"You need any help?" asked Pops getting to the point. "Want someone to talk to the coach for you?"

"No, but thanks for asking," said B. A. "Things have a way of working themselves out for the best. At least, that's what my dad used to say. He always said hard work and patience would solve most any problem. He was always such an optimist."

"A little optimism can be a good thing in a lot of situations. How about doing a little something for me?"

"Sure," said B. A.

"I've got a twelve-year-old niece who wants to be a pitcher. She's got a strong arm and a lot of ambition, but she needs someone to show her the finer points. Would you take a look at her sometime?"

"Sure, I'll be over when the weather gets a little warmer," smiled B. A. as she turned to leave.

"One more thing," added Pops. "How about showing me your high, hard one, so I know you've still got it. I don't want to waste my time on an old has-been."

B. A. knew a challenge when she heard it. She turned and motioned for the ball. Pops dropped his broom and bounced it to her. B. A. backed up to about forty feet between them. She shook her arm to loosen it up. Pops got down into a semicrouch.

"Don't hold back just 'cause I'm old."

B. A. had no intention of throwing it directly at him. It wouldn't look good if she knocked the janitor out with a basketball. She aimed about a foot to his right, took a big stride, and let it fly in a smooth, underhand motion. The smaller women's ball came out of her hand and sped straight at her target. Pops reached out with both hands and succeeded in knocking the streaking sphere down, but that was it.

"Yep, you've still got it," he said shaking the sting from his hands. "I'll tell my niece. She'll be real excited to hear a legend will be giving her some pointers."

B. A. gave him a "whatever" wave and headed for the gym door. She didn't see Coach Devers watching from behind the bleachers.

—◆—

Friday night's game was more of the same for B. A. She cheered Chip on as she shot over a screening Jenny Olsen several times. The little guard hit more than she missed. Both of B. A.'s protégées showed remarkable improvement. B. A. was pleasantly surprised, as were the rest of their teammates. When Chip came out for a breather, B. A. went in to spell her. They weren't even on the floor at the same time. Coach Harbison gave B. A. a forlorn look and shrugged her shoulders. B. A. forced an appreciative smile. She really was grateful that Coach Harbison was making an effort to make things right. The Lady Eagles lost by twelve in spite of Chip's twenty-four points. Jenny was rebounding tougher and had ten points herself, including a shot from the baseline that came off a fake pass with the ball held high. B. A. gave her a thumbs-up as she ran by.

Tammi was back to her old self. She acted like her eight points and five rebounds had just won Reston the state championship. She was all smiles and sang at the top of her lungs with the rest of her flock as the bus headed toward Reston. B. A. didn't think their behavior was all that great for a team that had just gotten its tail whipped.

Chip was fuming on the bus ride home. The satisfied feeling that she felt from her high-scoring effort had already worn off.

"What's wrong with Todd?" she asked her two teammates as they sat in their usual spot at the back of the bus. "With B. A. playing the other forward, we would have won by twenty."

"She's right," agreed Jenny. "I love my sister, even if she is wacko when it comes to sports. She's not nearly as good as she thinks she is and shouldn't get all the playing time she does. Not that I'm a pro or anything. I did try to show her some of the stuff that B. A. has been teaching us, and she said that you are just trying to get more playing time by being a kiss-up. Sometimes I just can't figure her out. I hope she snaps out of it. Life would be a lot more fun if she was with us instead of fighting us all the time. I think we've got a chance to be really good."

"She'll grow out of it someday," said B. A. "She's just a little insecure, that's all. She even called me and told me to stay away from you. I don't hold it against her, though. I'm a new kid who she sees as a disruptive force—more like an enemy than a teammate. And a teammate is all I really want to be. Heck, I'd be happy scoring five points a game if it meant we were awesome and a conference contender."

"I can't believe she told you to stay away from me," said Jenny. "I'm gonna confront her when we get home, and she better do some explaining. I'm tired of her trying to run my life as well as hers."

"Let it go," said B. A. digging her headphones out of her bag. "It's no big deal. By the way, you played really well tonight. It was your best game by far this year."

"Thanks. The stuff you've been showing us has really helped."

B. A. leaned back and turned up the volume on her MP3 player. She wondered if she should have been more aggressive at the beginning of the season. She could have dominated the scrimmages and would have been the team's starting forward and high scorer by now. But would she be as good a friend to Chip and Jenny if she had taken that route? Probably not. And what would have been the reaction of the rest of the team? They would respect her for her abilities, but she wanted more than that. She wanted friends who liked her for who she was, not for how many points or rebounds she was good for. Her thoughts wandered to Rod and their relationship, or lack of it. What was up with him lately? She thought they were the best of friends. Maybe she should have acted more like a lot of the other girls did around guys. Naw—hanging all over him and acting goofy wasn't her style. She didn't think Rod went in for the airhead act anyway. She had not worked out or thrown to him for two weeks. When they talked on the phone, he always had an excuse why they couldn't get together. Maybe she just wasn't his type after all. He had probably met some college sweetie who wanted to be more than just a workout partner. Her basketball and her relationship with Rod were all messed up. What else could go wrong?

The bus was just pulling into Reston when B. A. felt something poke her in the ribs. Chip had pulled something out of her bag. B. A. took off her headphones and tried to focus on the object her friend was holding. She squinted in the darkness and then her eyes went wide as she recognized it. The little guard was holding a doll in her hands. This wasn't just any doll. It looked like Coach Todd, right down to the same warm-up suit that she always wore at practice.

"Where did you get that?" asked B. A. in a whisper.

"At the store, of course," responded Chip. "It looked a lot like her when I bought it, but I still had to customize it a little. I had to carve on the cheekbones and sharpen up the nose and wham, a little Toddster. The hairstyle was a piece of cake."

"What are you going to do with it? You better be careful, if she finds out about it, you could get into big trouble. I thought you were kidding when you said you were going to make one of Tammi."

"I decided to go right to the source of our problems," whispered Chip as she looked over at Jenny who appeared to be sleeping. "Tammi is small potatoes. I'm not sure what I'm going to do with it yet. I need to read up some more on voodoo. This could be the answer to all our problems."

"You better get rid of that," said B. A., stealing a glance at Jenny, who was starting to stir.

"Anything you say," said Chip. "Should I throw her under the bus or flush her down the toilet?"

"No, nothing like that. You might be messing with unknown forces that we don't know anything about."

"So you think there's something to this voodoo stuff?" asked Chip with raised eyebrows.

"I don't know, and neither do you. Just put her away somewhere."

"Jeez, I didn't know you were so superstitious," said Chip, jamming the doll back into her bag.

• ◆ •

B. A. couldn't believe it. After she dropped her two friends off at home, she started laughing so hard tears started running down her cheeks. If this was what "normal" was all about, it wasn't so bad. She knew she shouldn't have led Chip on like that, but she was so serious about her creation. And it did look just like Coach Todd. As long as no one else found out about Chip dabbling in the black arts, what harm could come from it? All that voodoo stuff was just superstition anyway.

Chapter 9

Scrimmage

Mrs. Fullerton busied herself around the kitchen while her normally energetic daughter, Melinda, sat quietly reading the evening paper at the kitchen table. Chip had asked her mom to make her favorite meal—butterfly pork chops, green beans in some kind of special sauce, and baked potatoes. She wanted everything to be just right because B. A. was coming over for dinner. Chip was worried about her new friend. She rarely participated in any of the social activities at school, and now she and Rod must have had some kind of fight. On Chip's suggestion, B. A. asked Rod to a school dance two weeks ago. He had some lame excuse as to why he couldn't go. Chip also knew that B. A. hadn't talked to Rod since just before the dance. She went with Luke, of course, but it wasn't much fun without B. A. there.

"I should call that big goon of a cousin and give him a piece of my mind," said Chip to her mom. "He is ruining everything. I can't figure out why he is being so mean to B. A. They used to work out every Tuesday and Thursday, and I just found out they were playing basketball on Sundays, until the weather turned bad. Did you know that it's rained the last five Sundays in a row?"

"I didn't know it was that many in a row," answered her mom as she peered into the oven. "But I do know why Rod has made himself scarce lately."

"He better not have some college girlie on the side," said Chip. "If he does, I'm gonna thump him good."

"That would be a sight to see. He's more than twice your size. My sister tells me he really likes B. A."

"So, what's the problem? Is he afraid of girls or something? He wouldn't go to the winter formal with us—I mean, her. And I know he can dance. I mean, he's no Red Adair or anything, but he does have some coordination."

"You mean Fred Astaire, don't you? Red Adair put out fires."

"You know what I mean, Mom. Why is he being so difficult?"

"It's something he has to work out for himself. That's all I can tell you. And it would be best if your little nose, no matter how good your intentions might be, stayed out of their business."

• ◆ •

The talk around the dinner table ranged from sports to music to college. Chip warned her parents, and Luke, not to quiz B. A. too much because she didn't want them to appear nosy. She, on the other hand, posed as many questions as she could come up with. Chip was surprised at B. A.'s answer when she asked her what she intended to do after she graduated from high school. B. A. said she might find the band and travel with them for a while. Then she could learn more about her late father. Chip had assumed she would want to go to college and play a couple of sports. She had already fantasized about the two of them playing together in college. Her spirits were dampened for a few seconds until her dad asked B. A. about softball. B. A. told them she was an outfielder and the cleanup hitter on her high school team last year.

"With your luck the softball coach will probably make you play a position that you're not familiar with," said Chip.

"Right," said Luke. "She'll probably want you to pitch. Boy, would Tammi the Great be mad. It would serve her right, though. It might knock that chip off her shoulder."

"Why would Chip be sitting on Tammi's shoulder?" kidded Mr. Fullerton.

"Real funny, Dad," said Chip. "B. A.'s softball position isn't the issue here. We've got to find a way for her to show Coach Todd what she can do against the big girls underneath the hoop. And I think I just came up with an idea."

"This idea doesn't involve explosives, extortion, weapons, or witchcraft does it?" asked Luke trying to add a little humor to the seriousness of Chip's demeanor.

When Luke mentioned witchcraft, Chip and B. A. exchanged worried glances. Mr. Fullerton shook his head and snorted.

"No," answered Chip. "But I need to make some phone calls before we go out for a cruise. Thanks for the great dinner, Mom. I really like the green beans in that special sauce that you whip up."

"It's just mushroom soup, dear," said her mom as Chip and Luke began to clear the table.

"That stuff is mushroom soup?" asked Chip.

"Yep."

"But I don't even like mushroom soup."

"Well, you do when it's on green beans," said her mom.

Chip looked at her dad, who was taking it all in.

"You know what I always say, Dad. If you don't learn something every day, you're not getting any smarter."

B. A. and Luke looked at each other and rolled their eyes. After the dishes were done, Chip made her phone calls from the sanctuary of her room and then the three teens went out for a ride in the "punkin'." She never mentioned to whom she made her calls or what they were about. When pressed for information, she said, "Just wait and see."

•─◆─•

B. A. sat on the gym floor with her back to the wall before practice the next day and watched the two team managers scurry around. Carla and Sherry did a great job and were underappreciated, as a lot of team managers were. B. A. wondered what all the excitement was about. She was just about done lacing up her shoes when Chip came hustling over.

"This is gonna be a great practice," said Chip, full of excitement.

"Why is that?" asked B. A.

"Coach Harbison talked the Toddster into a scrimmage," answered Chip. "We're going to use the clock and keep the book and everything. It will be just like a real game, with officials too."

"Why are we doing this on a day before a game? This doesn't make sense."

"You ask too many questions," said Chip with a gleam in her eye. "Let's go with it and have some fun, okay?"

"I don't know," said B. A. dejectedly. "I think I'm all 'funned out' on basketball right now."

"Oh no," said Chip, bouncing a ball off the wall just above B. A.'s head. "I had to do a lot of talking to set this up for you. We don't need to blow it with a creepy attitude."

"I don't know what your scheme is, but count me out," said B. A., with her knees drawn up to her chest. "And stop bouncing that ball by my head."

"I don't believe I'm hearing this," said Chip through clenched teeth. She continued to snap off two-handed chest passes about two feet above B. A.'s head. "This is our chance to make a statement. We've only got about ten games left, and we've only won five games all season. What about all the stuff you have been showing Jenny and me? You've got to admit, we are getting better. C'mon, how about showing us some of that legend stuff that Dr. Snyder was telling us about after the Ferguson game. He wasn't exaggerating just a little, was he?"

B. A. stared ahead as Chip continued to bounce the ball off the wall. Her little friend was right, and she knew it. She didn't expect it to be the same here in Texas as it was back home, but this was turning into a real joke. The coach barely acknowledged her existence, and she only had two good friends on the team. She'd only had a couple of friends on the Jones Ferry team, but that was because of jealous and shallow teammates. Chip was also right about her and Jenny improving. She had just recently showed them the finer points of a pick-and-roll, and they clicked immediately. The secret was to set the pick, seal your opponent, and then roll to the hoop. She showed them a drill that helped Jenny to get the seal part right. Chip and Jenny looked like Stockton and Malone on the pick-and-roll—well, almost. They rarely got a chance to work on it during a game because of the motion offense that Todd had them running. Motion offenses were only effective if all five players could handle the ball and had good court sense. The makeup of this team was not conducive to that type of offensive strategy. All the good intentions that she had when she rolled into Reston had not helped her much. The team was below 500, and she was miserable. She was beginning to get real angry, which made her eyes start to leak.

B. A. thought back to last night. She had been lying there in the dark talking to her favorite baseball card. Actually, it was her only baseball card. The Roger Maris card had been given to her by her dad when she was in the seventh grade. He told her the whole story about what a great player and person Roger was. During the 1961 season Roger and Mickey Mantle had this great home-run race. They were both chasing Babe Ruth's record of sixty homers. They kept passing each other in total homers; first Mickey was in the lead and then Roger would pass him. It should have been a lot of fun, but the press and the Yankee fans turned it ugly. They didn't want Roger to break the record, because he hadn't been with the team as long as Mickey, and Mickey was a crowd favorite. When the press wouldn't let up on him, Roger was so stressed out that he started to lose his hair. He persevered, though, and he broke the record on the last day of the season. A lot of people said it shouldn't count because Roger played in more games that year than Babe did back in 1927. The fact that he had three fewer at bats when he tied Ruth with his sixtieth didn't seem to matter to them. And then, it only took him seven more at bats to break the record. She knew it was silly, talking to a baseball card, but it made her feel better. What would Roger do in her situation? She knew exactly what he would do. Go out and give it her best effort, and let the people say whatever they wanted to say. And do it with class, the way Roger did.

Chip was still babbling, even though B. A. had tuned her out. It was obvious that Chip wanted this real bad. She might as well do the unexpected when everything looked the bleakest. As Chip's next pass zipped toward her, she quickly put up her left hand and stopped the ball's forward motion. It fell straight down into her right hand, which was waiting for it. She stood up in one fluid motion, tossing the ball back and forth between right and left hands.

"Okay, squirt, you win," said B. A. with a forced smile as she walked past her teammate toward the bench.

"All right," hollered Chip, beaming. "Hey, you dropped your hair tie."

B. A. watched out of the corner of her eye as Chip bent to retrieve the hair tie that she had conveniently left behind. She turned around and whipped the ball she was holding just as Chip bent down. She threw it high enough to clear Chip's head if she stood up too quickly. The noise was the important thing, anyway. The ball hit with a loud splat above the little guard's head, which made her drop to all fours with a loud yelp. B. A. turned back to see the rest of the team staring at them. She just shrugged her shoulders and smiled at them.

"That's the spirit," said Chip as she ran over to the rest of the group.

After a short warm-up, Coach Harbison blew her whistle and called them all to the center of the floor.

"Okay girls, this is going to be full-game scrimmage," announced

Coach Harbison. "We'll choose up equal teams. You will choose what kind of offense and defense you want to run. The coaches won't help you in that respect. This will be a good test for you to demonstrate how much you have learned and how well you can think and cooperate under pressure. Remember, you are playing against your teammates, so no rough stuff. You know Coach Todd and I don't believe in that stuff anyway. Are there any questions?"

The girls just stood there with blank looks on their faces. Why was Coach Harbison running the show today? And scrimmaging the day before a game was something they hadn't done before. The two girls who knew what was going on didn't say a word.

"Okay," continued Coach Harbison. "How should we choose up teams?"

"Let's let the twins do it," Chip blurted out.

"Good idea, Fullerton," agreed Coach Harbison. "Tammi, why don't you go first?"

"Uh, sure," said Tammi. "I'll take Missy."

"Chip," said Jenny.

"Kris," said Tammi, who now had three-fifths of the usual starting lineup.

"Rachel," said Jenny, smiling. Chip threw a questioning look at Jenny, but Tammi's twin knew what she was doing. There was no way her sister was going to take B. A. She was counting on it.

"Darby," said Tammi.

"Amanda," said Jenny.

"Juanita," said Tammi.

"Lu," said Jenny.

"Carmen," said Tammi.

"Mony," said Jenny. Chip looked at her in shock. B. A. was now the only one left. Jenny was blowing the whole thing. B. A. just stood there, not quite sure what this was all about. Jenny was smiling at her sister, enjoying the moment. Be unpredictable. Wasn't that what B. A.

was always telling them? Tammi stood staring at her sister, trying to figure out a way to keep B. A. off her team.

"Well," said Coach Harbison, smiling at Chip. "This doesn't look quite fair to have seven on one team and six on another. Coach Todd, would you consider playing so each team can have a sub? I know you don't want me playing and slowing everything down."

"Sure, I'll play," said Coach Todd, surprising everyone.

"I'll take Coach," said Tammi excitedly.

"I guess I'm stuck with Smith," said Jenny dejectedly. "C'mon, Smitty, we'll find a spot for you—somewhere."

"That was pretty slick," said Chip to Jenny as they walked over to their bench. "How did you know the Toddster would step in and play?"

"I just had a feeling," said Jenny. "Besides, you're not the only one who can make a plan come together, you know."

B. A. walked to the end of the bench and did some hamstring stretches. She still wasn't sure what was going on, but she was glad she didn't have to play with Tammi and her little group. It was obvious that Tammi felt the same way, so why worry about it?

"I hope you came to play," said Jenny as she took B. A. by the arm and steered her farther down the bench. "Because if you didn't, this will all be a waste of time."

"What do you mean?" asked B. A.

"What I mean is, all the pieces are in place, and it's up to you to get them straightened out. And I'll tell you one more thing. It's not going to happen if you keep moping around and feeling sorry for yourself. You're ten times better than anyone else here, and all you've been doing is going through the motions since the Ferguson game. We're getting better, and you are going in the opposite direction. I remember what you said about being different and not following the crowd, but this can't be what you were talking about."

"What do you want from me? I'm just trying to get along here."

"Oh no, that excuse doesn't work anymore," said Jenny. "We want your best game. No holding back, no stalling, and no worrying what others are going to think. It's time to stand and deliver. Now come on over here and tell us what to do. We're waiting for your words of wisdom."

B. A. and Jenny walked back to where the other four were waiting. She quickly explained how they would be playing a loose switching "man" defense after they scored, and when they didn't score, a two-one-two zone. They were to call out the screens on defense. On the out-of-bounds plays under the basket, they were to do them in this order, 6-4-2 against a zone and 5-3-1 against a "man." She would throw the ball in and would not call out a number, so they had to remember the order and set up for that particular play. On offense, they would use the pick-and-rolls that Chip, Jenny, and B. A. had worked on. Use a lot of hand-offs and fast break every time there was an opportunity. Keep everything upbeat, with no standing and watching. Screen away from the ball and use good court sense. Both guards should fly if it looked like B. A. was going to get the defensive rebound.

Jenny could tell that her little speech had worked. B. A.'s eyes were all watery, and her demeanor was totally different. The horn blew to start the game. The girls started out to center court when Pops and Coach Devers came out of the locker room in black-and-white striped shirts. B. A. turned and went back to her gym bag, which was lying two rows up in the bleachers. She stuffed the hair tie in her bag and brought out her red bandanna. She rolled it up and tied it around her forehead.

"Watch it, ya'll," said Tammi. "They've got Rambo on their side." This brought a snicker from the girls on Tammi's team.

Pops walked over to the scorer's table and got the game ball from Coach Harbison, who was keeping the clock.

"Hey, Coach Todd," hollered Chip good-naturedly. "How about a little something to make this interesting? It wouldn't be gambling if the losing coach bought pizza for the winning team, would it? If you win, Coach Harbison will buy, and if we win, you buy. Just to spice it up a little."

"If it's okay with Coach Harbison, it's okay with me," said Coach Todd, smiling.

"There's no way I can be part of this," said Pops, startling everyone. "No sir, can't do it. Not unless the officials and the managers get pizza too—no matter who wins."

The two coaches looked at each other and nodded agreement. The girls took their places, and Pops walked around the circle and faced the scorer's table. Tammi stepped in to jump against her sister. Jenny crouched down low with her hands at her sides and prepared to jump like an athlete. Tammi bent a little at the knees with her right hand extended above her head. Jenny, Chip, and B. A. exchanged knowing looks. It was obvious who would get the tip. B. A. looked across the circle at Rachel. When she made eye contact, B. A. darted her eyes a few times toward their basket. Rachel nodded. Jenny exploded when Pops tossed the ball up. She was clearly a foot higher than her sister when she tipped the ball toward B. A., who jumped toward the ball and slapped it without looking toward the spot where Rachel should be. Rachel caught the ball in stride and roared into the basket from the left side. Her layup was contested, and she put it up too hard. B. A. was sprinting right behind and caught it as it cleared the rim on the right side. She softly banked the ball off the board while still in the air.

Darby Quinn grabbed the ball as it came through the net and heaved it to Kris Ritter, who was standing at half-court. Chip easily cut in front of the pass, intercepted it, and made it to the three-point line in two dribbles. B. A. was in good rebounding position, so Chip let it fly. She didn't shoot a set shot like she used to. She shot the "spring shot" that B. A. had taught her. Since she wasn't strong enough to shoot a jump shot from that far out, B. A. suggested she jump but shoot on her way up. That way it was considered an action shot, which meant she could get it off quickly, and the added leg drive gave her the power she needed. The shot was good. With seven seconds gone on the clock, the score was 5 to 0.

After a missed shot by Tammi at the other end, Chip dribbled slowly across the center line and waved Jenny up to the high post. Chip changed speeds and dribbled hard to her left. B. A. came up fast from the baseline and took Chip's bounce pass through Coach Todd's defending hand. B. A. went by Coach Todd easily and dribbled hard toward the baseline. Tammi, who was playing her sister loosely, stepped over to help out. B. A. surprised everyone by continuing her dribble right under the left edge of the backboard and jumping over the end line and out-of-bounds with the ball. Jenny did exactly what B. A. was counting on. She waited for about one count when her sister left to help guard B. A., then she came fast down the lane. She caught B. A.'s backhand pass in stride and laid it in as her sister stood at the baseline, helpless. The two teammates glanced at each other as they ran down the floor. No high-fiving, no fist pumping, just a look of mutual respect for a well-executed play.

B. A. took over the majority of the scoring for the rest of the quarter. She ran Coach Todd through her repertoire of shots. She hit a couple of jumpers and two hook shots. Just before the end of the quarter, she got Tammi and Coach Todd off their feet in the middle of the lane. They both came down right on top of her. Sensing that she was about to get hammered, she threw the ball up with her left hand. The ball went over the top of the backboard, but it didn't matter, as Pops blew the foul. She calmly went to the free-throw line and sank both shots. The scoreboard read 23 to 8 at the end of the first quarter.

Tammi's team came out playing tougher defense in the second quarter. They stuck closer to their girl on defense and attempted to double-team B. A. every time she got the ball. Tammi and Coach Todd grabbed her and held her every chance they could. It didn't make a lot of difference. Chip motioned Jenny to the top of the key to set some screens, and it worked to perfection. The first time down the floor, Chip dribbled right up to Jenny and shot her "spring" shot right over her teammate's head. She was appreciating that shot even more, now that she was used to it. She could effectively shoot it off the dribble and got it off extremely quickly. A minute later, she drained another three over Jenny, who had her hands out to catch Chip, as the guard's momentum carried her right into the tall forward. The successful shots over the screener set up a series of pick-and-rolls that netted a couple of easy baskets for Jenny. The girls got some funny looks from Coach Todd as they ran back up the floor. Tammi's squad ran the predictable "motion" offense that the team had been running, all season.

B. A. was surprised at the quality of officiating provided by Coach Devers and Pops. Coach Devers did an acceptable job, but Pops was excellent. His last two calls of the half showed his knowledge of the game. With twenty seconds to go in the half, B. A. was at the top of her jump ten feet out from the basket. She twisted in the air and tossed the ball back to Chip, who had spotted up just behind the three-point line. Chip caught the pass in shooting position and tossed in her second three of the quarter. The ball was about three-quarters of the way to the hoop when Juanita aggressively boxed Chip out. She backed right into Chip and knocked her to the floor. Pops whistled the foul.

When Juanita complained, Pops asked, "How did she get on the floor? She didn't trip over her own two feet. She fell because you knocked her down. A shooter is like a kicker or punter in football. They are in a position where they can't protect themselves, so it's up to the officials to do it."

He wanted to continue and ask why you would aggressively box someone out who was twenty feet from the basket. All you had to do was stay in front of her and she wouldn't be a rebounding threat. Turning your back on them and sticking your rear into them that far out from the basket didn't make sense. The technique that B. A. had passed on was to put out a soft hand and make gentle contact with the person who had just shot. If you turned about halfway around, you could keep an eye on her, which would make it easier to stay in front of her. After about two seconds, you should then turn and locate the ball. Pops caught himself and didn't say any more because Coach Todd, like so many other coaches, taught her players to turn their backs to the shooter, even if they were way out on the perimeter, and aggressively box her out. That technique was fine if you were in the lane and worried about being pushed under the basket, but out on the perimeter a different technique was called for. Coach Todd bit her tongue and didn't comment.

Pops then surprised everyone by saying Chip would go the line to shoot one-and-one. Coach Todd did question this. Pops explained that the foul happened well after the shot, and since Jenny's team was in the bonus, it was a one-and-one situation. Most refs just call this a shooting foul, but it hadn't happened during the shot. It actually happened while the players were getting ready to rebound. Chip dropped them both, which amounted to a five-point play. Coach Devers just nodded in agreement.

Missy Springer scored for the opponents on a short shot with five seconds to go in the half. B. A. grabbed the ball as it came through the cords and whipped a quick pass out to Jenny, who took one dribble up the right side and threw the ball at her basket just before she got to the ten-second line. To her amazement, Tammi tried to block the desperation heave. You could hear skin on skin all over the gym, as Tammi whacked her sister on the forearm. Some refs would have let this foul go, which would have been a big mistake. When a player is hit on the arm when she shoots, whether it's from five or fifty-five feet, it is still a foul. Pops knew this and called the infraction. He looked at Tammi in disbelief as he blew his whistle. Tammi realized she had just committed one of the dumbest plays in basketball. She had fouled an opponent who was attempting a shot that they might make one time in fifty. And now, that opponent was going to shoot three free throws. She sat on her bench sipping her water bottle, as her twin sister made two of the three shots. The half-time score was 51 to 20 in Jenny's favor.

Jenny's team sprawled on the bleachers sipping from their water bottles. They watched Tammi's team as they sat under the basket to their right. They seemed to be having a heated conversation.

"What do you think they are saying?" asked Chip.

"They're probably discussing what press to use against us for the second half," answered B. A. "That and who is to blame for the lopsided score. Their only hope of getting back into this game is to press. Let's use our normal press-breaker with a few small adjustments. I'll take the midcourt position. Just throw it somewhere close, and I'll do my best to get it. Whoever is on the wing, as soon as the ball gets close to me, fly if the person guarding you is next to you, or if they turn their head. It will be like a backdoor play. Go hard all the way to the hoop, and if you don't get the ball, circle around. Don't stop and clog up the area around the basket."

Jenny's team had a spring in their step as they went out to shoot a few before the second half started. Even Mony Sharp, who usually hung around Tammi and her "disciples," as Chip called them, was friendly and listened to everything B. A. had to say. Chip even threw a verbal jab at her to test her. Mony had a quick comeback and even said it with a smile on her face. *This is the way a team is supposed to act,* thought Chip.

B. A. was standing by Jenny, watching her shoot.

"Your shot has really improved," observed B. A. "And it's a lot more effective since you got rid of that little step toward the basket."

"I know," said Jenny. "I quit doing it after listening to you explain to Chip why we shouldn't do it. It really wasn't that tough to change my technique. Once I made up my mind to do it."

"Stand and deliver," said B. A., repeating what Jenny had said to her just before the game started. "That's a good one. That's catchy enough to be a song lyric."

Jenny nodded in agreement, not mentioning that she had heard it in a song. It was in a song by Thin Lizzy and Metallica called "Whiskey in a Jar." Chip had told Jenny that B. A. was some sort of music expert, but this was one fact that B. A. obviously didn't know. She jogged over to the bench and joined the rest of "her" team.

"What do you have to tell us, Coach Smith?" asked Jenny.

"Well, we went over the press breaker. Be smart and keep moving to the open spot. No one's got more than two fouls, so we're not in any trouble there. If they zone us to slow the game down, which means they are throwing in the towel, move the ball around quickly, and nobody passes up a shot. Don't be too selective, just shoot. We'll try to get some offensive rebounds and some put-backs. Remember, long shots produce long rebounds. Chip, if it even looks like you've got an open shot against a zone, let it fly."

"I've got a few things to add," said Chip. "I know what you're thinking, B. A., and I want you to misspell any notions of taking it easy on them this half."

"You mean dispel any notions, don't you?" corrected Rachel, laughing.

"You know what I mean," countered Chip. "We're not trying to rub it in. We're just making a statement while we've got the chance. So let's get out there and rock and roll."

B. A. looked around the circle at her teammates. Their eager eyes were focused on her, waiting for her response. Jenny, Chip, Rachel, Amanda, Lu, and Mony had acted like real teammates, at least for the first half. Especially Mony, whose style of play and language was usually rougher than it should be, was acting like she was part of the team. Chip was right. B. A. had been thinking about letting up a little. She didn't like to run up the score on anyone, let alone her teammates. She locked eyes with Chip, who seemed to be pleading for her to finish the game the way they had started. B. A. decided to go for it. If the rest of them thought she was trying to take over the team, which she wasn't, that's the way it would go. It was time to really kick out the jams!

"Okay, what do you say we take it up a notch, at least for a few minutes?"

They all nodded.

"This is something I call Full-Tilt Boogie. Here's how it works. We're looking for threes only. The exception is if you have an uncontested put-back underneath the basket. There's no reason to pass up an automatic score. So, all other offensive rebounds will be thrown or slapped back out to the three-point line. The girls out on the perimeter need to put it back up as soon as you can. It's like a three-point shooting frenzy. Shoot as quick as you can, I don't care if it's from thirty feet, just get it up there. Screen for each other out there to help you get open. Jenny, don't get too close to the basket, because the rebounds will come out hot. What do you think?"

The rest of the team looked expectantly at each other. Big smiles broke out all over. That's all B. A. needed to see.

"Another thing. We have to press to pull this off. It's very intense, and there will be a lot of action, so we'll try it for about four minutes, or less if we get too tired. Amanda and Lu, you sit out, but come in after only two minutes for whoever wants a break. Oh, and one more thing. We're way up, and I'm sure they are not too happy with the way the first half went, so be careful, they might get overly aggressive. And no smiling or even grinning. Like Chip said, we're not trying to rub it in or taunt them. Questions? Okay, rock and roll on three."

Pops was standing outside their huddle as they put their hands in the middle and hollered, "Rock and roll." As he walked next to B. A. to the far side of the court, he said quietly, "Full-Tilt Boogie? Where did that come from?"

"I'm not sure. I think I just made it up. Wait a minute. It might be an old Janis Joplin song."

"It looks like this half will be even more interesting than the first. I hope you know what you are doing. It could turn into disaster, you know?"

"Time's getting short, Pops. If I'm going to crash, it might as well be going full speed ahead with my hair on fire."

"It's your decision. I'm anxious to see your shooting frenzy in action."

Pops didn't have long to wait. Chip took the inbounds pass from B. A. to start the second half. She calmly walked the ball up the floor and then let fly from about thirty-five feet out. To everybody's surprise, the shot hit the board and went in.

Tammi hollered, "No way!"

Jenny responded with an uncharacteristic, "Way!" She then proceeded to contest her sister's inbounds pass. The rest of the team had picked up their girl in a tight "man" press. Chip got a piece of a bounce pass and deflected it toward Mony, who picked it up and threw a crisp pass to Jenny. Jenny started to dribble toward the basket as her sister stood there waiting for her to get closer. She surprised her sister, when she turned and dribbled back to the three-point line and took a shot. B. A. watched the shot in the air and knew it had no chance. It was way too hard. What did they expect from a girl who had never shot a three in a game before? B. A. had positioned herself about six feet out from the basket as the ball came off the backboard after totally missing the rim. She slapped it back toward Chip, who was waiting. Chip had to scramble to get the ball, but she recovered quickly and made the shot.

B. A. and the rest of her teammates were surprised when Mony hit a three-pointer on their next possession. However, they weren't surprised when their opponents went into a full-court press. After Coach Todd scored over Jenny, they set up their press breaker. B. A. was standing at half-court with her back to her own basket. Tammi was right behind her. Mony stood off to her left, with Kris Ritter guarding her. B. A. noticed that Kris was standing between Mony and the ball, as it was being thrown in. She hoped that Mony was paying attention when she was talking about breaking the press. The pass came to B. A. at center court. She had to jump high to get it, but she never came down with it. B. A. caught the pass at the top of her jump and then tossed it softly backward over her head toward her basket. When the ball was halfway to B. A., Mony took a step toward Kris to get her back on her heels and then turned and sprinted toward her own basket. She gathered the pass in, and since there was no one around her, she took one backward dribble and shot a three. The ball hit the front of the rim and came right back to her. She caught it and dribbled in for a layup. The shooting frenzy lasted until Chip called a time-out with 4:10 to go in the third quarter. In that time, they had hit four three-pointers and had two put-backs.

The play for the rest of the half was fast and furious. Jenny's team was crushing their opponents, but Tammi's group wouldn't give up. B. A. admired them for that. Coach Todd stared at her a lot as if she was seeing her for the first time. B. A. never really noticed the stares because she was totally into the game. She was in her "zone" and rarely looked at the people she was playing, except for the person she was guarding. Her eyes were looking elsewhere, taking in the floor and constantly exploring options. Tammi and her crew started to push and shove a lot toward the end of the game. Most of it was out of pure frustration. Pops and Coach Devers stepped in and told both sides to "cool it," even though it was obvious who the culprits were. B. A. and Coach Harbison both thought it was a good move. Coach Todd just stood there quietly, looking winded and a little pale. B. A. wondered if Pops had ever officiated before. It seemed like he was always doing something to surprise her.

The last play of the game was a classic, and in B. A.'s mind it moved Chip one rung higher on the character ladder. The score was 98 to 41 with ten seconds left. B. A. knew the rest of her teammates wanted to hit the one hundred mark. She cleared Missy's three-point attempt from the board and threw the outlet pass to Chip at half-court. Chip dribbled hard toward the basket with Tammi in full pursuit. Tammi looked determined to stop the shot at all costs. The rest of the players just stood and watched as Tammi's long legs closed the distance between her and the little guard. Chip appeared to take one last dribble in preparation to shoot a right-handed layup. Tammi left her feet with both hands high in an attempt to smother her opponent. All she got was air. At the last possible instant, Chip darted to her right along the baseline still dribbling the ball and running the clock out. If she had attempted the shot, Tammi would probably have taken her into the wall.

Tammi's team begrudgingly complimented Jenny's team on a game well played. The girls headed toward the bleachers to take a well-deserved break. Chip turned to say something to Jenny, when her eyes went wide in disbelief. Coach Devers and Pops were kneeling beside Coach Todd, who was lying motionless on the floor beneath the far basket.

Chapter 10

Voodoo Child

B. A. pulled up in front of Kim's grocery store. She was out of the truck and through the front door before her two passengers could get their doors open.

"Hi, Mr. Kim," hollered B. A. as she spotted the store owner behind the counter. She waved toward her two passengers as they came through the door. "Have you met my friends before? This is Chip, and the tall girl is Jenny."

"Ah, basketball players," said Mr. Kim as he came around the counter with his hand extended. Jenny and Chip shook hands with the smiling Korean. Mr. Kim appeared to be about B. A.'s height and looked to be about fifty years old. He moved quickly, like an athlete. His most striking feature was his smile. When he smiled, which he did quite often, his whole face lit up. The girls decided immediately that they liked him. He seemed to be an adult who would listen to your opinions without judging you.

"How was practice today?" asked Mr. Kim.

"It was different," answered B. A. as she went to the cooler with juice in it. "We had a scrimmage and the coach got sick. They took her away in an ambulance. You're about out of orange juice, Mr. K. I'll put some up for you." B. A. disappeared into the back room as her two friends stood there and stared.

"She's a nice girl," observed Mr. Kim. "How did the scrimmage go?"

"B. A. scored thirty-five points," said Chip.

"And Chip had twenty-eight," added Jenny. "I think our team is going to surprise some people for the remainder of the season. We are really starting to play well."

"And B. A. is a good player?" asked Mr. Kim.

"Mr. Kim," said Chip in a low voice to make sure B. A. didn't hear her. "She is the best player that Reston has ever had and probably ever will have. And starting with tomorrow's game, everyone around here will know it."

"Yes," agreed Jenny. "Wait until you read the reports after tomorrow's game with Springfield."

"I would like to come and watch," said Mr. Kim. "But my wife is not feeling well, so I must stay and watch the store. I will come when she gets better."

"I hope your wife gets better soon," said Chip. "We've only got about ten games left to go in the regular season. Then the state tournament starts—if we make the play-offs."

B. A. came out of the storage room with three bottles of orange juice in her hands. She held them up so the storeowner could see them.

"Mark these down, please," she said as she headed for the door. "I'll be in Friday and Saturday to help out, if that's okay."

Mr. Kim gave his best smile, accompanied by a grateful nod. Chip and Jenny said their good-byes and joined her in the truck.

"What's the big hurry?" asked Chip as they headed west out of town.

"I'm taking you to a special place, and we've only got a couple of minutes to get there," said B. A. Jenny and Chip looked at each other. They both had several questions on their minds. Jenny elbowed Chip to indicate that she should start the inquisition.

"Okay," said Chip. "Where are we going? Who was that nice Japanese guy and why did you go into the back room of his store and do the self-serve thing? Do you think the Toddster will be all right? Do you think you will get to play forward tomorrow night? And, oh yeah, how come we got juice instead of sodas? Do you think this afternoon's scrimmage was a fluke? I mean, we could have scored a hundred points! Is that it, Jenny?"

Jenny nodded in silent agreement.

"We're going to my favorite spot," said B. A. as she turned north onto a paved road just outside of town. After about a mile or so, the road turned to gravel. B. A. turned right into a shallow ditch a few hundred yards farther up the road. It was actually a grass path that led to a locked gate. She eased the truck right up to the gate, which got the back end of her vehicle off the road.

"Ram it," said Chip half-kidding. "It's just wood. It'll give way."

B. A. looked at her, shaking her head in disbelief. She reached behind her and grabbed a blanket that was behind the passenger seat. B. A. was out of the truck in an instant and deftly hopped into the truck's bed. She quickly spread out the blanket. Her two passengers sat in the truck, watching her out the back window. They didn't have any idea what was going on.

"Well," said B. A., sitting on the tailgate, "come on back and bring the drinks."

Chip and Jenny joined B. A. in the back of the truck. There was just enough room for them to sit side by side.

"Okay," said B. A. as she sipped her juice. "I'll try to answer your questions. This is where we're going. Mr. Kim is Korean and not Japanese. I've been helping him out at the store because his wife is sick. He's a real nice man. I think Coach Todd will be all right. She must have eaten some bad food or maybe she just got superexhausted. I'll ask my mom when she gets home. We need to stop drinking so many sodas and start drinking something healthier. And, let's see, no, I don't think the scrimmage was a fluke. Y'all have improved so much. I can't believe how fast your skills have developed."

"You scored thirty-five points," said Chip.

"Shhh," whispered B. A. "Watch the show."

"Show, what show?" asked Chip, looking at Jenny for an explanation.

"She means the sunset," said Jenny, looking out over the field toward the west. "It's beautiful."

The three friends sat quietly and sipped their juice as the sun dipped lower and lower toward the horizon. B. A. was surprised at how close they had become in such a short time.

"I've been coming here for a few weeks," said B. A. as the sun was halfway down. "Mr. Daggert, the guy who owns this property, came by on his tractor once, and we just sat here together watching. I was sitting on the road, and he said to pull in here for a better angle. He's a pretty cool guy. He said he always stops what he's doing so he can watch the sun set. It sure is peaceful out here, isn't it? Did you know that the sun will burn for another four billion years? After that, we're out of luck."

"How do you know that?" asked Chip.

"She pays attention in class," explained Jenny.

The girls sat and talked about basketball and other things for another half hour. They wondered how good they could really be. They talked about how to win Tammi and her followers over. Jenny was not very optimistic. She had tried for years to get her sister to stop worrying about her popularity and her image. So far she had not been very successful. Jenny explained that it wasn't like she was a bad sister or anything. When it was just Tammi, Cassie, and her, Tammi let her guard down and was a pleasant person to be around. But as soon as other people were around, she had to be the center of attention.

"Wait a minute," said B. A. "Did you say Cassie?"

"Yes," said Jenny. "Tammi isn't my only sister. Cassie is the youngest. She's one of the girls that you have been coaching in the park. She just raves about you, which makes Tammi mad."

"I get it now," exclaimed B. A. "When Tammi told me, on more than one occasion, to stay away from her sister, she was talking about Cassie, not you."

"Obviously. How could you stay away from me? We have three classes together, we eat lunch at the same time, and we're on the same basketball team."

"I didn't know Cassie was your sister until now. That's hilarious. Tammi needs to work on her communication skills."

"Among other things," added Chip.

* ◆ *

B. A. dropped her two friends off at their houses and headed for home. She had a short workout to do in her room, some studying to do, supper to fix, and a phone call to make. She made up her mind to call Rod and ask him what the deal was. Were they ever going to do anything together again or were they through as good friends? The few times she had talked to him lately the conversation had been short and strained. It was like they hardly knew each other anymore. She couldn't figure out what was going on, so she decided to ask him point-blank. It was apparent to her that he had a college girlfriend and was afraid to tell her. Well, if he wasn't going to volunteer the information, she was going to extract a confession. Why did guys have to be so weird?

* ◆ *

B. A. had just finished her chores when she reached for the phone to call Rod. It was 8:45 and her mom would be home in about forty-five minutes. She knew exactly what she wanted to say, so there was no reason to put it off any longer. She picked up the receiver on the house phone, but there was no dial tone. "Hello?" she asked timidly.

"B. A.?" Chip asked in a voice that was mostly a whisper. "How come your phone didn't ring, and why didn't you answer your cell?"

"I was just going to make a call, silly. I picked it up before it had a chance to ring. My cell must still be in my truck. What's up? Is something wrong, you don't sound so good?"

"Uh, we got problems," said Chip. "Is it okay if I come over?"

"Now? It's getting kind of late."

"Yeah. My mom says it's okay if I get back by ten. I'm lucky she gave me permission. Luke pulled a stunt a month or so back and I got into big trouble."

"Sure," said B. A., sensing that something was really wrong. "Do you want me to come and get you?"

"No, I'll drive over. See you in a couple of minutes."

B. A. sat at the kitchen table and waited for Chip to show up. She hoped it wasn't anything serious. It was hard to tell with Chip. She could be overly dramatic at times. Whatever it was, she had never heard her use the voice she had just used on the phone. It sounded like she was scared.

"I need something to drink," said Chip as she sat down.

"Juice or water?" asked B. A. as she went to the fridge.

"Something with a little more character, please," said the little guard.

"How about we split a soda?"

"Now you're talking."

B. A. served the drinks and sat down across from her guest. She waited for Chip to start.

"First of all, I want to admit that this whole thing is all my fault," said Chip in a remorseful tone. "And I know that I will probably go to jail for this. I never meant for anything serious to happen. It was just another project. You know, something to do, to add a little excitement to things. Luke and I do it all the time. He's in the clear on this one, though. I take full responsibility for everything. They're probably going to put me away for a long time."

"What the heck are you talking about?" asked B. A., finally breaking in.

"Look," said Chip as she reached into her gym bag and took out the little doll that she had fashioned in Coach Todd's image. She laid it gently on the kitchen table. There was a straight pin sticking through one side of the doll's lower abdomen. B. A. just stared at it for a moment.

"So you stabbed her," whispered B. A., trying to stay serious.

"It was an accident," wailed Chip. "I would never do something like that intentionally. I should have never messed with such dark and potent powers."

"Maybe it was a suicide attempt," said B. A., reaching slowly for the pin.

"Don't touch it!" hollered Chip. "If you take it out, she could get a collapsed lung or something. It could make things worse. I learned that in health class."

"Her lungs don't go quite that far down," said B. A. trying to stay in control. It was all she could do not to laugh or make a joke, but Chip seemed so serious, it probably wouldn't have been a good idea to make light of her.

"Tell you what, my mom will be home in a few minutes. Why don't we ask her for an opinion? She's a nurse, and she might even know how Coach Todd is doing. They probably took her to the hospital where she works because it's the closest one to Reston. If it looks bad for you, then the three of us can plan your getaway."

"You're making fun of me, and this is a serious matter," said Chip, leaning back and crossing her arms. "We're talking jail here. I don't know if I'm equipped for jail. I hear the food is awful."

The two athletes sat and talked until Martha Smith came through the back door. She looked a little tired, as she often did after a tough shift in the emergency room. Martha could have had a less exciting job in one of the other departments at the hospital, but she was a self-professed action junkie. She loved it when things were hectic and bordering on out-of-control. She also received a lot of self-satisfaction knowing she played a big part in saving people's lives.

B. A. hugged her mom at the door and walked her over to her chair at the table. As usual, she had a hot cup of tea waiting for her. It was normally a time where they would sit and tell each other about their day. But tonight there was more serious business to tend to. Chip put the doll back in her gym bag when Mrs. Smith came through the door. B. A. stood behind her mom rubbing her shoulders as Chip began to explain the events leading up to the doll's "accident." The more she talked, the faster she talked, until she was almost incoherent.

"Mom," said B. A. as she came around and took the chair across from Chip. "Let's see if I can clear this up. Did Coach Todd come to your hospital tonight?"

"Yes," said Martha, still trying to figure out what Chip was talking about.

"What was the matter with her? She passed out at the end of practice today."

"Her appendix almost ruptured," explained Mrs. Smith. "It was lucky she got there when she did. You never know about those things. Actually, no one even knows what the appendix does. But you can relax. Your coach is fine. She was out of surgery when I left, and there appeared to be no complications."

"That still doesn't let me off the hook," said Chip dejectedly. "I'm glad she's okay, but it's still all my fault."

"What is this girl talking about?" asked Martha, looking for some sort of explanation.

"She thinks she caused Coach Todd's appendicitis attack," said B. A., winking at her mom. "Will you show her where your appendix is, Mom?"

"Well, it's right—"

"No, Mom," said B. A., laughing. "Chip has a model you can show us on."

"A model?" asked Mrs. Smith, still confused and trying to make some sense of what was going on. She looked from Chip's sullen face to her daughter's mischievous one.

"Show her 'Exhibit A'," said B. A., looking across the table.

Silently, which was not easy for her, Chip reached into her bag and brought out the doll. She laid it carefully on the kitchen table.

"What's this?" asked Martha, not expecting an answer. "This looks like your coach. It's almost an exact replica. Did you make this?"

Chip shook her head, staring at the doll.

"Will you show her where the doll's appendix is—that is, if she had one?" asked B. A.

Martha put her little finger on the lower right side of the doll's abdomen, just over from the hip bone. She left her finger there and glanced up at the two teens.

"What's this straight pin doing here?" asked Martha as she pulled it out.

"Careful!" exclaimed Chip.

"I think I know what's going on here," said Martha holding up the pin and looking at it. "You think you caused your coach's health problems by sticking this pin into the doll. Well, that's impossible. You can't hurt someone by doing something to a figure that looks like them. Besides, the pin is on the wrong side for what happened to your coach. The appendix is on the right side. Did you make this doll hoping something would happen to Coach Todd?"

"No, not really," explained Chip. "I was just messing around. I wouldn't do anything to hurt someone on purpose. I guess I was a little frustrated because of the way the coach was treating B. A., but I didn't want anything to happen to her. You believe me, don't you?"

"We believe you, dear," said Mrs. Smith, patting Chip on the hand. "Now that you know it wasn't your fault, you two should get ready for bed. Don't you have a game tomorrow?"

"I have to go home," said Chip. "I have my dad's car. So, you really think I'm in the clear? Man, I thought I was a goner. Thank goodness for appendicitis. I mean, I'm glad it wasn't something serious. I mean, I'm glad everything is all right. You know what I mean, don't you?"

B. A. just stood there and shook her head. She slowly stood up with an understanding look on her face and guided Chip to the back door.

"One thing I don't believe," hollered Mrs. Smith as she headed down the hall. "The pin sticking wasn't an accident. It was stuck in way too far. I believe you when you say you didn't stick her, but someone did."

The two ballplayers stopped in their tracks at the back door. The same thought occurred to them at the exact same time. They looked at each other and simultaneously exclaimed, "Luke!"

Chip was waiting for Luke the next morning at school. He was barely out of his car when the fiery little guard started in on him. She followed him all the way to his locker and then to his first-hour class. The teacher told Chip to get to her own class and to find some other time than school time to berate her boyfriend.

"Boyfriend!" exclaimed Chip to no one in particular as she hurried down the hall. "I owe him big-time. Vengeance is nine-tenths of the law, or something like that. No, wait. Vengeance is mine, said somebody real important. Yeah, that's it. I'm gonna lay low for a while, and when he least expects it—wham! It will be payback time."

Chapter 11

Mojo Rising

The Springfield gym was only about one-quarter full the next night when the Lady Eagles from Reston came to town. It was Friday night, and apparently a girls' high school basketball game was not in the plans of most of the Springfield inhabitants. As a result, they missed a great performance. Not by the home team, but by the visitors, who took up right where they left off from the previous day's scrimmage. Springfield was three games over 500, and they figured that, because of their record, Reston would be an easy win. They were unpleasantly surprised.

"All right, girls," said Coach Harbison just before the team was ready to take the floor. "We'll go with Fullerton and Ritter at the guards, Smith and Jenny at the forwards, and Espinosa at the post. Play an up-tempo game, pushing the ball up the floor as much as possible. They like to work the ball into the middle and—you know what? I don't think we care what they like to do. How about we do what we want to do for once? Pass a lot, shoot a lot, and don't hurt anybody, including yourselves. That's it. Let's get after it from the opening tip."

Chip was a bundle of nervous energy. She jumped to her feet and ran out the locker room door. The rest of the team followed, shaking their heads. It was the strangest pregame talk they had ever heard. Coach Harbison's pregame speech might have been out of the ordinary, but it got results. The Springfield Lady Rams kept looking over to their bench for help as Reston scored fast and scored often. Unfortunately, their coach was just as surprised as they were. He called two time-outs in the first quarter to make some changes, but nothing slowed down the visitors. They weren't prepared for Chip's two three-pointers in the first quarter. And they definitely weren't prepared for the shorter of the two forwards, who scored over, under, around, and through their front line. Where was this girl when Springfield beat Reston the first time around in Reston's gym? She must have been sick or something. Reston's play wasn't the only thing that surprised the home coach. The conduct exhibited by the visitors made him think of his playing days a few decades earlier. There was no high-fiving or goofy gestures. When Springfield committed a traveling violation, the Reston girls didn't signal traveling, as if they were refereeing. This was something he could not get his team to stop doing. At times, they seemed more interested in making calls than in playing. He thought to himself, *Man, would I like to coach these girls.*

The Reston starters communicated well with each other. It was obvious that their point guard and two forwards were the core of the team. Most of the time they acted as if the Rams didn't even exist. They talked quietly among themselves during dead balls and went about their business. They were acting like—well, pros. No, pros wasn't the right word. Professionals, men and women, were among the worst at grandstanding gestures and all the other nonsense that comes with the professional game. Pro ball was supposed to be entertainment, but, somewhere along the line, modern players had decided that they had to do more than just play the game. These girls, especially their three leaders, were playing with a touch of class. The Springfield coach appreciated the way they handled themselves, and he told them that when he shook their hands after the game. Everybody from the Reston squad played a lot of minutes, or they would have been in triple digits on the scoreboard. He wasn't even sure if their board could display a score of 100 or more. He looked at the scoreboard as he headed to the locker room to talk to his team. It read: Rams 41 Visitors 84.

Martha Smith and Helen Fullerton sat and watched their daughters play for the first time this season. Chip always told her mom not to bother coming, because the team was so bad, and it made her nervous. When Chip found out that B. A.'s mom had taken half a day off to go to the Springfield game, she told her mom to call Mrs. Smith so they could go to the game together. As their moms filed out the gym doors into the cool evening air, they couldn't help but overhear the home-team crowd talk about their respective daughters.

"Was that little guard a quick shooter or what?" asked a middle-aged man.

"She was quick," said another. "But what about that Olsen girl? She had two put-backs in the first two minutes. Boy, was our coach mad."

"Where did that Smith girl come from?" asked the first man. "She was a scoring machine. I think she was in double figures before the first quarter was over. I hope they can keep it together for tomorrow night's game with Ferguson. That Miller girl can be rough."

"They'll handle Ferguson. They already beat them once, and that was at Ferguson. Heck, they would have scored a hundred on us if they hadn't substituted so much."

The two moms didn't say much on the short trip home to Reston. They were both deep in thought about what wonderful daughters they had. And it wasn't just all about basketball ability. They had also noticed the sportsmanship that their girls exhibited. Their combination of ability and behavior was something a parent could be proud of.

* ◆ *

Chip sat at the kitchen table watching her mom make breakfast the following morning. Her dad had already hustled off to work, as usual.

Saturday was always a big day at his hardware store. Chip was going to go in and help her dad later, as he had a big sale going on. She liked helping her dad. He wasn't really into sports. Tools were his thing. Working occasionally at his store was quality time that they could spend together. She had been doing it since she was in eighth grade.

"Wasn't that a great game last night?" asked Chip as her mom set their plates on the table. "B. A. pretty much did it all last night. You know, I've learned a lot from her these past few months. And I don't mean just basketball."

"What else have you learned?" asked her mom as she sat down and began to butter her toast.

"It's just her whole attitude, Mom. She never complains, and she's so nice to everybody. I've never seen anyone my age who cares as much as she does about the people around her. She has been helping Jenny and me after practice and Cassie Olsen's group once in a while at the park. And I just found out she's helping Mr. Kim at his store. She probably gets it from her mom. She's a nurse, you know?"

"Yes, I do know," replied Mrs. Fullerton. "I had a nice, long talk with her at last night's game. I checked her out real close, and I believe she really is B. A.'s mother. In case you're wondering about her being a government agent or something."

"I told you that Luke's theory on the witness thing was all wrong. We're way past that now. I don't know if I told you this before, but she does a thing I've never seen another kid do. She picks up trash all the time. I mean off the floor, in the street, and in the locker rooms. Anytime she sees trash, she picks it up and throws it away. She's even got Jenny and me doing it now. I actually kinda like it. Is that strange or what?"

"I don't think it's strange. We need people to clean things up, even if they weren't the one that made the mess. Otherwise there would be trash all over the place. Apparently she has figured that out at a young age, and she's doing something about it. Good for all three of you."

"Well, I'm going to help dad at the store. You're not going to use your car, are you? I can get Luke to take me if you need it."

"No, I've got this week's books to take care of. Don't stay too late. You should rest before tonight's game. I'm sure this 'Judo Jane' will be a handful tonight. Especially after what happened the last time you played them."

"It's "Crazy Jane," Mom, but I like your description too. She probably would give someone a judo chop if she thought she could get away with it. Oh, by the way, did you know there is no such thing as a judo chop? Luke says there's no hitting or punching in judo. You wanna know something funny? He reads these adventure books where the author has the hero giving judo chops to the bad guys. Luke says the author has probably never seen a judo match. It's actually an Olympic sport."

"I didn't know that. Your boyfriend is a veritable sports expert."

"Mom, he is not my boyfriend. We're just good friends, that's all."

"You keep saying that, but it sure looks like it to me."

"It's obvious you know very little about modern boy/girl relationships. I should be going. Dad doesn't like it if I'm late. See you around supper time."

With that, Chip bounded out the door muttering something about what a big jerk Luke was. She was still planning her revenge for his involvement in the doll incident.

●◆●

The game with Ferguson was not anything like the first game at their place. One difference was the huge presence of Reston rooters. Word had gotten out about their recent success, and the locals wanted to see if there was anything to it. It didn't take long to figure out that there definitely was something to it. Reston took a first quarter lead of eight points and continued to add to it for the rest of the game. Two things happened that surprised both B. A. and Chip. The first thing was when

Carmen Espinosa came up to B. A. in the locker room before the game and asked her for her advice on what she should be doing on the floor. B. A. told her where and how she should set screens. She also told her to try to set four screens on every possession. Carmen was 6'2" with wide shoulders and was capable of setting a pretty mean screen. Miller found that out in the second quarter when Jenny cut around Carmen and ran Miller right into the big center. Carmen barely flinched, but Miller was rocked pretty hard. She didn't know it was coming because not one of her teammates opened her mouth to call the screen out. B. A. wondered if they kept quiet on purpose or just forgot to warn their star. For the remainder of the game, Miller played hard, but without the antics and loud chatter for which she was famous.

The second surprise was the play of Xiu Lu. The junior guard played a bit role and usually didn't get much playing time. Lu, as everyone called her, was a quiet girl who played basketball to keep in shape for her one great love—distance running. She was already the school record holder in the 1600 meters. When Lu came in at the end of the second quarter, it was the first time she had played in the first half all year. Coach Todd, if she played her at all, would put her in with a minute or two to go. Coach Harbison, on the other hand, tried to get everybody in as early as she could. When Lu came on the floor for Kris, she motioned to Chip that she would guard Ferguson's second-leading scorer. The girl who played the number two spot for Ferguson was fairly quick and a good shooter. Her one big drawback was no jump shot. She was strictly a set shooter. Because she couldn't go one-on-one with a defender, she had to work real hard to get open. Lu stuck close to her and dogged her every move. Lu got so low on defense that her fingers actually touched the floor. Her defense was so tenacious that Coach Harbison left her in for the rest of the half. She completely shut down the opponent's second-leading scorer. She never even got a shot off. B. A. and Chip both patted her on the back as they went in for the half-time break. Lu had a big smile on her face. It appeared she had found her niche, just as Carmen had. A successful team is made up of many components and two more for Reston had just fallen into place. The final was: Reston 72 Ferguson 51. "Crazy Jane" had nothing to say and didn't appear to be very happy as she headed for the visitor's locker room. She was glad that she would not have to see the Reston girls again for the rest of the season.

Chip looked up at Luke as she left the floor. He usually gave her a thumbs-up or some sort of gesture of approval. This time he didn't see her at all, as he was huddled extremely close to Clarice, his protégée. They were obviously concentrating on something and didn't bother to acknowledge the team as they left the floor. She was hoping for something from him, as her twenty-five points was second only to B. A.'s thirty-one. She didn't take the snub very well, even if it was from a guy who was *not* her boyfriend. Chip wasn't the only Reston player with a concerned look on her face. With Coach Harbison running the show while Coach Todd was recovering from her appendicitis surgery, it didn't look good for the self-proclaimed star and leader of the Reston squad. Tammi was on the outs, and she realized there wasn't much she could do about it.

● ◆ ●

B. A. was feeling pretty good about the way things were turning out. The team was coming around, and it was a beautiful Sunday afternoon in northern Texas. She had spent the morning with her mom and even packed her lunch for her while Martha took a nap before heading off to work. Her mom had Mondays and Tuesdays off, so she got to see a lot of her four days in a row. They didn't see each other much for the other three days of the week. It was almost as if B. A. had her own place from Wednesday to Friday. This Sunday was going to be an interesting day. She decided to confront Rod after her mom left for work. She called his cell phone but got no answer. She decided to drive over to his house to ask him what was going on. They hadn't lifted or played ball together for several weeks. The last time she had talked to him, he seemed to be in a big hurry to hang up. She was tired of not knowing where she stood. As she was on her way out the door, Doc Snyder called her to check on things. They talked for fifteen minutes before his pager went off, and he had to go. Before he hung up, he mentioned something about anxiously waiting for the box scores from her games. As she headed out the door, she figured out what he was talking about. Doc Rupert was faxing the team's box scores to Doc Snyder. What a nice man he was, to be so concerned about her. Sometimes people didn't realize how lucky they were to have so many people care about them. She made up her mind to recruit Chip and Jenny to go with her on a special trip she had been planning.

•◆•

B. A. pulled up in front of Rod's house and went to the front door. Rod's mother answered the door, and her face lit up when she saw B. A. Grace Foster was Karen Fullerton's sister. Grace was much taller than Chip's mom. She was about 5'8" with blonde hair. If you saw the two women together, you probably wouldn't have guessed that they were sisters. They were the best of friends, in childhood and as adults. When Karen's husband mentioned moving to Fort Worth to be closer to the hardware store, she vetoed the idea. No way was she going to move, even twenty miles, away from her sister. In the interests of family harmony, he dropped the idea. As a compromise, he convinced her to quit her job at the bank and do the store's books for him. The arrangement worked out, and everyone was happy.

"Hi, Mrs. F. Is Rod around?" asked B. A.

"Hi, B. A.," said Mrs. Foster smiling. "I think he is in the garage with his weights. I haven't seen you for a while. What have you been up to?"

"Just going to school and playing basketball. Oh, and I put in a few hours at Mr. Kim's store a few days a week. Do you ever shop there? It's a nice store, and he's got more stuff than you'd think. It looks small from the outside, but it's crammed almost to the ceiling with food and other things."

"I do shop there once in a while. I like him and his wife, but I haven't seen her in a while."

"That's because she's been sick. Mr. Kim doesn't like to talk about it, but I think it's pretty serious."

"I'll stop by and ask about her. I don't think they know very many people in town. Maybe I'll take them some of my famous beef stew."

"That would be great. He's a real nice guy. I'm sure they could use the business, and the food would be a nice gesture. It was nice seeing you. I have to talk to Rod, if it's okay."

"Sure. Just go on back. You know the way."

B. A. walked around back of the house to the garage. She knocked on the side door and walked in.

"Hello," she hollered. "Are you in here, Rod?"

Standing by one of the benches was a girl who appeared to be a couple of years older than B. A. She looked like she had just gotten done doing a set of bench presses. The girl was reasonably attractive with long, blonde hair. She smiled at B. A. and offered her hand.

"Hi, I'm Beth," said the stranger.

B. A. offered her hand in return.

"I'm B. A.," she said. All sorts of thoughts were going through her head. So this was why Rod had been avoiding her. Rod had found a girl more his own age. *I've should have known*, thought B. A. *Why didn't he just come out and tell me? I thought he had more character than that. Hey, maybe this is his cousin or something. I doubt it. Neither he nor Chip ever mentioned another cousin. I'm not even sure what to say to her.*

"Uh, is Rod around?" was all she could come up with. It was still a shock to see this girl doing what she used to do on that very bench. This was awful. *I can't believe Rod is that kind of guy. He's always been so nice and considerate. Maybe it was all an act. No, he's not that good an actor. There has to be an explanation.*

"He's back there with Carl, my boyfriend," said Beth, pointing to the corner of the garage. "They're looking at Rod's car. He's got some serious problems."

Rod and Carl came around the corner talking and laughing until Rod saw B. A. He stopped in his tracks and looked at the two girls. It didn't take him long to assess the situation. It also didn't take him long to figure out that he had made a big mistake. Avoiding B. A. while he tried to figure things out was not the right approach to solving his dilemma. The look on her face gave him an uncomfortable feeling in the middle of his chest. He had been mentally wrestling with the idea of liking a high school girl. When he was in high school, the guys always made fun of other guys who went after the younger girls. They called it "dropping down in class." Senior boys would go after freshman or sophomore girls, because a lot of the girls liked the older guys. And, in a lot of cases, it was the only date they could get. For the girls, it was something of a status symbol to go with an upperclassman. But it was usually because the older guys could do stuff that guys their age couldn't. They could drive, they had a lot more freedom, and they usually had money to spend. He even remembered a girl in his freshman class who was seeing a guy in his twenties. What kind of guy that age would date a fifteen-year-old girl? It was creepy.

Carl was a mechanic, and he had come over to check out Rod's car. As he suspected, Rod needed a rear U-joint. Carl looked at B. A. and then back to Rod.

"Is this the girl that you've been telling us about?" he asked. He walked over to B. A. and introduced himself. "I heard you are some kind of basketball player. Beth was a starter on her high school team. Maybe we can catch a game soon. When do you play again?"

"We've only got two more," said B. A. "Tuesday at home and Friday at Lakewood."

"What do you say, babe—Tuesday or Friday?"

"Friday would work for me," answered Beth.

"Okay, Friday it is. I want to see what this big guy has been raving about," said Carl, gesturing toward Rod. "I'll be over sometime next week, as soon as I can get the parts. I'll give you a call, okay?"

"That would be great," said Rod. "Thanks a lot."

"Nice meeting you," said Carl as he and Beth headed for the door.

"Me too," said Beth. "I'm anxious to see a legend in action."

"It was nice meeting you two," said B. A. "I wouldn't put too much stock in that legend talk. Rod tends to exaggerate a little. We do have a real sharp point guard. She's quite a character and a lot of fun to watch. She's Rod's cousin."

"Hey, I know her," said Carl. "Haven't seen her for years, though. All right, it's a date then. See you Friday. We expect a major show, B. A."

Rod and B. A. both waved to them as they let themselves out.

* ◆ *

B. A. sat down on a bench and looked at Rod. He gave her that shy look that she remembered from the first time she had met him. The look that said he wasn't very experienced with the opposite sex. It was one of the first things that she liked about him. She wasn't into the cocky, "Look at me, I'm special," kind of guy.

"So, what have you been telling people about me?" she asked, trying to make small talk before the real issue was brought up.

"Oh, just guy talk," responded Rod. "That you were a great basketball player and a wonderful girl. And the kinda girl that some big goof should appreciate more."

She started to say something, but he held up his hand to stop her.

"Look, I'm sorry for avoiding you for the past month or so. When I was in high school, we made fun of guys who hung around the younger girls. You know, looking for dates because they couldn't get girls their age to go out with them. Well, some of the guys starting kidding me about spending so much time with a high school girl, and I thought maybe I was turning into one of those guys we used to look down on. You know, the desperate type."

B. A. smiled as she stood up and took a step forward. It was all coming into focus now, and she felt herself forgiving him faster than she thought was possible.

"Is that so?" she asked holding back her emotions. "I don't like you for your status or anything else—and definitely not for your car. I pushed it once before, you know. And now you can't even drive it. Let's be honest. My truck is nicer than your car."

She had hoped to get a smile out of him with her last statement, sensing that he was having trouble with his thoughts.

"I know you're not one of those types, Annie. I guess I was just all mixed up about things. I really like you, and not just for a lifting and basketball buddy. Does this make any sense at all?"

"You have cleared some things up," said B. A. "How about we forget the past weeks and start over." She stepped forward and offered her hand to him. "Hi, I'm Annie Smith, and I'm a junior at Reston High School. And you are?"

"I'm Rod Foster," he said. "Sophomore at the University of North Texas and sometimes not the sharpest knife in the drawer. I just turned twenty, so I'm asking for a little leniency for past indiscretions. I'm feeling like I need a little more than a handshake. How about a hug?"

"You just turned twenty?" she asked. "Our ages aren't that far apart. You're only about two and a half years older than me. I'm thinking a little more than a hug is in order. You can either bend down, or I'll stand on this bench."

Rod bent down and took her in his arms. Their lips met in their first real kiss. They both decided that it was something they would be doing a lot more from now on. They separated, looked at each other, and then kissed again. This one lasted even longer.

* ◆ *

Rod and B. A. were sitting on his front porch swing together when Chip and Luke pulled up in the "punkin'." They chuckled when the orange car came to a stop and chugged a bit before it finally shut down. It was hard not to laugh at Luke's vehicle. Rod had his arm around B. A. and she was comfortably snuggled into him. Chip's eyes opened wide when she got close enough to see what the situation was. She had what appeared to be a slip of paper in her hand.

"Okay, this has got to stop right now," she hollered, pointing at them. "No lovey-dovey stuff, B. A. It just gets in the way. We've got two big games coming up and then the state tournament. I can't have you looking up in the stands and batting your eyes at this big ogre. Get your arm off of her, cuz. I'm serious. This could ruin our team chemistry. Right, Luke?"

Luke thought the matter was rather humorous until he was called upon for his opinion.

"I don't know, lots of girl athletes have boyfriends, and it doesn't seem to affect their performance."

"That shows how much you know," continued Chip. "She's going to start worrying about her hair and all sorts of goofy stuff, just trying to impress him. We've got basketball to concentrate on. I've seen it a hundred times. Now let go of her. I thought you didn't like her anymore, the way you've been avoiding her."

Rod had hugged B. A. even tighter as Chip ranted.

"Relax, mighty mite. We made up, and you are just going to have to get used to it. Why are you here, anyway? Are you spying on us? Is this your latest project?"

"What? No. My mom asked me to bring this recipe to Aunt Grace. I had no idea I would witness the destruction of all the hard work we've put in to get things straightened out. I think I'm going to be sick."

"C'mon, Chip," said B. A. "Don't you think you're overreacting just a little bit? This is going to have no effect on my play or our team chemistry. I promise."

"I'm holding you to that, sugarlips, or whatever pet name he has for you. Here, lover boy, please give this to your mom. I don't think I can face her under these circumstances."

She tossed the recipe on the swing and headed back to the car with Luke in tow. Luke turned back and looked at them, shrugging his shoulders in a classic "What can I do about it?" gesture. Chip sat in the passenger seat staring straight ahead with her arms folded across her chest. She was the picture of indignation. When Luke had trouble starting the car, B. A. and Rod looked at each other and snickered. Those two were always good for some sort of entertainment.

"She'll get over it," said Rod. "But just to be sure, you better have an awesome game on Tuesday. Otherwise, I'll never hear the end of it. Twenty years from now when the family gets together at Thanksgiving, she'll still be blaming me for the team crashing and burning."

"I'll do my best," said B. A. "I was planning on getting my hair and nails done before the game on Tuesday. I've got a boyfriend to impress, you know."

They looked at each other and laughed again.

⚬⬥⚬

Luke looked over at Chip as she continued to stare straight ahead with furrowed brow.

"Don't you think you laid it on a little thick back there? Do you really think B. A.'s relationship with Rod will make any difference in how she plays?"

"We'll see," answered Chip. Her mind was racing, and she didn't quite know what to make of it. If her idol could cozy up to her guy, maybe there was no harm in it. She better do something before Luke did something rash with that little redheaded freshman, Patrice, or whatever her name was. Everything was starting to fall apart—and just when their mojo was beginning to rise.

"Okay," she said, looking over at Luke. "At the risk of blowing my whole high school sports career, I guess it's all right if you and I hold hands, but not in public. I mean, if you want to."

Luke couldn't believe what he was hearing. He should have jumped at the opportunity, but he couldn't pass up a chance like this, even if it was something that he had been hoping for.

"I don't know. I've got quite a list of admirers. They probably wouldn't like it if I limited myself to just one girl. I have to think about my rep with the ladies."

"I wouldn't call junior high girls ladies, stud muffin."

"Ouch, that hurt. You've got a sharp tongue, and you're a bit feisty for my taste. But you do have some good qualities, down deep inside. What the heck, I'll give it a shot, as long as it's a private thing between you and me."

He reached over and took her hand. She clasped it and smiled at him.

"Thanks for putting up with my feistiness," she said.

"Actually, I wouldn't have it any other way," replied Luke, realizing that his breathing rate had just doubled. It was fortunate for him that Rod had made up with B. A. This was one of the best days of his young life.

Chapter 12

Sportswriter

As the Fullerton family was eating their Monday night dinner, Chip stood up and lightly banged her spoon against her glass. John and Karen Fullerton were used to this sort of behavior, so they weren't surprised in the least. They just continued eating as if nothing out of the ordinary were happening.

"Mom, Dad, how about a little courtesy here," said Chip. "I have an important announcement. Okay, Mom, this is what you've been hinting at for the longest time. Luke is now officially my boyfriend."

Chip's parents were calmly eating their soup as if Chip weren't even there.

"Hello, this is a major happening here. How can you be so nonchaliced? A major event has just occurred in your only daughter's life. How about a little parental concern?"

Her parents looked at each other, and then back down at their soup.

"I don't believe this. Do ya'll need hearing aids?"

Mrs. Fullerton reached over and took her daughter's hand.

"Sit down, dear. Why are we supposed to get excited when you state something so obvious? Luke has been your boyfriend for as long as we can remember. It's about time you realized it."

"Yeah," added her dad. "That guy eats here as much as I do. What's the big deal? And I think you meant nonchalant. You know, like we don't care. Well, we do care, and I'm glad you finally came to your senses. You could do a whole lot worse, like that Cooper kid. Now he's a real piece of work."

"C'mon, Dad, Stench Cooper? Yes, that's his nickname. Everybody calls him that. You can't be serious."

"What kind of nickname is Stench?" asked her dad. "What's the story behind that?"

"Trust me, you don't want to know. I'm finished here. Can I be excused?"

They both waved at her and went back to their soup.

"This is incredible," she wailed, pushing back her chair. "My own parents. I'd just like to say that I'll be going out a little later because my boyfriend and I have a heavy make-out session planned. Any objections?"

They both looked up, trying to hold back grins.

"No problem here," said her mom. "Just make sure you've got all your homework done first."

"You two are impossible," she hollered, stomping off to her room.

* ◆ *

Chip sat down at her desk and looked over her assignment book. It was an easy night, so she sent Luke a text to see what he was up to. He responded by telling her to turn on her computer. He was sending an e-mail with his latest article for the school paper. She put her ear buds in and punched in a couple of Grand Funk Railroad songs. Grand Funk was a group she had never even heard of a few months ago. B. A.'s influence was definitely changing her. The music she listened to, the way she played basketball, and her general outlook on things. She decided it was all for the better and decided to thank her again for moving to Reston. Luke's e-mail appeared, and she clicked on the attachment.

SMITH AND FULLERTON LEAD LADY EAGLES TO VICTORY

By Luke Slowinski

The Lady Fighting Eagles are coming together at the ideal time. With one more regular season game to go, they are playing like a team possessed. Led by B. A. Smith and feisty point guard Melinda "Chip" Fullerton, the Lady Eagles scored 84 and 72 points in their last two games. The team was averaging in the thirties before Smith was moved to the number three position, which is her natural spot. With a little detective work, this reporter has learned that Smith was a first team all-conference player at Jones Ferry High School in Arkansas last year. She was also named to the third team all-state squad. She's not the type to toot her own horn and did not volunteer this information. Jones Ferry's loss is certainly Reston's gain. Smith has scored thirty-five and thirty in the team's last two victories. She outplayed Ferguson's star, Jane Miller, in every category for the second time this season.

Chip Fullerton has also shown great improvement in the second half of the season. Her three-point shooting and quick shots off the dribble have proven to be very effective. Between her and Smith, they have been recently been averaging a combined total of over fifty points per game. These two like an up-tempo game, which makes it very exciting to watch. If you have not seen the Lady Eagles lately, you should make plans to visit Lakewood this Friday. It's the last regular season game for the girls. Lakewood is only about twelve miles away, so it's a short trip to see some excellent basketball.

Other players who have greatly improved their games are Jenny Olsen, Kris Ritter, and Xiu Lu. Olsen has been rebounding up a storm. In the last two games she has totaled fifteen defensive boards and seven offensive ones. She has also scored in double figures for the last four games. Kris Ritter is doing what needs to be done to complement Fullerton. She plays well without the ball and does the little things that are necessary for a successful team. Ritter had a season high of twelve points at the Springfield game. Xiu Lu has fast become a defensive standout. She has seen limited playing time, but when she is on the floor, she is a defensive force. Ferguson's number two scorer, Lindstrom, found that out last Tuesday. If this team keeps scoring and playing defense the way they have, there's no telling how far they will go.

On a side note, Coach Todd will probably be out for the rest of the season, as she is recovering from a recent emergency appendectomy. Coach Harbison has risen to the occasion and has the girls working together. They have morphed into an exciting, high-scoring outfit.

Chip was incensed. If Luke put this in the school paper, B. A. would never speak to him again. What was he thinking! "With a little detective work—feisty point guard." Was he insane? She had better straighten this out face-to-face before he ruined the team and her friendship with B. A. He was only officially her boyfriend for a few days, and he was already causing trouble.

Chip walked into the living room where her parents were watching television. She grabbed the remote and muted the sound. Her parents looked at her and didn't say anything. This was also typical behavior in the Fullerton household.

"I would like to announce that I have officially gone into crisis mode and need to use the car. There is a problem that has to be taken care of immediately."

"Does this have anything to do with the heavy make-out session that you mentioned earlier?" asked her dad.

"Absolutely not," she responded indignantly. "It could turn into a punching-bag session if somebody doesn't come to his senses. Let's just say he is trying to ruin everything. Can I have the keys, please?"

Her dad reached into his pocket and threw her the car keys. He motioned for her to give him the remote.

"Take a deep breath and calm down, dear," said her mom. "Don't go storming off. That's how some people get speeding tickets. Luke only lives about a half mile away. You'll get there soon enough."

"Hey," her dad hollered as she was heading for the back door. "We better not have to call Rubio again to track you two down."

She turned to face them.

"Listen, that was an honest mistake. We did fall asleep. Nothing was going on."

"We believe you, Melinda," said her mom in a quiet voice. "He's just saying to think twice before you do anything. People who make rash decisions often live to regret them."

"If you do punch him," added her dad holding up his hands like a boxer, "work a few combos in. They're very effective."

Chip's only response was a loud "aaaggghhh." She turned and headed out the door. It was time to straighten out one cocky sportswriter before her whole life went into the tank.

• ◆ •

Luke's mom answered the front door. She was a smaller version of Luke—same hair color, same dimples, and same facial expressions.

"Hi, Mrs. S.," said Chip. "I need to see Luke right away, please."

"Hi, Chip. He's in his room studying. Go on in. Knock first. He might be on the phone with his other girlfriend."

What? Everyone's suddenly a comedian. First my parents and now

Luke's mom. She stopped at the door to Luke's room and knocked loudly. Before he could answer it, she pushed the door open.

"Okay, Mr. Super Sportswriter. Are you trying to ruin everything?"

Luke was sitting on his bed reading a sports magazine.

"What are you talking about? I was just sitting here minding my own business."

"That stupid article. That's what I'm talking about. You can't put it in the paper."

"Why not? Everything I said in there is true."

"That's not the problem, Luke," she said softening her tone. She had to admit, she really did like the guy, despite all his faults, which were numerous. "Okay, sit down. We're going to have a serious talk, and you can never repeat anything I tell you. Agreed?"

"So, you're saying this is off the record?" he asked. He didn't mention that he was already sitting down. He knew the safe play was to just go along with her, especially when she was agitated, which was a good deal of the time.

"I'm saying it was never said, and you won't repeat it if you value your health. I'm talking to you as—as someone who likes you, okay?"

Luke put the magazine down and gave her his complete attention. No wisecracks. No interruptions of any kind. He was a master at dealing with her when she was like this.

"I'm just gonna close this door," she said, getting up from his desk.

"I wouldn't do that if I were you," said Luke. "It's against house rules."

"All right. Jeez, why is everything so difficult? Never mind. Here's the story on B. A. that was just supposed to be for my ears and now probably her new sweetheart's too, as much as that still annoys me. But you weren't supposed to hear it. When she came here, the plan was to fit in like a normal kid. Back in Arkansas, her teammates and the press weren't very nice to her. I know it's hard to believe, but it's true. She told me all about it a couple of weeks ago while we were out at our favorite spot watching the sunset. Apparently, her teammates were jealous of a sophomore getting so many write-ups in the paper. And because of this, she didn't like to do interviews and didn't say much when they asked her questions. She figured this would draw less attention to herself. Well, it pretty much backfired on her. They rumor mill spread the word that she was full of herself and thought she was better than everyone else. Actually she is, in many ways, but that's beside the point. So, where was I? Oh yeah. When her mom told her that she had a chance for a better job in Texas, she told her mom that it would be okay with her if they moved. It would be a chance for both of them to start over."

Luke sat still and gave her his strict attention. He nodded occasionally to show that he was following her. He had recently learned that's what good communicators do. Not only were they good at speaking, they were good at listening too.

"So, on the way here," continued Chip, "she formed a plan to try and fit in as a regular high school student. Which you and I know is pretty much impossible, considering her basketball ability. Early in the season, when basketball wasn't working out for her, she was willing to go along with the status quo. I had to push her to be the player she really is, and look at us now. We're better than I had ever dreamed. The bottom line is she doesn't want the attention. I know that's hard to believe in these times, with people doing almost anything to get on TV. She knows she is real good, and it's impossible for her to hide it. But she doesn't want people to make a big deal about it. Does that make sense to you?"

"I guess so," said Luke, trying to digest all the information. "It sounds like B. A. got some rough treatment from the press up in Arkansas." Her story also reminded him of a news story he had read when he was in eighth grade. Some students on a high school paper had printed a story about a teacher that was falsely accused of a serious crime. The teacher was eventually exonerated but bringing up the story and putting it in print again totally ruined his teaching career. They had their facts straight and stood by them, knowing that it would do irreparable damage to the teacher. It had nothing to do with his relationship with the students or his ability to teach. Still, they went ahead with the story, claiming it was something the public needed to know. Luke knew that reasoning was total nonsense. It was just a way to embarrass someone that they were trying to get even with. The teacher had probably given one or more of the writers a detention or a low grade on a quiz. Too many people, no matter what age, seem to hold grudges when they think someone has done them wrong. Most of the time the best strategy was to just get over it and move on. He shook his head and looked at Chip. She was saying something, but he didn't catch it.

"Are you still listening? It looked like you were zoning out on me."

"Okay. I'll rewrite the article."

"Just like that? No argument? For real?"

"Yup, you've convinced me that the story would do damage to someone who doesn't deserve it. I wouldn't want to be part of something like that."

"Wow, thanks. This boyfriend/girlfriend thing has merits. Other than the obvious, of course."

Chip got up and went over to Luke.

"I really do appreciate this. I knew deep down that you would understand. Oh, yeah. How about not saying much about me, either? I don't need any trouble from the rest of the girls, especially since my boyfriend writes the articles. Thanks."

With that, she leaned down and gave him a quick kiss on the lips. The timing couldn't have been worse, as Mrs. Slowinski was walking down the hall and saw the whole thing. She cleared her throat to get their attention as she stood there in the doorway doing the raised eyebrow thing.

"Mrs. S.," said Chip, "this is not what it looks like. Your son has just done a wonderful thing, and I was congratulating him."

"Well," Mrs. Slowinski said with a straight face. "I know he can be wonderful at times. I guess there's no harm in a little smooch now and then. He did follow the house rules with the door."

They looked at each other as she headed down the hall. They simultaneously mouthed "smooch" at each other and stifled a laugh. *Parents, what can you do?* As Chip headed for the door, she turned and asked, "Is 'nonchaliced' a word?"

Luke put his thinking expression on and replied, "I've never heard of it, why?"

"Oh, just something my dad said. You know how he is. See ya."

• ◆ •

Tuesday's game against the Staunton Lady Cougars was not your ordinary game. The Staunton coach, Fred Simmons, knew all about Reston's recent changes, and he wasn't about to let these small-town girls run over his squad. His school and town were almost twice the size of Reston. Staunton was 13 and 8 for the season, while Reston was one short of the .500 mark, at 10 and 11. Reston got a small mention in the papers when they beat Ferguson, at Ferguson. The info his scouts brought back from the following Springfield game gave him reason for concern. They raved about Smith, Fullerton, and Olsen. In a free-flowing game, Staunton had little chance. The scouts didn't feel his squad could run with the Lady Eagles. Coach Simmons decided to slow everything down and use his superior height. His front line went 6'2", 6'1", and 6'0". His personnel were not conducive to a running game anyway, but he was going to take it one step further. It would be a night that turtles would appreciate. Everything was going to be in slow motion. When Smith was in the game, they would play a two-one-two zone, collapsing on her at every opportunity. The one thing he didn't count on was that Reston's Smith had seen this tactic before. It was nothing new to her.

•◆•

Chip, B. A., and Jenny stood next to each other as the last few notes of the national anthem faded away. There was a fairly large crowd in the stands. It was Reston's last home game, and it was senior night. Since Kris, Missy, Amanda, and Darby were the seniors on the team, Coach Harbison was going to start them. When they were introduced, their parents walked out with them and each girl was given a bouquet of flowers. The four seniors and Chip made up the starting five.

B. A. was sitting on the end of the bench. As the teams took the floor, she turned to Jenny and said, "Our job is to help out the girl on the floor who plays our position. You know, act like a bench coach, hollering encouragement and advice at times. Don't holler too much, but just enough to let them know you're supporting them."

Jenny nodded, but B. A. was surprised when Carmen, Rachel, and Lu were all listening and also nodded in acknowledgment. *This is awesome*, thought B. A. *If these girls all buy into solid basketball principles, and we all get along, next year is going to be a great year. I guess most things work out if you just show some patience.*

Chip did a good job of getting her teammates in the right place. It was obvious that they weren't used to this particular combination. The girls on the bench cheered their counterparts on the floor. They were especially helpful in calling out the screens. Kris saved Chip twice from nasty collisions, as she followed her girl through the lane. Coach Harbison called a time-out with four minutes to go in the quarter and surprised everyone by sending the same girls back out. The score stood at: Reston 8, Staunton 13. B. A. approved of the move. Coach Harbison was showing respect for her players by not playing them for a token few minutes before the "real" players came into the game. They worked hard in practice and games just like the regulars did and deserved the attention of the crowd and the admiration of the little girls sitting in the front row. Cassie Olsen and her crew had missed only one home game this year. B. A. looked over and waved at them and they all waved back. She noticed that their numbers had increased from the start of the season. She guessed there were about fifteen of them now. It was good to see so many little girls take an interest. If you're going to have a strong program, you have to start early.

With three minutes left in the quarter, the coach put Jenny in for Darby. Darby got a huge ovation from the home fans. For the rest of the quarter, she subbed the regulars in at thirty-second intervals. B. A. was the last to come in, and everything immediately changed. As Chip dribbled down the floor, she recognized the change and hollered out, "Zone." There was no reason to send someone through the defense to see what they were doing. It was obvious. Up to now the game had been fairly fast-paced. B. A. gained an appreciation for the visiting coach. He wasn't going to run with them when the regulars were on the floor. This was going to turn into a chess game. The only problem was they had to play eight minutes before they could get into the locker room, where they could go over some major changes. Reston was down 17 to 9 at the end of the first quarter. During the break, much to Tammi and Missy's disgust, the coach let B. A. do the talking. B. A. ignored the snarky little comments they made under their breath.

"We need to attack their even front with an odd one," instructed B. A. "Let's start with just Chip and maybe go to three out front if that doesn't work. I'll come out with the two guards, if we make that change. Chip, split the two out front, and if they have trouble deciding who's going to guard you, shoot. Straight on is the best three-point shot in the gym. We need to push it hard up the floor, even if they want a slow-down game. The best way to get shots against a zone is to get down there before they can set up. From the looks of them, they're not a running team. Let's see if we can get their tongues hanging out before the half ends."

"Like tired dogs?" asked Chip. There was nervous laughter in the huddle. This start was more like the first half of the season, and some of them were thinking their run might be over. Maybe it had been too good to be true.

"Yeah, something like that," said B. A. "C'mon ladies, this is going to be a challenge, but we're up to it. Right?"

Most of them hollered in the affirmative. Tammi and Darby exchanged grins. It's too bad some people will do anything to see someone else fail, even if it means losing themselves. That sort of thinking was purely self-destructive, but losing doesn't matter to them when they're so determined to see the other party fall on her face.

There was a reason that Staunton had a winning record for the season. They weren't just tall; they played tough, and they used their height to their advantage. With two more six-footers on the bench, they didn't mind a little rough stuff. When one of the starters was tagged with her third foul, the sub who came in was just as tall. Pushing the ball up the floor was effective for Reston, but they couldn't stop the big girls underneath. Chip's first three-pointer of the game closed the gap with eight seconds to go in the half. The home team went into the locker room down by five, 30 to 25.

Coach Harbison briefly went over some things they were doing well and some things they needed to improve on. Then she asked B. A. if she had anything to add. The whole team turned their heads in her direction. B. A. hesitated for a few seconds. With a couple of exceptions, her new teammates were looking for guidance. She decided to take charge, regardless of what the two malcontents thought. They were who they were, so why worry about them?

B. A. took the marker from her coach and drew up a simple play on the board. Before she told them what it was, she complimented everyone who played in the first half on some aspect of her game, even Tammi.

"Okay, this will help us get some good shots against their zone. I drew it up with the ball starting on the right, but it will work from either side.

We need the four to come way out, top of the key extended. They'll let you have the ball out there because they don't think you will shoot from that far out. It also helps to have the ball in a taller girl's hands. You need to throw it all the way over the top of the zone to Chip in the corner, on the opposite baseline. She will be open because I will screen the girl who has corner responsibility. I can't hold her forever, so if Chip doesn't have a shot, she needs to get it to me as quick as she can. I'll turn and post up as soon as the defender gets by me. Chip, the baseline girl will come charging out at you, so do a volleyball pass or whatever you have to do to get it to me. If I can score on them, they will react and clamp down hard. That will leave Chip and the number two guard open. Kris, or whoever is playing number two, as soon as you throw the ball to the forward on the right, sprint over to the left side of the floor, just past the free-throw line extended. We'll do a little triangle action, passing it between us. It should get us a lot of shots. Remember, sports is usually about establishing something. Once we establish that we will get good shots off of this, they will react to try and stop us. When they react, it will open up other options."

"What about the rest of us, superstar?" quipped Tammi. "Do we get to play too, or is it just you three?"

"Of course," responded B. A. ignoring the dig. "We're going to move the ball around a lot, which means everyone handles it. Overhead passes will work best on the perimeter. Jenny, remember shooting from the passing position? Coach, we need our best shooters and ball-handlers in there, especially at the end. I don't think we can stop them from scoring, so we need to just flat outscore them. If we get too far behind, say double digits, we can try the shooting frenzy that you saw in the scrimmage. Any questions? Oh, one more thing. Screens work against a zone. You just can't drive off them. Shoot directly over the top of the screener like Chip does or go one or two steps by and put it up. One-on-one moves work against a zone, too. You're just somewhat limited in what you can do. Don't pass up any shots. The more we pass it around, the greater the chance for us to throw it away."

No one had anything to say, so they joined hands.

"Let's take it to these ogres," said Chip. "No offense, Carmen."

"None taken," said the 6'2" center. "Ogres drool, Eagles rule, on three."

Everyone laughed. If you were watching the Reston Lady Eagles come out of their locker room, you would have thought they were winning by a huge margin.

· ◆ ·

The first time they tried the diagonal pass, Chip was open and got off a three-pointer. It hit the front of the rim and bounced back to Kris who had hustled over to her spot. She took it right back out front and started over. *Good job*, thought B. A. *Way to show some discipline.* Jenny threw the pass to Chip again. B. A.'s screen held the baseline girl just long enough for Chip to get her shot off. She connected this time. The Staunton coach hollered at his girl to get out there faster and cover the corner. Staunton walked the ball down the floor and worked it in for a basket. The two teams played even until the end of the third quarter. The screens were working well, as there was no defender to switch off as long as the player with the ball stayed right by the screener. Chip hit several shots over the top of her screener, and Kris had a couple.

With 1:30 to go in the third quarter, Tammi and Missy came in for Jenny and Carmen. The first time down the floor, Tammi came out to the wing, where she was supposed to make the diagonal pass to Chip. Instead, she faked the pass and shot a long three-pointer. The ball missed the rim entirely and hit the board, coming down right into B. A.'s waiting hands. She powered it back up and was fouled hard. The ball bounced around and fell in. Her free throw tied the game. As the clock was winding down, Tammi had a second chance with the ball on the wing. This time she made the pass, but threw it too hard. Chip leaped in the air and tipped it back as she was falling out of bounds.

B. A. caught the pass and looked over her left shoulder, faking a hook shot. When her defender left her feet to block the shot, B. A. did a neat little step-through and banked the ball in. The crowd erupted, as Reston had its first lead. Tammi ran down the floor with her fist in the air looking at the crowd. It didn't seem to matter to her that she had just shot an air ball and had thrown a terrible pass. In her exuberance, she wasn't watching where she was going and she ran right into Staunton's big center. Both girls went down and then started to wrestle right at midcourt. It wasn't a full-blown fight, but it was enough to get both girls ejected from the game, and a double foul was called. There was only one second left in the quarter, which was probably a good thing. Staunton wasn't happy about losing one of their starters.

At the quarter break, the Reston huddle was very quiet. Jenny was totally embarrassed. Her sister had made a fool of herself before the largest home crowd of the season. She stood with her head down. The rest of the team offered words of encouragement, but to no avail. Coach Harbison subbed for her so she could get her feelings under control. B. A.'s respect for the assistant coach was growing with every game. Maybe her expertise wasn't in X's and O's, but she sure knew how to handle young athletes.

As they stood sipping from their water bottles, B. A. asked a question.

"Hey, Coach. How about we show them something they haven't seen before?"

"What have you got?" the coach asked, her face breaking out in a huge grin.

"Well, a couple of games ago, we did a two-fly with our guards, right? Remember, they would sprint the floor as soon as one of the front line got the defensive rebound. I would like to see how they react to a four-fly."

"Are you serious?" asked the coach.

"Why not? It will be totally unexpected and might just break this game wide open."

"All right, what do you think, girls?"

They looked around the huddle at each other. They were being asked to make a team decision. This was something Coach Todd had never done. At this moment, they felt more like a team and not just a bunch of girls playing basketball together. They could see it in each other's eyes. It was a different feeling—a feeling of being part of something successful. Heads nodded. The coach nodded toward B. A. to continue.

"Here's how it works. If it looks like I'm going to get the defensive rebound, everybody else sprints down the floor. Just take off and don't worry about helping out. Watch your spacing. They have been harassing the rebounder with two defenders all game to slow us down. That will give us at least a four-on-three advantage even if their other three hustle down the floor. Also, watch for some weird passes. They might not be right to you. If not, go get it. No hesitation, ladies. You've got to believe in yourselves."

Chip stuck her hand in the middle and whispered, "Cougars cry, Eagles fly." Then louder, "Fly on three. One, two, three!" They enthusiastically broke their huddle and headed out for the fourth quarter.

In the stands, the Reston's principal turned to the athletic director and commented, "Whatever Harbison is doing, it sure is effective. I've never seen such a turnaround in all my years watching high school basketball. This is not the same team I saw at the beginning of the season. Did you know that Smith was this good when she transferred in?"

"No," said the athletic director. "I'm ashamed to admit that I didn't even know who she was until a couple of weeks ago. I don't know how she slipped by me, but she did. Did you notice that she has done most of the talking during the time-outs?"

"I did notice that," said the principal. "This is very strange, but you've got to admit, it's exciting."

The home team started the last quarter with Chip, Kris, Missy, B. A., and Rachel. Reston was up by two, and they had the ball to start the fourth quarter. Staunton surprised them by coming out in a "man" defense. They must have figured out that the zone and slow pace weren't working. Since the Reston starters came back in late in the first quarter, they had outscored Staunton by ten points. That, plus Reston's momentum, forced the Staunton Coach's hand. Maybe a defensive change would give his girls an advantage and confuse Reston enough to get the lead back.

B. A. immediately saw the switch in defense as she threw the ball in to Chip at midcourt. Following her pass, she ran right at Chip and took a return hand-off. Her defender had turned her head to follow the pass and didn't realize that B. A. was heading down the floor with the ball until it was too late. Rachel was under the basket and she did just what B. A. hoped she would do. She just stood there. When her girl left her to pick up B. A., she received a bounce pass for an easy bucket. The Staunton coach slammed his clipboard on the bench loud enough so the whole gym heard it.

B. A. got her first defensive rebound of the quarter a minute later, and the rest of her team sprinted down the floor, leaving her to fend for herself. Two tall Staunton girls were on her immediately. She dribbled hard for the sideline and threw a waist high pass that looked more like one of her hook shots. Chip saw it coming and went back to get it. Two dribbles later and a bounce pass to Missy got them an easy basket. Jenny stood up and hollered something from the bench. A few plays later, B. A. gathered in her second rebound and surprised everyone when she rolled the ball hard down the sideline. Kris scooped it up and dribbled to the middle. Reston had a one-girl advantage and used it to get a short bank shot by Rachel. Jenny couldn't take it anymore. She went and sat by the coach.

"Coach," she hollered over the noise of the crowd. "Can I get in for just a couple minutes? I want some of this."

Coach Harbison saw the fire in her eyes and told her to report in for a tired-looking Missy.

Jenny came onto the floor looking like her old self. She called for a quick huddle.

"We're still going to four-fly," she explained. "If B. A. or I get the rebound."

Jenny had to jump as high as she could to get her first defensive rebound. She jumped right back up and rifled the ball to Chip. Chip went to the middle of the floor and made a smooth pass to B. A., who could have cruised in for an easy layup. Instead, she waited for Kris, who was coming fast down the opposite side. B. A. faked the shot and passed to Kris, who laid it in. The Staunton coach immediately called time-out. Kris looked at B. A. with a strange expression as they walked over to the bench. B. A. just said, "Senior night." Kris showed her appreciation with a modest five on the down low.

The Reston girls stood by their bench and listened to the Staunton coach holler at his team. They were down by twelve, and the visitors were aware that, barring a miracle, the game was out of reach. Staunton was not a quick-scoring team, and they knew it. They fouled several times in the last two minutes to get the ball, but it backfired too. With a minute to go and a thirteen point lead, Coach Harbison put her seniors back in. The crowd roared and stomped their feet for the rest of the game. Like the principal said, it was exciting basketball.

When the horn sounded, B. A. went over to Coach Harbison and hugged her.

"What was that for?" asked the coach.

"For being such a great coach and believing in us," said B. A. "And for standing up for me with Coach Todd."

Neither of them knew it, but Coach Todd had slipped into the gym in time to see the whole fourth quarter. She didn't know what to think about her team's recent success.

Tammi stood waiting for them as the team filed into the locker room. They were still hollering and slapping each other on the back. Tammi lifted her arms for silence.

"I want to apologize for fighting out there," she said somewhat remorsefully. "I don't know what got into me. And I'm sorry for embarrassing you, Jenny."

Jenny went over and hugged her sister. The Lady Eagles started hollering all over again.

Life is good, thought Chip. *Maybe Tammi will change. Naw, I doubt it. Anyway, we are now a .500 team and on the move. I can't wait to hear what my boyfriend has to say about this game. I don't even care if he's sitting close to that redheaded freshman. I am an open-minded woman and certainly not the jealous type.*

Chapter 13

Equipment Failure

B. A. was waiting for Chip and Jenny when they pulled into her driveway. Thursday's practice was a short one. They went through their shooting drills and then the scout team simulated Lakewood's offense and defense. Lakewood played a "man" defense and tried to fight through all screens. Apparently their coach wasn't big on switching. Their offense was simple, with four or five set plays. They were 15 and 7 for the season with some big wins over some pretty good teams. It was obvious that they knew what they were doing, and they could execute. They had beaten Staunton by ten a few games ago. After about an hour into practice, the coach surprised the team by telling them to go home and rest, after they did their homework, of course.

The early out from practice played right into B. A.'s plans. She had switched vehicles with her mom, so the three of them could ride comfortably. Her truck was an extended cab, but not good for the eighteen-mile ride they were going to take. When Jenny and Chip pulled into her drive, she motioned for them to get in to her mom's car. Chip jumped in back so Jenny could stretch her legs out in the front seat. As instructed, both girls were wearing their basketball warm-up jackets. B. A. had hers on too.

Chip looked over at the cardboard box sitting next to her in the back seat.

"Hey, what's in the box?" she asked as she started to lift up a flap.

"Stay out of there," warned B. A. "It's a surprise."

"Why did you ask us to wear our warm-ups?" asked Jenny. "We're not doing a TV interview are we? I thought you didn't like that sort of thing."

"I can't go on TV. I don't have any makeup on," laughed Chip.

B. A. decided to string them along a bit.

"They have a makeup department at the station, silly. Just be yourself. That will be entertaining enough."

"Are you kidding me?" asked Chip excitedly. "We don't have anything prepared. What are we supposed to do, just stand there like goofs? You are kidding, right?"

B. A. looked in the rearview mirror and smiled at Chip.

"You better get used to it. You're a fast-rising star, and the people want to know more about you. Your favorite shows, food, and how many boyfriends you have. You know, all the juicy stuff. Jenny and I are the support crew. You're the main show."

"I'm not believing this for a minute. You probably switched cars with your mom because you didn't want to drive to the city alone. We better get a free meal for our efforts."

"Yeah," said Jenny making a haughty gesture with her hands. "No fast food. We demand a real fancy place where warm-ups are the style and they serve Viking food. "

Chip was still questioning her when B. A. pulled into the hospital parking lot. She found a spot and got out. Both girls had questioning looks on their faces. B. A. opened the back door and grabbed the box.

"C'mon, ladies," she said. "We've only got about an hour before we have to head back. And I've got a test to study for."

Without waiting for a response, B. A. headed for the main entrance. Once inside, she went right to the elevators. Her two teammates followed along, speculating on what they were doing here. The third-floor elevator door opened to a smiling face in hospital garb. It was Martha Smith.

"You're right on time, girls," she said. "Follow me. I have to head right back to the ER, so I'll just introduce you to the head nurse on duty."

Jenny and Chip still hadn't figured it out until they saw a five-year-old in the hallway sitting in a wheelchair. They looked at each other.

"Little kids," whispered Chip. "We're here to visit little kids. Awesome."

B. A. put the box on the nurse's counter and opened it. It was full of little Reston Eagle basketballs. They were the balls that the cheerleaders would sometimes throw to the fans at games. She gave each girl a fine-point Magic Marker.

"Stuff some balls in your warm-up pockets," she said. "I'll leave the box right here if you have to come back for more. Make sure everybody gets one."

B. A.'s mom came back with a tall woman who looked like she might have played some basketball in her day. The girls shook hands with the head pediatric nurse and listened while she gave them instructions. None of the children in this wing had a communicable disease. Most of them were postsurgery, but there were some cancer patients. They knew the Lady Eagles were coming, and they were real excited. The nurse said it would be best if they split up and visited the patients one at a time. She also said to talk quietly and not to excite them any more than they were already.

"What are we supposed to do?" asked Chip.

"Tell them who you are," said B. A. "They'll have plenty of questions for you. And be sure to ask them about themselves. Sign the ball and give it to them. If they already have a ball, just sign it for them. Y'all go to opposite ends of the hall. I'll start in the middle. Remember we only have about an hour before visiting hours are over. Have some fun with them. It will be a great experience for you and the kids."

B. A. headed down the hall juggling three of the balls and humming. No matter how many times she had done this, it always gave her a feeling of tremendous satisfaction. She hoped her friends would feel the same way.

Chip and Jenny watched her walk down the hall. They looked at each other nervously. Jenny shrugged her shoulders and headed to the other end. Chip headed the other way and into a room where a seven-year-old boy was waiting. Despite of the tubes connected to his body, he lit up in a big smile. She took a deep breath and introduced herself.

* ◆ *

"I can't believe what we just did," said Chip as the girls got back in the car. "It was totally magnificent. Those little guys are so brave. It was tough to hold back the tears. Did ya'll feel the same way?"

"I know I did," said Jenny. "I could have sat with that little redheaded boy the whole time. He was quite the little trooper. He said he had a hernia operation earlier that day. Do you know what a hernia is?"

"Yes," said B. A. "My mom's a nurse, remember?"

"How about you, Chipper?"

"I just know it hurts a lot," responded Chip.

"The little guy showed me with his hand," continued Jenny. "He spread his fingers apart and said when flat muscle tissue is strained too much it will sometimes spread apart. Then another body part gets stuck in there. He put a finger from his other hand through to demonstrate. He was so cute. Like a little doctor explaining it to me. Then he looked up with a serious expression and said the pain was an eleven on a ten-point scale. I wanted to give him a hug, but I remembered the nurse said only to shake hands."

"Good thinking," said Chip. "A big hug from you might have sent him right back into surgery."

The girls laughed and chatted all the way home. It was a night that they would all remember for a long time. It finally dawned on Chip as they pulled back into B. A.'s drive.

"Hey, where did you get all those little basketballs?" she asked.

"I know a guy," said B. A. She wasn't about to reveal her source.

"A guy. What guy would that be?"

"Just a guy. You sure are nosy."

"She's always been like that," said Jenny. "Even when she was in elementary school. She had to know what everyone was doing."

"How are you supposed to learn?" asked Chip. "You can't learn if you don't ask questions. I think Einstein said that."

"Yeah," added Jenny. "Gerald Einstein. He used to live over by us but moved away in sixth grade. Remember, Chip, he used to eat the paste from the big jar in the art room?"

"I remember him," said Chip. "He's not the guy I was talking about. I meant the famous guy, Englebert Einstein."

"You're kidding, right?" asked B. A. as she closed the rear door on the driver's side.

"Of course I was kidding. I know who Edward Einstein was."

Jenny and B. A. rolled their eyes and laughed. As Jenny backed out the drive, Chip hollered out the window, "E=MC², baby."

B. A. smiled as she let herself in the back door. It was sometimes hard to tell whether or not Chip was kidding. She was on the high honor roll, but that could be due to her diligence on assignments and good test-taking skills. If she was really bright, she did a good job of covering it up. Not that she was an airhead or anything. It was just some of the off-the-wall ideas she would come up with. B. A. did think there was more to Chip than she let on. Anyway, she was a lot of fun to be with. She imagined some of the hilarious conversations that Chip probably had with her recently acknowledged boyfriend. B. A. would have been surprised to know she was quite often the main topic of those conversations. Before Jenny dropped Chip off at her house, Chip had figured out where B. A. got the basketballs. And she also figured out there was no such thing as Viking food.

* ◆ *

While the three girls were making their trip to the hospital, Luke was working on his own project. He had decided to get as many fans as he could to come to the last regular season game at Lakewood. He had been on the phone for over an hour, calling Reston residents and telling them about the girls' team and their accomplishments. He hit pay dirt when he got ahold of Mary Lou Crimmins. She was the one who was responsible for getting the girls' basketball program started in Reston. Luke hung up after a twenty-minute chat with Mary Lou. She was almost as excited as he was. She also happened to belong to several community organizations, and she volunteered to contact as many as she could before the next night's game.

* ◆ *

Luke and Clarice were seated right behind the Reston bench watching the fans file in before the start of the fresh-soph game at Lakewood. At first they were pleasantly surprised. Their surprise turned to shock when the Reston half of the gym was full as the first quarter ended. They just kept on coming. Luckily, Lakewood had a beautiful modern gym that held several thousand fans. Luke looked at the basket to his right and gave Clarice a gentle elbow. She followed his gaze to the balcony area behind the basket. There were two long tables set up and some guys were scurrying around checking cables and their connections.

"Radio stations," said Luke. "It looks like two of them."

"Did you call any radio guys?" asked Clarice. "I know I didn't."

"No, but maybe Mrs. Crimmins did. She told me she knew a lot of people. One thing is for sure. This is turning out to be more than I expected. It will be a good test for our girls when they get into the state tournament. When they start to win, they will have to face the Fort Worth schools, and there will be big crowds then."

The Reston varsity was sitting in the first two rows of bleachers by their locker room. They couldn't believe the crowd. All that was missing was the television cameras.

"I know this is senior night," said Jenny, "but this is ridiculous. Something else must be going on."

"Maybe they're raffling off a Harley Davidson, and tonight they're announcing the winner," said Chip. "Did you buy a ticket, B. A.?"

"I forgot," said B. A. "I wouldn't mind cruisin' around on a big bike if I knew how to drive one. One of my dad's friends gave me a ride around the block once. It was pretty scary for a seventh-grader."

Jenny looked at Chip and grinned. She put her arm around Chip's shoulder.

"If you won, little Chipster, they would have to come up with a little smaller version of a regular size bike. Like one of those minibikes that circus clowns ride around on."

Several of their teammates snickered.

"Funny," retorted Chip. "I liked it better when you were the quiet, shy type—like when we were back in second grade. You're quite the comedienne now. And there's no such thing as Viking food. And I know what you're thinking. I didn't look it up on the Internet, either."

"Hey," said Kris pointing to the far entrance. "Is that guy carrying what I think he's carrying?"

The whole team turned their heads toward the main entrance just in time to see a guy set a huge camera down on the floor.

"They're here to get the Harley winner on film," said Chip excitedly.

"There's no Harley raffle," said a fan behind them. "They're here to get some highlights for tonight's sports on television. We thought our Lakewood team was big news, but y'all apparently are a bigger story. I haven't been to a girls' high school game since my niece played about five years ago. Where are Smith and Fullerton? I came to see those two in action. It's not often that two girls average over fifty points a game between them. I expect that's what this big crowd is all about."

The Reston girls looked at each other. They knew that Chip, B. A., and Jenny were doing most of the scoring, but they didn't realize the actual numbers that the first two had been putting up.

Chip turned to the man and started to answer his question. When she opened her mouth, she saw B. A. with a troubled look on her face.

She quickly altered her response. "I'm sure the papers are building it up to be more than it is. It's still five-on-five out there. Some score and some do other things that are just as important."

"Nice recovery," whispered Jenny as she leaned closer. "I think he bought it."

"I was being sincere," said Chip, also whispering. "I've actually been listening when B. A. tells us stuff. I'll tell you what, though. I don't think she likes all those cameras and reporter types here."

"Well, she's going to have to get used to it. Like that guy said, you two are a big story."

"What about you?" asked Chip. "From the time that B. A. was moved to forward, aren't you averaging double figures in rebounding and scoring?"

"You're right. Remind me to ask Harbison to take me out with a few minutes to go in the game. I need to sneak back into the locker room to do some personal grooming. I can't do an interview looking all sweaty like I just played a basketball game. My fans deserve more."

The varsity squad stood up and cheered the fresh-soph as they ran on to the floor for the second half. They were only down by four, so they were making a game of it. Once they were all out of the locker room, the girls that the big crowd had come to see went in to change. This was going to be a totally different experience. To one of them it was like déjà vu all over again.

⁕ ◆ ⁕

Coach Harbison had just finished her pregame talk, and it was too early to go out to the floor, so the girls started stretching. B. A. put her leg up on a bench and slowly started to stretch her hamstring. Chip looked over at her shorts and noticed something. She reached out toward her teammate.

"B. A., you've got a loose string. Hold still. I'll get it for you."

She grabbed the string and yanked hard on it. The whole string came out down the back seam of B. A.'s shorts. Chip's eyes went wide.

"Ruh oh. This is not good. The whole back of your shorts is open. Lucky we pack extras for road games. Have a seat. I'll find Carla."

Chip came back with a serious look on her face.

"Carla checked the equipment bag, and she only has one pair of extra game shorts. They're double X. She said she took the others out to wash them and forgot to put them back. What are we going to do?"

"Let's go, girls," hollered Coach Harbison from the hallway. "The fresh-soph game has just ended."

"We'll be right with you, Coach," said Chip. "We've got a small equipment problem here."

The rest of the team filed out the door to a gym that was standing room only. A huge roar went up as their opponents took the floor first. The Reston fresh-soph girls came in and stared at B. A. as they quietly went to their end of the locker room. They had been outscored 16 to 4 in the last quarter. They knew this was their last game of the season, and they didn't want to go out looking liked they had given up. They did battle, but the other team was a lot deeper, and it had finally caught up with them.

"If we had a needle and some thread, we could repair them," said B. A. "Do you know how to sew? I don't."

"No," said Chip. "I'm taking sewing class next year. Hey, why don't you borrow a pair of fresh-soph shorts?"

"They're not the same as ours," said B. A. "They must be hand-me-downs from a few years ago. I'm sure the rules won't let me wear different shorts than the rest of the team. Their shorts aren't even red anymore. I don't know what color you would call them."

"I'm sorry, B. A." said Carla came hustling back into the locker room. "I took the extra shorts home to wash them and forgot to bring them back. How about this—we switch shorts with one of the subs, find some thread, and sew them up. She'll be back on the bench before the first quarter is over. Maybe their sewing teacher is here, and she can open up her classroom. It would only take a few seconds if we could use a sewing machine."

"Don't worry about it, Carla," said B. A. "We'll figure it out. But I don't think I can ask a teammate to give up her shorts. It would seem like I'm more important than she is. No, I couldn't do that. I do like your idea about using one of the machines in the sewing room—if they have one. How about this? Find the gym supervisor and explain our predicament. He or she will know how to get into the room with the sewing machines. Chip, you better get out there and warm up."

Chip nodded and followed Carla out the door. They almost ran into Jenny as she came bursting through.

"What is going on in here?" she asked frantically. "The place is packed to the rafters, and they want to see Reston's high-scoring dolls."

"B. A.'s shorts are ripped," said Chip. "You can see her undies."

"What!" exclaimed Jenny. "Here, switch shorts with me. Carla can go find a needle and thread. Somebody in this crowd is bound to have some in their purse. I'll just wait here and sew them up when she comes back."

"You can sew?" asked Chip.

"Of course," responded Jenny. "What? You can't?"

"Forget about that," said B. A., bringing them back to the problem at hand. "I'm not switching shorts. You two go out and warm up. I'll be out as soon as Carla gets us into the sewing room. Now go."

Chip and Jenny hurried back out to finish their warm-up. There was five minutes until game time. They met Coach Harbison at the door.

"Everything's under control, Coach," said Chip. "It's a long story. B. A.'s shorts had a malfunction. She'll be out as soon as they can be repaired."

"I hope it's quick," said Coach Harbison. "The crowd is going crazy. Where are the spare shorts?"

"I told you, it's a long story," answered Chip as she turned her coach by the shoulders and directed her back out to the floor. "No time to explain it now."

Carla came running back into the locker room.

"Give me your shorts, B. A.," she said, out of breath. "The janitor will get us a needle and thread. He said to have one of the moms in the stands sew them up. It will be faster that way."

B. A. took off her game shorts and handed them to Carla. She went over to her bag and pulled out a pair of practice shorts. After putting them on, she started to do her own warm-up. Jumping jacks, squats, and stretches were about all she could do in a cramped locker room. The fresh-soph girls were peeking around the lockers and whispering. All of a sudden several pairs of shorts came flying over the top of the lockers.

"Funny," hollered B. A. as she scooped up the shorts and tossed them back. They were all still laughing when the fresh-soph coach came in and told them to quit messing around. B. A. laughed quietly to herself as she thought about how silly her predicament was. Her dad had always said that if you couldn't laugh at yourself, you were wound a little too tight.

* ◆ *

The packed house was buzzing like a mad hornets' nest. No one was sure as to what was going on. Where was Reston's big star? And why were some of the players leaving the court and going back in to the locker room? The coach even went back. Somebody must be sick. It must be Smith, because she was the only player they hadn't seen yet.

Luke gave Clarice a concerned look. She shrugged her shoulders with her palms facing up, signifying that she had no opinion. Something strange was going on. As a good reporter, Luke was going to get the story. He stepped onto the court as the horn blew. Carla almost ran into him. She was carrying a pair of game shorts and what looked like a needle and thread.

"What's going on?" he asked Carla.

"We have to get someone to sew up B. A.'s shorts," she replied, holding them up for him to see.

"Let's get out of the way," he said, guiding her back toward the end of the bleachers.

The starting lineups were being introduced. The Reston fans screamed and clapped for their girls. Tammi had taken B. A.'s spot and was hamming it up. She tried to chest bump Carmen, but instead of reciprocating, Carmen caught her in the air and set her down gently. The gesture sent a huge message to Tammi and the rest of the team. *We're going to play the way the new girl wants us to play. Play with class and no showboating.*

Luke stood next to Carla with hand over heart as the national anthem was played. When the teams went back to their huddles, he surveyed the crowd. He was looking for a logical sewing candidate. His gaze stopped when he came to Mary Lou Crimmins. He quickly formed a plan. It would be embarrassing to walk up through the crowd with the shorts in hand. He decided to take the other route—underneath them.

"Give them to me and wait here" he told Carla. "I'll be back in a couple of minutes."

Luke worked his way under the bleachers until he was close to where Mary Lou was sitting. He knew he could find her, since she had told him on the phone that she would be wearing her lucky red socks.

The gym grew quiet, indicating that the game was about to start. Luke walked slowly, checking out the feet of the Reston fans. He figured she was sitting about seven feet up, which would make it easy for him to hand her the shorts. Finally he saw them. He heard a huge cheer right above him. He assumed that Reston must have gotten the opening tip. He reached up and tapped Mrs. Crimmins on the foot. She let out a yelp and jumped up from her seat. She sat back down and looked through the bleachers to see who was touching people on the feet.

"Mrs. Crimmins," announced Luke. "It's Luke Slowinski. I'm the guy who called you about tonight's game. We need your help. Can you sew?"

"What are you doing down there, young man? Scaring people like that. And yes, of course I can sew."

"B. A. Smith is waiting in the locker room for these shorts. Will you please sew them up for her?"

"So that's what's going on," said Mrs. Crimmins. "Hand them up. It will only take a couple seconds."

Luke handed up the shorts, followed by the needle and thread. Shirley Jones, a classmate of Mary Lou's, was sitting next to her. She started to laugh when she saw what her friend was doing. Luke was perplexed as the crowd had stopped yelling. He couldn't see through their feet to make out what was going on. Mary Lou finished the sewing in record time. She handed them back down to Luke, who thanked her and scurried back to Carla.

"What was that all about?" asked Shirley.

"You know how I petitioned the school board years ago for them to let us start a girls' team?" asked Mary Lou.

"I remember. You were relentless. You started the petition and bugged the board constantly. And I also remember, you weren't a very good player," said Shirley. "I was better than you, and I was awful."

"Well," laughed Mary Lou. "I might have done more for the team in the last minute than I ever did when I actually played."

* ◆ *

The crowd's mood had changed. It was a strange sound for a basketball crowd. In a word, it sounded like confusion. Hurrying under the bleachers, Luke could make out a few of the louder voices. It seemed like they were mad or agitated about something. He reappeared and gave Carla the shorts. She immediately turned and headed through the door back to the locker room.

* ◆ *

There were two radio stations covering the game. One was the small Lakewood station, and the other was from Fort Worth. Both of the play-by-play guys knew exactly what was going on, and they thought it was brilliant.

Bill Hall from the Fort Worth station looked over at his partner.

"Can you believe this strategy, Ed? We've played over a minute, and only one shot has been taken."

"It looks like they're waiting for their other star to join them," observed his partner. "I've never seen a team call three time-outs in less than a minute."

"The Reston coach's strategy is extremely risky," said Bill. "They might need those time-outs as the game progresses."

A fan sitting behind Clarice made the same observation. Clarice turned around and looked him in the eye.

"Trust me, sir," she said in a serious tone, "we won't be needing them."

* ◆ *

Luke had to wind his way through the fans standing in the aisle to get back to his seat. Both teams were huddled on the sidelines, so he figured it must be a time-out. He looked up at the clock and was shocked to see the time. There was 6:40 left in the first quarter. They had only played one minute and twenty seconds. How could that be! He asked Clarice for an update.

"There's not much to tell," reported Clarice. "Tammi threw a pass out-of-bounds on our first possession, and Lakewood went down and scored. After that, Chip has called two regular time-outs and a thirty-second one. It appears they don't want to do anything until B. A. gets here. She is going to play isn't she?"

"She'll be out any second now," said Luke. He was going to say something else, but a huge roar from the Reston crowd drowned him out.

The Lakewood radio announcers weren't looking at the floor when the cheer went up. They looked over at the Fort Worth guys, sensing that they had missed something. Bill Hall covered his mike and hollered over to them.

"Smith just walked into the gym. And I think you're in big trouble."

Reston had just broken their huddle when B. A. walked in. She was going to sit inconspicuously on the end of the bench when Coach Harbison stepped out where B. A. could see her and gestured for her to enter the game. The coach called Tammi back, and the wannabe star made a disgusted face.

"All right, we're saved," hollered Tammi. "The superstar has just made her grand entrance."

Jenny walked over to her sister and spoke to her in a low voice.

"Sis. When are you going to see things as they really are? I sure wish you would join us. You could be a big help. But not with that kind of attitude."

Tammi was speechless. She stalked over to the bench and plopped down.

The radio announcer was only half-right about Reston's strategy. It was risky all right. But it was Chip's idea and not the coach's. Right after she called her third time-out, Lakewood's best player, Cheryl Williams, walked by and said, "Gutsy move, Fullerton."

B. A. reported in and went over to the official with the ball. He was standing at the top of the key extended in Reston's frontcourt. Kris Ritter was in the backcourt in case there was trouble throwing it in. Carmen Espinosa was down by the basket but started walking toward the opposite sideline where Jenny was standing. The official handed the ball to B. A. Chip broke toward B. A. from the baseline and received the pass. The girl guarding B. A. turned to see where the pass went. B. A. sprinted right by her, took a return hand-off from Chip, and scored easily. This was a play that they had worked before. There were two key factors in this play. B. A. had to be guarded tightly when she threw the ball in, and the opposing center had to follow Carmen when she headed to the other side of the floor. This left the ball side of the floor open and uncluttered. The crowd exploded with approval.

The play for the rest of the game was upbeat and exciting. B. A., Chip, and Jenny did most of the scoring for Reston. Cheryl Williams had a great game for Lakewood. Jenny played her tight before fouling out halfway through the fourth quarter. Williams tallied twenty-two for the home team, but she was no match for B. A.'s thirty-two and Chip's twenty-four. At the end of the game, Williams ran over to Chip and B. A. and gave them both a hearty handshake. She told them how much she enjoyed playing against them and wished them good luck in the tournament. The big surprise of the game was Tammi's play when she spelled Jenny. She hustled, and her behavior was acceptable, for her. Maybe her sister's little comment at the beginning of the game had gotten through to her. Only time would tell on that issue.

* ◆ *

Bill Hall and his partner were packing up their cables. The gym was just about empty.

"Can you believe that game, Ed?" he asked. "Smith would throw her outlet passes to midcourt. And double-teaming her didn't make much difference. It's too bad the television guys left so early. They didn't get the behind-the-back pass Smith threw to Olsen."

"Olsen's pass to Fullerton was also a thing of beauty," commented Ed. "The Lakewood coach took a time-out after that one. How long do you think it took to him to figure out he was totally outclassed?"

"In more ways than one," replied Bill. "Reston played with a lot of poise. When was the last time you saw a female player shoot a jump hook from ten feet out?"

"Don't think I've ever seen it," answered Ed. "Why do you think we couldn't get Smith or Fullerton to do an interview after the game? I didn't believe their coach's explanation for one minute. Fullerton has a stuttering problem, and Smith is too shy. I don't think so."

"Whatever. It was a great game. Eighty-two points is a lot for a girls' game. Most of the regulars are juniors too. And when's the last time Lakewood has been beaten by twenty points in their own gym?"

The guys were just about finished when the Reston varsity came out of the locker room and walked across the gym floor. They waved at the girls, and the gesture was returned. Jenny Olsen was in the lead, and she hollered up at them.

"Thanks for doing our game, guys. I think it's the first time this year that we've been on the radio."

"You're welcome," said Bill. "You certainly made it worth the trip. Where are Smith and Fullerton?"

Jenny turned around and surveyed the rest of the team. Chip and B. A. weren't with them. She mentally kicked herself for not staying behind. She knew what they were doing. She nodded to her coach and then she jogged back toward the locker room.

"I'll go check on them, Coach," she said over her shoulder.

Jenny came through the locker room door and saw her two teammates doing exactly what she thought they were doing—cleaning up the room. B. A. had told them earlier in the season that they should leave the locker room in better condition than they found it.

"C'mon, y'all," said Jenny. "The bus is waiting."

"We're coming," hollered Chip. "We don't want them to think that Reston girls are a bunch of pigs, do we? You could almost eat off this floor now."

"That's disgusting," said Jenny. "Hey, I'm sorry about fouling out. I've never done that before. That Williams girl was pretty good."

"I liked her attitude," said B. A. as she went over to the sink and washed her hands. "She wished us good luck in the state tournament. How many times do you hear that from someone who has just lost a home game?"

"She was pretty cool," said Chip. "I wouldn't worry about fouling out, Jen. You almost kept up with her in scoring, and I know you had more rebounds."

"Thanks, Chipper. Now I feel bad for what I said to the radio guys. You know, when you wouldn't do an interview."

"What did you tell them?"

"I said your command of the English language wasn't the best, and you were afraid you would embarrass yourself and the team by talking on the radio."

"You told them I was too stupid to talk?"

"Yeah, something like that," laughed Jenny.

"You two are incorrigible," said B. A. as they walked out the door and headed for the bus.

"I might agree if I knew what that meant," said Chip.

"I rest my case," hollered Jenny.

Chapter 14

The Incident

Chip, Jenny, and B. A. sat at the kitchen table watching Mrs. Fullerton make supper. The little guard had invited them over to discuss their strategy in the upcoming state playoffs. She'd figured they would have three fairly easy games until they ran into a real strong team. Roosevelt was 18 and 6, with some wins over bigger schools. They were the toughest team in the area.

"It looks like you have this all figured out," said Jenny. "Have you come up with any trick plays for us? How's this for a crowd-pleaser? Carmen gets down on her hands and knees and then you—"

"The barking dog play has already been used," interrupted Chip.

"No, that's not what I'm talking about. You step on her back and leap into the air as B. A. lobs it to you. If you get a good run, you might get high enough to dunk it."

"Do you see what I'm working with here, Mom?" asked Chip. "We need to talk some serious strategy, and they want to talk about illegal plays. That's gotta be illegal. Isn't it, B. A.?"

"Maybe not," said B. A. "What if Carmen fell flat on her face as she was in the process of getting up? Then it would look natural, like we didn't set it up beforehand. We would have to give a verbal signal to let everybody know what was going on, though. It would have to be something that would stand out over the crowd noise."

"How about a loud call that a crow would make?" asked Mrs. Fullerton joining in. "Something like this—caw, caw."

"All right, Mom," exclaimed Chip. "These two jokers don't need any encouragement. What are you cooking over there?"

"It's red beans and rice, with a little sausage thrown in."

"It smells awesome," said Jenny.

"We have it a lot," said Chip. "My dad lived in Louisiana before he moved here. They eat that kind of food all the time. You know, stuff that comes out of the swamps. We had gator tails just last week. Mom can grill up a mean gator."

"Not hardly," said her mom. "The sausage is actually made from turkey. But don't tell your dad. We're trying to eat healthier. You two are staying for supper, right? I've got plenty."

Jenny and B. A. looked at each other for a sign.

"It's actually quite good," said Chip sensing their hesitation. "Dad even eats it for breakfast. Although I've also seen him eat chili for breakfast, so I guess that doesn't say much."

"That would be great," said B. A.

"Yeah," said Jenny. "We need to broaden our culinary horizons. Do you want us to do anything, Mrs. F.?"

"Chip's job is to set the table and then do the dishes," answered Chip's mom. "She's still banned from cooking."

"Banned from cooking?" asked B. A. sensing a humorous story. "Why?"

"It's a long story," said Chip. "I might add that the punishment was way too severe for the crime. We didn't even have to call the fire department. This house has a lot of harsh rules. A couple of months ago I was grounded for two weeks. All I did was, uh—never mind."

Chip covered herself when her mom turned around and gave her a peculiar look. It probably wasn't a good idea to explain the events of the night that Chip and Luke fell asleep spying on B. A.'s house.

"Let's eat," said Mrs. F. "Your dad will be home late, so there's no need to wait."

The talk around the dinner table turned to the upcoming playoffs and how good their opponents would be. Chip mentioned that the Arlington team would be a likely opponent down the road. They had a talented player named McIlroy. She was about six feet tall, so Jenny would probably be guarding her. B. A. said not to worry. Coach Harbison would have their future opponents scouted.

The girls made quick work of the dishes and then headed out to the country to watch the sun set. Chip was in the backseat and B. A. was riding shotgun.

"I just want to get this straight," said Chip. "The play you talked about is illegal, right?"

"Yes!" said B. A. and Jenny at the same time.

Jenny backed the car into their usual spot. As they got out, B. A. saw Mr. Daggert, the owner of the property, in the distance. She had seen him in the crowd at their last home game but hadn't gotten a chance to talk to him. She hoped he would drive his tractor over to talk for a bit. She couldn't explain it, but she really liked to make connections with older people. She gave him a big wave, hoping it would get his attention.

"B. A. and I will sit on the fenders," said Jenny. "Chippy, you probably only weigh about forty pounds, so you can sit in the middle."

"I'll have you know I weigh exactly one 110 pounds," said Chip proudly. "How much do you weigh, B. A.?"

"More than 110," she responded. "Shh, the show's about to start."

As they watched the sun go down, each girl was caught up in her own thoughts. Jenny was thinking about her sister and her improved demeanor during the last game. B. A. was thinking about how she would get out of interviews if they won a few games in the state playoffs.

Chip was picturing herself leaping off Carmen's back and slamming it through the hoop. It was an awesome two-handed stuff that came at the end of a cool 360-degree helicopter spin.

As the girls were about to get back in the car, Mr. Daggert pulled up on his old tractor.

"Hi ladies," he hollered over the noisy engine. "I had no idea that you three were such sports celebrities. The whole town is talking about you. Think y'all will win the state title?"

"That's a long way off, Mr. D.," said B. A. "But we'll give it a shot."

"Can I drive your tractor sometime?" asked Chip.

Jenny and B. A. looked at her like she was crazy.

"Have you ever driven a big rig like this before?" he asked.

"No. But it looks easy enough."

"I don't think your feet will reach the pedals. You better stick to shooting jump shots."

"If you change your mind, let me know. I'm sure I can handle it."

He throttled up and headed down the fence line, giving a wave over his shoulder. Jenny and B. A. stared at Chip as she got into the backseat.

"What?" she asked in response to the funny looks she was getting. "Haven't you ever wanted to drive something big like that?"

"It never crossed my mind," said Jenny. "Apparently a lot of strange things cross your mind. And, by the way, you don't have a real jump shot, ya know."

"Here we go," hollered B. A.

"Tell you what," said Chip. "Next game, I will drain a real jumper just for you. B. A., is it admissible to point at her as I run down the floor? You know, after I connect on a 'J' with perfect form?"

"As long as it's discreet," said B. A. "Let's leave the theatrics after made shots to the pros. They do enough of it for everybody."

"Yeah," added Jenny. "After a dunk, they act like they have just saved the world or something."

"Did you know that the dunk is the easiest shot in basketball?" asked Chip. "I mean, as long as you're tall enough to do it."

"Where did you come up with that?" asked Jenny looking in the rearview mirror.

"It's all math, babe. What's the shooting percentage on dunk shots? It's got to be in the upper nineties. I don't know if I've ever seen one missed on TV."

"She's got a point," added B. A.

• ◆ •

Luke sat in front of his computer looking at what he considered to be the finest sports article he had ever written. It described everything the reader needed to know about the Lakewood game. The strategy, the plays, and the personal stories were all in there. Even if you were at the Lakewood game, the incredible insight he exhibited would make the article worth reading over and over again. The reason for B. A.'s late appearance had made its way through the crowd by halftime. Luke gave Mary Lou Crimmins a lot of credit for her sewing expertise. He also explained the efforts she'd had to go through to get a girls' program started in Reston. He looked at his efforts on the screen—and then he deleted most of it. The history paragraph was good, so he kept that. Otherwise, the accolades of the three main characters were replaced with basic facts and a few highlights. Now that the team was doing so well, the last thing he wanted to do was start trouble.

Luke marveled at the influence B. A. had over her teammates. Not only were Chip and Jenny following her lead, but Kris, Carmen, Lu, and Rachel all seemed to be very comfortable with B. A.'s philosophy. Luke considered himself a traditionalist when it came to sports. He often applauded a good play by the opponent. And he also realized that every close play shouldn't go to the team he was rooting for. He wondered if the girls would have followed B. A.'s teachings, mostly by example, if she had only mediocre talent—probably not. Any way you looked at it, from the moment B. A. was moved to forward, she'd had a tremendously positive influence over the girls' basketball program at Reston. In his last paragraph he mentioned that Coach Todd would be back on the bench for the state tournament playoffs. Her recuperation period was longer than usual because of a mild case of pneumonia. *This will prove to be very interesting*, he thought.

* ◆ *

The Reston girls' varsity sat on the first two rows of bleachers waiting for the coaches to come out of their office. They had no idea what Coach Todd was going to say. They talked quietly among themselves. Would she revert to the style and personnel that she had used for the first half of the season? If she did, the postseason would probably be a short one. She had to realize that they were a very different team from the beginning of the season. Tammi's group was down to her and Darby, and at times Darby didn't appear to be all that gung ho on Tammi anymore. They were somewhat surprised when Coach Devers and Pops walked out of the boys' locker room and directly toward them.

"All right—listen up, ladies," said Pops. "We've got a situation here that needs to be discussed. Coach Todd will be out in a few minutes, and she's not sure how she will be received. She's human, and she knows that mistakes were made. We all make mistakes. There's no denying that. How we handle those mistakes is a huge factor in determining the kind of life we lead."

"Pops is right," added Coach Devers. "I've made some doozies in my coaching career. The point is, if you make the right decision here today, you will look back on this time with great pride—regardless if you win any more games this year. Pops and I just wanted you to think about that before your coach comes out here to talk to you. It will not be easy for her. You can be a huge help, or you can make the situation worse."

Pops and Coach Devers turned and walked quietly away as the two female coaches came out of their office. Pops gazed intently at B. A. for a couple of seconds before he left. She knew what he was trying to communicate. *It's up to you. You and your two friends are the leaders of this team now. Do the right thing.*

Coach Harbison and Coach Todd approached the bleachers and stood for a minute. It was obvious that Coach Todd was having trouble with what she wanted to say. Jenny nudged B. A. with her elbow. B. A. took the cue and did what a team leader was supposed to do. She stood and started clapping. The rest of the team stood with her and joined in. Two players were a little slower standing than the rest. Tammi couldn't figure B. A. out. This was her chance to stick it to the coach for the way she treated her. Tammi had finally admitted it to herself that B. A. was tons better than she was. Heck, her own sister was now better than she was, and she never thought that would happen.

Coach Todd put her hands up for them to stop. Tears were running down her cheeks.

"Girls, you have no idea how much I dreaded this moment," said the head coach. "I just want to say that I'm sorry for some past decisions and hope you will understand. Coaches don't always know what's best for the team. That being said, I would like to add that you have come together to accomplish more than anyone in this town believed you could. I can't begin to tell you how impressed this whole area is with your play. B. A., I—"

"Don't worry about it, Coach," interrupted B. A. "Newbies have to pay their dues just like everybody else."

Coach Devers and Pops were standing around the corner of the bleachers, eavesdropping.

"Did you know she would do that?" asked the coach.

"I had an idea," replied Pops. "There's more to Smith than just basketball skill."

"Well," said Coach Devers as he slapped Pops on the back, "I sure could use a few like her on the boys' team."

◆

The practice that afternoon was by far the best all year. They went through their drills as though it were the first day of the season. There was a feeling of togetherness. Tammi made a few of her usual comments, but no one seemed to be paying attention to her. She would be glad when the basketball season ended, and she was back on the softball field. Then she could take her rightful place as the star of the team.

◆

The three team leaders squeezed into B. A.'s truck for the ride home.

"I saw Tammi talking to you after practice," said Chip, looking at B. A. "What was that all about?"

"She said that I should enjoy all the attention while it lasted," said B. A. "Once basketball was over and we started playing softball, I would be just another player and not a big star."

"I don't know where she gets that attitude," said Jenny. "It would be nice if she would change her outlook. She could be a big help out there on the floor, on defense and rebounding. I don't know about offense, though. Lately, when she gets in, all she wants to do is chuck it up."

"Chuck it up?" asked Chip. "Did you just make that up?"

"Naw, I heard it somewhere. I think it was in a newspaper article about you."

"No way. B. A., would you consider me a chucker?"

"If you are," responded B. A., "keep doing it. You are one of the best outside shooters I've ever seen."

"There you go, smarty," said Chip smugly. "The best player in the whole area thinks I'm a great shooter. Now let's talk about the secret play where I jump off Carmen's back."

Jenny and B. A. broke into loud laughter.

"By the way," added Jenny. "You do know that this truck is not equipped for three adults to ride in the front seat?"

"Why are there three seat belts, then?" asked Chip.

B. A. saw where this was going and bit her lip, trying to stifle a laugh. Jenny could get Chip going like nobody else. She started to shake and was having trouble concentrating on her driving.

"B. A.," said Jenny in a very serious tone. "This is your truck. Will you please explain the reason for the middle seat belt?"

B. A. tried hard to hold back the laughter that was struggling to get out. She was shaking and her face was all scrunched up. She took a deep breath and got control of herself.

"It's for—" that was as far as she could get. The laughter finally escaped. She had trouble catching her breath and driving at the same time. Jenny was looking out the passenger window, afraid to make eye contact with Chip or B. A.

"Oh, I get it," said Chip. "It's for a little kid, isn't it? Funny. You're both lucky I have such a good sense of humor. Otherwise I would be offended."

"I'm sorry, Chipster," said Jenny. "I didn't know our driver was going to totally freak out."

"Hey, no worries," responded Chip. Silently she added both of their names to her payback list. She had mentally started the list when Luke messed with her voodoo doll.

* ◆ *

The next two games went exactly as planned. Reston rolled over their opponents, which made them district champions. Everything was clicking. Coach Todd and Coach Harbison were like co–head coaches.

They must have come to an agreement between themselves. The players liked the idea of Coach Todd getting the respect she deserved, and they were glad that Coach Harbison had been elevated in status.

The next game for the bidistrict championship did not go as planned. Reston was up by six halfway through the third quarter when "the incident" happened. At least that's what Chip called it when she explained it to her parents.

It all started in the second quarter. Washington High School was from north of Arlington, which was the next district to the east. Their coach was real animated, jumping off the bench when his girls scored and pumping his fist like this was the last game that would ever be played on earth. Chip kept looking over at him when he went through his act. It was all she could do not to laugh. Jenny told her to forget about him and to stay focused on the task at hand. This was hard for Chip to do. Jenny was shooting two free throws and Chip was standing just past half-court when she looked over at him again.

"Hey, 22," hollered the Washington coach. "You know that little step-through move you made earlier was traveling, don't you? You got away with that one."

Chip couldn't believe it! The other coach was taunting her. She just smiled at him and shook her head from side to side. He said something else, but she didn't quite catch it. Coach Todd stood up and called time after Jenny's first free throw.

"What's going on between you and their coach?" asked Coach Todd as they gathered in front of their bench.

"That dude's wacko," said Chip. "He's hollering stuff at me. Can he do that? He said my step-through move was traveling, and I got away with it."

"Okay, just forget about him," said Coach Todd. "Don't let him turn this into something other than a basketball game. If he keeps it up, I'll say something to the officials."

The Washington coach didn't say anything more to Chip until the third quarter. He just stared at her a lot. She knew he was trying to get into her head, which she thought was pretty childish for an adult. Especially an adult who was responsible for teaching young women sportsmanship. She was standing only about ten feet from him waiting for B. A. to throw the ball in. Two subs were entering the game, so there was a lull in the action.

"Hey, 22," he said. "We're about to press. I hope you can handle it."

B. A. was standing off to the side, and when she looked at him, she didn't see Chip's response. It was obvious that he saw it. Chip considered blowing the coach a kiss but decided against it. In this day and age, it was probably not a good idea. Also, she knew that B. A. would not approve. So she decided to do something that she had seen B. A. do from time to time. She winked at him. The wink brought him up off the bench and out onto the floor. Chip stepped back a few steps, not sure what was about to happen. His face was turning red, and he was hollering something to the ref and pointing at Chip. He was very much out of control. The ref immediately hit him with a technical foul for coming out onto the floor without being beckoned by an official.

B. A. went to the line and made both free throws. On the ensuing play, Chip hit her fourth three-pointer, and Washington was toast. Chip sat out the rest of the third quarter and half of the fourth. Coach Todd said they would talk afterward about what had happened. One of the big keys of the game was Xiu Lu's play. Her knuckles-to-the-floor defense had totally shut down Washington's high-scoring guard. She picked her up at three-quarter court and stuck to her everywhere she went. It was obvious that her opponent was extremely frustrated. With twenty seconds to go she was called for traveling, and she slammed the ball to the floor. This should have been another "T," but the refs wanted to get it over with. It was probably a good choice because the Washington crowd was not happy, and they were letting everybody know it. Reston played the subs a lot and still won by fifteen.

* ◆ *

The team sat in the locker room, anxious to get an explanation of the incident with the opposing coach. Chip was slouched between Jenny and B. A. when the coaches walked in.

"Okay," said Coach Todd. "I told the newspapers there would be no comments until I get this straightened out. Chip, what the heck happened out there?"

"Coach, uh, Coaches," started Chip. "That dude was harassing me for most of the game. Half the time I couldn't figure out what he was saying. Just before he went crazy, he was saying something about us not being able to handle their press. Right, B.A?"

"She's right, coach," offered B. A. "He was acting real weird. For some reason, he was focused on Chip. She is a cutie, but he's way too old for her."

B. A.'s comment brought snickers and lightened the mood a little.

"I'm only going to ask once, and I'll believe what you tell me," said Coach Todd. "Did you make any gestures toward him?"

"What do you mean by gestures?" asked the little guard, somewhat confused.

"She means," said Jenny. "Did you show him the bad finger?"

"What? You mean flip him off? Is that what you think, Coach? No way. I just gave him a little wink. It's something I saw a teammate do once, and I thought it was the appropriate response for the situation."

Both coaches stared at Chip for about five seconds. Then smiles started to crack their stern demeanor. The smiles were followed by raucous laughter. The rest of the team joined in. Through the wall, the Washington team heard the laughing and carrying on. They wondered what it was all about. Their coach, however, didn't hear it because he was in a serious conversation with the school superintendent. The 'super' had been seated across the floor during the whole game and had witnessed everything. His head girls' coach had a lot of explaining to do.

Chapter 15

The Big Get-Even

The team sat around Coach Harbison's living room eating spaghetti and talking about their upcoming game with Crockett High School of Arlington. Crockett was a basketball powerhouse in the area. They had lost only four games all season and were the pick to play in the regional quarterfinals. They were led by a trash-talking, cocky, power forward. She was notorious for her rough play and general all-around bad sportsmanship. Somewhere along the line, she had convinced herself that to be successful you had to play the game that way. Coach Harbison put in a DVD with a recent Crockett game on it, and the girls quieted down.

"The redhead is McIlroy, right, Coach?" asked Chip

Before the coach could answer, B. A. spoke up.

"Her name is McCoy."

"What? You know her?" asked Chip.

Coach H. stopped the DVD. The whole team looked to B. A. for an explanation.

"I played against her once," said B. A. "Outside, at the UNT courts. She plays rough and will look for an advantage at every opportunity. I'm just saying—we need to be careful not to get caught up in her type of game. If we do, it will favor them and certainly not us."

Coach Harbison looked over at Coach Todd.

"What's that old saying, Coach? Never wrestle with a pig—you both get dirty—and the pig likes it."

◦ ◆ ◦

On their way home, Chip, Jenny, and B. A. continued their discussion of Crockett's players and playing style. McCoy wasn't their only player who liked to mix it up. They had a little guard who took aggressive defense to a whole new level. On more than one occasion, they could plainly see McCoy and the guard holding their opponent's jersey. The officials only called it once for the entire game, and even then, it wasn't an intentional foul, as it should have been. Her teammates asked B. A. why she thought it should have been an intentional foul. She described the five main goals for a defensive player. If, as a defensive player, you weren't trying to accomplish one of those goals—you were just fouling on purpose. She reminded them about the foul drill she'd put them through several weeks earlier. The one where they practiced fouling in case they had to, at the end of a game. The best way to foul an opponent was to make it look like you were going for a steal. If a defensive player swiped at the ball and subsequently made contact with the offensive player, a foul was almost always called. If a defender just grabbed her opponent, it had nothing to do with playing defense—it was just plain fouling for the sake of fouling. B. A. went on to explain that if the refs would call more intentional fouls, maybe the coaches would teach their teams how to foul properly. Until then, players would continue to grab their opponents when they needed to foul—sometimes with disastrous results.

"I hate to say this," said B. A., "but the outcome of this next game will depend a lot on the officials. If they let Crockett get away with all the nonsense we saw on the video, it will put us at a huge disadvantage.

We've never played against a team that does all that stuff, at least not to the extent that they take it. For some reason the players, and obviously the coach, seem to think that to play at a high level you need to resort to dirty play. And, if the officials start calling fouls on them, they will squawk about it, big-time. My point is—if it looks like we have enough skill to beat them, they will try to turn the game into something totally different. More like a brawl than a high school basketball game."

"Shouldn't we get good officials?" asked Chip. "I mean, these are real important games. Since the better teams are still in the tournament, shouldn't the better officials be doing the games?"

"Let's hope so," added Jenny, deep in thought.

* ◆ *

B. A. dropped off her friends and headed over to Rod's place. They were going to relax and watch a movie together. She also wanted some advice on how to play against Kay McCoy. This time she couldn't fake a sprained ankle. As much as she detested Kay McCoy's approach to the game, she had to stand up to her.

* ◆ *

Game day couldn't come soon enough for Reston. The psychological part of the game came earlier than anyone had expected. Both coaches and several members of the team received phone calls at home before school started. The coaches were also called during the school day. The calls were from various newspapers and two radio stations. They all had the same question—did you see Kay McCoy's comments in the paper? Coach Harbison was the only one receiving a call who had actually read the article, and she was livid. McCoy had spouted off about how Crockett would totally shut down the two high-scorers from Reston. She went on to say that she thought Chip and B. A. didn't have it in them to compete at a higher level. She pretty much called them chokers, and her real concern was the following game for the area title. The word *overrated* had come up several times.

B. A. would have been proud of her teammates if she could have heard their responses to the reporters. Everyone who was called said, "No comment." Coach Harbison did say that talk was cheap, and the contest that evening wasn't going to be about who could talk the best game. After she hung up, she had misgivings about what she had said. She hoped her response wouldn't make things worse. Both coaches wished they could protect their team from this sort of nonsense, but that wasn't possible. They would all have to deal with it. It would definitely be a test of character for the Reston team.

* ◆ *

Rod and B. A. pulled into the Reston High School parking lot. As B. A. got out and headed toward the big yellow bus, he leaned over and hollered through the passenger window.

"Just do what you do best, babe. You know what she can do, but she has no idea what your best game looks like."

B. A. smiled and waved at him. She had come to the conclusion that this game would be a defining moment. One of the moments that would be looked back upon and discussed over and over by anyone who was there. She hoped that for her and her teammates it would be a proud moment and not a disappointing one. A win was not the only goal today. If the team played with class and exhibited true sportsmanship, it would make the day memorable, regardless of the outcome. If that type of thinking made her a sports geek in this day and age, then so be it.

Luke pulled into the lot with Chip and Clarice. He was glad that Chip hadn't objected to picking up Clarice. She appeared to be cool with the saucy redhead. At this moment, he didn't need any complications. He was about to cover the most important girls' game of his career.

He had also received early calls. Two newspapers, one from Dallas and one from Fort Worth, wanted his write-up on the game. This was a big opportunity for him, and he wanted to stay focused and objective. How many juniors in high school get their work printed in a major newspaper?

"Hey," hollered Clarice as Chip got out of the car. "I just want you to know that all the redheads in Texas are rooting for you today. That girl gives us a bad name. Go get her."

Chip flashed them a thumbs-up and headed for the bus.

Jenny and Tammi were the last to make an appearance. Tammi had filled Jenny's ear all the way there with talk of B. A. taking over a team that had played together as little girls. She went on and on about B. A. being a ball hog and headline seeker. It was obvious that Tammi's enthusiastic efforts at practice the other day were just a cover-up. As usual, Jenny just tuned her out. It didn't do any good to argue with her sister when she was like this. She just hoped that someday Tammi would see things as they really were. Apparently, that day was quite a ways into the future.

•◆•

The three Reston stars sat in their usual spot at the back of the bus.

"B. A., can I ask you a question?" said Chip.

"Isn't that a question already?" responded B. A.

"Yeah, I guess it is, but not the one I have been wanting to ask for a long time. How did you learn so much about basketball and, you know, all that other stuff that you have been teaching us?"

"Well, I had just started eighth grade when my dad died. My mom worked second shift at the hospital, and my sister was already away in college. So I went to the neighbor's house three days a week after school. But once basketball season started, I went from my practice at the middle school to the high school to watch the boys practice. Coach Thomson was awesome. He asked me if I wanted to do stats for the team. To make a long story short, if I wasn't playing in a game, I was watching the boys practice or doing the varsity stats at games. Coach Thomson was where I learned most of the basketball stuff. He actually let me participate in some of their drills. Riley Buelow was a sophomore on the varsity, and he always took me home. He was a great player, and he sort of took me under his wing. He was always looking out for me. His mom and my mom were high school classmates. I learned a lot about life and competition from him, and from my parents, of course."

"So you were like a child protégée," said Chip. "Very cool."

"Yeah, something like that."

B. A. didn't add that Coach Thomson had called her out of the stands at practice on more than one occasion to demonstrate a move that his guys were having trouble with. "The wheel" was one of the moves that he'd had her demonstrate. She had it down to perfection. She would drive hard to the hoop with her opponent right on her shoulder. After a jump stop and a shot fake, she would spin to the outside and shoot a soft hook. It was hard to defend if you did it right. She could do it right, and with either hand. If her opponent saw the move coming and tried to block the hook shot, she countered with a step-through and a bank shot.

⬦

As the teams walked out for the opening tip, Kay McCoy said something to B. A. about not getting hurt this time. B. A. couldn't make it out exactly because the gym was packed with loud, boisterous fans. They were screaming all during warm-ups and got even louder when the game started. It was definitely the big-time for the girls from the little town of Reston. On their first offensive possession, Chip threw a nervous pass that was about to sail out-of-bounds when a Crockett player tipped it. That's when the chanting started.

"Overrated, overrated," shouted the Crockett side. And they continued to shout it every time Chip or B. A. touched the ball.

It was obvious that the Reston team was rattled. They had expected some grief from the Crockett players but never imagined that the crowd would be a problem. With two minutes gone in the first quarter it was six to nothing, and it looked like it was going from bad to worse. Chip's first three-point attempt was almost an air ball. This got another huge response from the crowd. A few groans could also be heard from the Reston fans. Todd signaled for a time-out.

Everybody but B. A. was talking in the huddle. Opinions and a few complaints were being passed back and forth. B. A. stood in the middle, bent over with her hands on her knees. To the outside observer, it looked like she was winded already. She wasn't winded. She was thinking.

"Hey, superstar," said Jenny as she leaned in close. "We could really use your help here. You've got to stop this before it gets out of hand. We know you can do it. What do you want us to do?"

"Okay," said B. A. as she stood up, wiped her eyes, and addressed her teammates. "Ya'll don't mind if I take a few shots, do you?"

"How about you take all of them," said a dejected Chip.

"Don't get down, girls," said Coach Harbison. "Two minutes is only a small fraction of the game. We've got thirty minutes left. Let's get out there and take care of business. Now, TCB, on three!"

The girls broke the huddle and walked toward the official with the ball. He was standing at half-court waiting for them. As he handed the ball to B. A., he heard what she said to Chip.

"Watch this first one," she said, smiling. "You're gonna love it."

B. A. threw the ball in to Chip and took a return pass. She dribbled at half speed down the left sideline and took a fifteen-foot set shot right in front of McCoy. McCoy jumped high and slapped the ball about ten rows up into the bleachers. She almost blocked it with her elbow. The crowd went berserk as McCoy egged them on with raised fists. As she waited for the ball to come back, B. A. looked at Rod, who was sitting about three rows up with a bunch of his UNT buddies, including Butch McCoy. He gave her a sympathetic smile. She locked eyes with Rod and gave him a little wink. He broke into a huge grin and gave her a clenched fist.

From then on, every time B. A. faked a shot, McCoy was off her feet trying to duplicate her first spectacular block. B. A. got the tall redhead off her feet and scored twice in succession. The next time down the floor she got off the shot of the game. She had the ball about three feet out on the left side. She pump faked and McCoy jumped high to block the shot. Sensing that the defender was going to come down right on top of her, she waited until the last instant and then threw up a desperation hook shot with her left hand. She didn't expect to make it. She was just looking for the foul and the two free throws. The ball kissed the very top of the board and came back down through the hoop. B. A. bent down after the shot, preparing for the collision. McCoy came down hard on her back, and they both went to the floor. The Crockett crowd was dismayed when B. A. offered McCoy a hand up, and she swatted it away.

"Luckiest shot I ever made," she told Jenny as they waited for the towel girls to wipe the floor.

"I won't tell anyone," responded Jenny. "Just make the free throw. It might shut these guys up for a few minutes."

B. A. didn't make the free throw, but Jenny gathered in the rebound and took it back up strong. She banked it in, and the foul was called. The Crockett center wasn't trying to block her shot. She was sending a message that there would be no close shots without a little pain attached. The ref who called the foul told her to cool it. When she didn't acknowledge his comment, he got right in her face and repeated it. The Reston crowd loved it.

McCoy was relentless. She kept up a line of smack talk for the entire game and slipped in an occasional elbow whenever she thought she could get away with it. It didn't dawn on her until late in the game that her fans were slowly changing their allegiance. When the individual point total was announced at half-time, there was a smattering of applause from the Crockett fans. B. A. had scored twenty-five of Reston's thirty-one points. Reston was only down by one.

In the locker room at half-time, the Reston team was uncharacteristically quiet. They were somewhat embarrassed that B. A. had to do practically everything. Both coaches talked to them about the many parts of a successful team. The value of defense, passing, screening, and rebounding was not diminished just because you weren't scoring your usual number of points. Chip didn't realize it, but she was on her way to setting a school record for assists in a game. She was in total awe of her teammate. They were walking shoulder to shoulder on their way out for the second half when she looked over at B. A.

"What do you call that?" she asked, referring to B. A.'s first half point production.

"Warm-up," said a determined B. A. as she looked her teammate.

The foul that B. A. was hoping for came at the start of the third quarter. She was about five feet from the hoop on the right side this time. Chip was dribbling around Jenny's screen on the opposite side of the floor. B. A. felt McCoy grab her jersey, so she took off for the sideline. This surprised McCoy. She didn't let go quickly enough, and her arm was stretched out to its full length. The one official who B. A. thought was the strongest was standing about six feet away. He blew his whistle and crossed his arms. Intentional foul! McCoy and her coach went ballistic. The official said he didn't have time to explain to them why holding someone's shirt wasn't part of playing defense. The ref couldn't believe the Crockett players and fans. Their team was being totally outclassed, and they didn't even realize it.

McCoy's fourth foul was a thing of beauty. B. A. knew McCoy was playing a little more cautiously, so she had to come up with something totally unconventional. She was on the left side with the ball, standing on the lower box. With her back to McCoy, she looked quickly over her left shoulder toward the hoop, then spun the other way with a quick dribble. Instead of a fade-away jumper or a hook, she came underneath with a two-handed scoop shot. It was the type of shot that you might have seen in the early sixties. Even though she knew she had three fouls, McCoy couldn't pass up the opportunity for an easy block. She wouldn't even have to leave her feet for this one. She miscalculated just a little and her arm came crashing down on both of B. A.'s wrists. The same ref who had called the third one blew his whistle for foul number four. B. A. thought she heard him chuckle as he headed for the scorer's table to report it. What he really wanted to do was high-five B. A., but his job was to stay unbiased. So far he was doing a good job of it, but with McCoy's style of play, it wasn't an easy task.

With three minutes to go in the game and Reston up by ten, McCoy drew her fifth foul and stormed off the floor. She was the second one to go, as the Crockett center had already fouled out earlier in the quarter. Surprisingly, the nasty little guard from Crockett wasn't much of a factor, mainly because Chip had only taken five shots the entire game. Her job was to get the ball to the superstar, and she did it efficiently. She did make three of her five shots. The high-scoring duo still racked up over fifty points between them because B. A. had fifty-two all by herself. The final was Reston 76 Crockett 65.

The press had gotten smarter. They were standing between the Reston players and their locker room. There was no way Smith and Fullerton were going to get by without a comment. To their surprise, the girls had no problem talking to them. They answered their questions simply and straight to the point. If the writers were looking for a few zingers at the Crockett players or fans, they were disappointed. The only celebration they saw from the two Reston stars was a subtle fist bump as they headed for the locker room.

One of the writers in the gym didn't even try to get close to the girls after the game. Luke knew he would get an exclusive interview with both of them when they got back to Reston. It was one of the perks of having your girlfriend and her best friend as the stars of the game.

Back in Reston there was a huge crowd waiting for the victors in the high school parking lot. It looked like the whole town had turned out. The throng of people was getting anxious because the bus was way late getting there. Luke and Clarice pulled into the lot in the "punkin'." He opened his door and stood looking over the hood of the car. The crowd quieted down when he whistled and waved his hands at them.

"The Lady Eagles would like to invite you all to the Pizza Palace for a celebration," he hollered.

The crowd cheered and headed for their cars.

"Dang," said Luke as he pulled onto the road and headed for the Pizza Palace. He had received a phone call from Chip telling him of the team's plans and was told to go extend the invitation to their fans. "I hope they didn't get the impression that the team or I was buying pizza for everyone."

"I don't think so," said Clarice sarcastically. "I think they're smart enough to figure out that a man who drives a car like this can't afford much of anything."

The celebration lasted for a couple of hours. The fans rehashed almost every shot B. A. had made and every rebound that she and Jenny had pulled down. The rest of the team also got their due. *Carmen must have set over a hundred screens out there. Could you believe the defensive job Lu did on their guard? She held her to ten points under her average. And what about Tammi's block at the end of the half? She got a piece of it, came down with the ball, and started a fast break. That's a lot smarter than slapping it into the stands and giving the ball back to the offense.* They also praised the girls' composure. It would have been easy to throw in the towel against a team that played like that.

The team also impressed their fans by getting up and walking through the crowd, thanking them for being so supportive. It would have been easy to sit there and let the crowd come to them, but that wasn't B. A.'s style. She asked Chip and Jenny to go with her, and once the rest of the team saw what they were doing, they got up and mingled too. It was a new experience for all of them, and they loved it.

• ◆ •

B. A. was lying in bed thinking of the day's events. She and Chip had given Luke an exclusive interview for the two papers he was writing for. They were very excited for him. She was about to turn out the light when her phone rang. She didn't recognize the number. It was tempting not to answer, but she did anyway.

"B. A.?" came the voice from the other end.

"Yes," was all she said.

"You probably don't remember me. This is Cheryl Williams from Lakewood."

"Of course I remember you, Cheryl. How's it going?"

"Good. But not as good as ya'll are doing. I listened to your game on the radio. Fifty-two points might be a record around here. Nice job of putting that arrogant McCoy girl in her place. The radio guys said she stalked out of the gym in a huff when she fouled out. She just headed to the locker room. I don't think I'd want her for a teammate. Anyway, the reason I called is I have a proposition for you. My uncle is a basketball coach in Michigan, and he runs a series of summer camps for high school and junior high girls. I'm going up there to work this summer, and I was wondering if you and Chip Fullerton might like to join me. I told him about you two, and he was all for it. You know, it's not nearly as hot in Michigan as it is in Texas, and there's a lot to do other than basketball. I know you've got a lot of things on your mind right now, so just think about it."

"Okay," said B. A., somewhat shocked. "I'll mention it to Chip."

"Thanks. We'll talk later if you're interested. Good luck in the Area Championship. Ya'll are awesome ballplayers. Bye."

"Bye," responded B. A.

Her thoughts as she was falling to sleep were of leaving her mother for a while. She also thought about what it would be like spending part of the summer with Chip on a daily basis. She would definitely come back with more "Chip stories" to add to the growing file. Would they be staying in the same room? Would Luke and Rod be able to come and visit them? How far away was Michigan? She closed her eyes. These were questions for another day. They had more basketball games to win.

* ◆ *

Fortune did not smile on the Reston team before the Area Championship game. Jenny looked terrible at Friday's practice. It was obvious that she was catching a cold. B. A. went directly from practice to Mr. Kim's store. He was really worried about his wife and stayed by her side, so B. A. ran the store by herself for the rest of the evening. Then she got a call at five a.m. asking her to come back in and open up at seven. Mr. Kim had taken his wife to the hospital. B. A. couldn't get back to sleep after the call. Too many images were running through her mind.

* ◆ *

B. A. found the key where Mr. Kim had left it and opened up the grocery store. He was worried because two big deliveries were coming, and he couldn't afford the extra money he would have to pay if someone wasn't there to receive them and they had to go back into storage. B. A. busied herself around the store, checking out customers and stocking the shelves. She called Chip around eleven. She wanted to know how Jenny was doing. Chip said she didn't sound very good on the phone, but she was still coming to the game. B. A. told Chip her situation at the store, and the little guard came right over.

"I'm glad you're here," said B. A. "Watch the register, please. I have to use the restroom."

"How's Mr. Kim's wife?" asked Chip when B. A. came back.

"He called about an hour ago and told me she had a kidney infection."

"Ouch. I've heard they're painful."

"They can be. At least they know what to treat her for. She's been sick for quite a while. Maybe they can find out what the problem was before this latest setback. It's no fun being sick."

"I'm sure Jenny is thinking the same thing right about now."

"Mr. Kim said I can close up as soon as the second delivery gets here," said B. A. "I would have called Rod to take over, but he's doing an all-day lab or something at school. This is like bad timing all the way around. What is Luke doing?"

"He had a family thing over in Dallas," said Chip. "He's going from there right to the game. I'd call my mom, but she's helping dad at the store. She said they'd be there right up until game time. It's inventory weekend. I've helped with inventory before. It's brutal."

"It looks like we're on our own," said B. A. "My mom is taking a refresher class at the hospital before her shift starts, so she can't help us, either."

"Hey, what do you have to eat around here?" asked Chip.

"Look around, silly. You're in a grocery store."

"Oh yeah. Well, let's find something to eat. I'm starving."

* ◆ *

The bus was scheduled to leave at six o'clock. B. A. had been told that the second delivery would definitely show up by four o'clock. This would give them time get it in the cooler, get home to get their stuff, and then get back to the school. The reefer truck showed up at 4:20. The only problem was that their stuff wasn't right by the door. The driver explained that his last delivery had a refrigerator breakdown, so their product had had to stay on the truck. He told them that if they all pitched in, they could move the stuff by the door and get Kim's stuff into the store in about an hour's time.

The two athletes surprised the driver with their work ethic. They pitched right in and worked like troupers. That's more than could be said for the driver. His pace was getting slower and slower as they went.

"Are you all right?" asked B. A.

"I just need to take a short break," said the driver. "My back is tightening up. I've been lifting all day. We unload our big accounts by fork truck, but we have to do the smaller ones by hand. Today is small delivery day. Don't you two have boyfriends we could call?"

"I'll try again," said B. A., pulling out her phone and walking away for privacy. "Mine's at school in Denton. He should be on his way back by now."

"I'm anxious to get this delivery done," said the driver as he sat down on an empty crate and wiped his forehead with a red bandanna. "There's a big girls' basketball game tonight, and my niece is playing. She starts for Dunbar. Hey, we're playing Reston tonight. I hear y'all are pretty good. Actually, I'm really looking forward to seeing Smith and Fowlerton play. Do you know either of them?"

Chip just stared at him. *Fowlerton*, she thought. *It's obvious this dude has trouble with the English language.* B. A. came back with good news.

"Rod is only a couple of minutes away," she announced.

"We've been working next to this guy for over an hour, and we haven't introduced ourselves," said Chip to B. A. "You first."

"I'm sorry," said B. A., sticking out her hand. "I'm B. A. Smith."

"And I'm Chip F-u-l-l-e-r-t-o-n," announced Chip.

"I'm Don Stubblefield. Hey, are you kidding me? You're Reston's two hotshot ballplayers? What are you doing unloading produce right before an important ball game?"

"It's a long story," said B. A., looking over his shoulder at Rod's car as it pulled up into the lot. "Here's my boyfriend. He'll help you finish up here. We have to go."

"You two are good workers," said the driver, standing. "I hope you boyfriend isn't the wimpy type. There's still a lot of lifting to do."

"I think I can handle it," said Rod, walking up behind the driver.

The driver turned around to see Rod standing behind him—all six feet seven inches and 250 pounds of him.

"Yeah, I think you'll do," said the driver, smiling. "Do you know what a celebrity your girl is in the Dallas/Fort Worth area? Her name comes up on the sports shows all the time. Oh, and they talk about you too, Chip."

Chip snorted as B. A. handed Rod the store key and gave him a big hug. The two ballplayers said good-bye and jogged to their vehicles.

"Let's get this stuff put away," said Rod as he turned and looked at the little guy standing next to him. "I've got a ball game to go to."

"You and me both, big guy."

❖

If the scoreboard was all a fan went by, the game with Dunbar didn't appear to be all that impressive. Jenny never got in. She sat on the end of the bench and blew her nose a lot. Chip played with arms that felt like they were made of lead and had no feel whatsoever. B. A. was just plain fatigued. But they battled for all they were worth. With four minutes to go, they were only down by five but couldn't get any closer. Tammi and Lu played the best games of their young careers. Carmen set some awesome screens, and Kris had a personal best in scoring and assists. It was a real team effort that their coaches and fans were proud of. And they let them know it. They were led back into town with police and fire trucks blaring. The girls couldn't believe it. Not in their wildest dreams would they have come up with the season they just had. And it all started because their assistant coach put the new girl in at forward. They'd had no idea who she was. They also had no idea that her initial goal was to stay out of the limelight and live like a regular high school student.

B. A. ended the season the way a true student of the sport would want to end it. One paper said she was "magnificent in defeat." She scored thirty-two points and brought her team back to make a game of it more than once. In the end, she just ran out of gas. When interviewed, she sincerely praised Dunbar for their play and sportsmanship. She also praised her teammates and coaches for their efforts all year. The rest of the team followed suit. Roger Maris would have been proud of them.

◦ ◆ ◦

Luke's article drew a lot of attention in the Dallas/Fort Worth area. He was up most of the previous night, thinking about what he wanted to say. He decided on making it more of an editorial than a game summary. There would be plenty of game summaries written up by other sports journalists. He admitted to himself that he was also influenced by B. A. Chip had relayed to him a lot of the stuff that B. A. had taught her and Jenny. Luke was amazed at B. A.'s insight into the game and her sportsmanship. Being a tough competitor had nothing to do with the faces you made when you were photographed or when you were looking at your opponent during a contest. The only way to prove your dedication to your sport and your ability to compete was how you conducted yourself during the game. All that other stuff, the gesturing and the gyrations, was just window dressing. To true sports enthusiasts it's usually just annoying. It seems like the modern fan and athlete, whether they approved or not, have just grown to accept the attention-drawing actions of the game's participants as part of the game. He didn't want to lay it on too thick, as it might alienate a lot of folks. His intent was to educate his readers, not to chastise them.

RESTON FALLS TO DUNBAR IN AREA
CHAMPIONSHIP (68–58)

By Luke Slowinski

Do you think you've seen it all in girls' basketball? If you do, then you haven't been following the Reston Lady Eagles this year. After a lackluster start, one simple position change enabled the Reston girls to run off a string of eleven straight victories. When B. A. Smith was moved to the small forward position, several pieces fell into place for the Reston squad. Their new up-tempo style proved to be very effective as they mowed down their opponents—usually by wide margins. During their eleven-game win streak, they averaged seventy-five points per game. Smith and point guard Melinda ("Chip") Fullerton were good for two-thirds of that total.

Last night, Fort Worth's Dunbar finally put a stop to the Lady Eagles' remarkable run. But they didn't go down without a fight. On paper, Dunbar looked like they would have no problem with the team from the small town to their north. The Dunbar coach, Mike Weathers, told his girls before the game that this could be the toughest team they would play this year. He was talking mostly about mental toughness. Reston has found a way to make up for their lack of size. Smith (5'8") and Fullerton (5'3") were joined by three other starters: Tammi Olsen (5'11"), Carmen Espinosa (6'2"), and Kris Ritter (5'4"). Rachel Moon and Darby Quinn would spell the two starting forwards, while defensive specialist Xiu Lu would come in to shut down the opposition's high-scoring guard. Jenny Olsen, who averaged a double-double (points and rebounds) for the streak, was sidelined for last night's game because of illness.

The Reston girls knew their roles and played them for all they were worth. They did all the things that a team needs to do to be successful: pass, rebound, defend, and most of all—implement solid game management. And they did it with a sense of class. They did not celebrate when they made a spectacular play on the floor—and there was certainly a lot to celebrate. Instead they chose to go about their business with a low-key attitude that is very refreshing in this age of absurd fist-pumping gestures and the "look at me" mentality that permeate today's sports from junior high to the pros. There were a lot of smiles from Smith, Fullerton, Ritter, and the rest of the Lady Eagles. They proved that a player can be tough without the "check this out, I'm bad" attitude that usually goes with it. They were just being themselves. Being himself worked out just fine for Hall-of-Famer Magic Johnson. Besides, it's a whole lot more fun to play just for the sake of competing and discovering what you are truly made of. I have to believe that if Magic had been at last night's game, he would have been one of the first ones to congratulate the nonwinners. Notice that I didn't say "losers" because that word does not describe the Lady Eagles efforts or their character.

When Fullerton and Smith were questioned after the game, they said they thought they had played well but that Dunbar had definitely played the better game and deserved to move on. They also were very complimentary of Dunbar's sportsmanship. Coming from these two, that is very high praise indeed.

Coaches Todd and Harbison heaped praise on the whole team, especially their two leaders, Smith and Fullerton. The best way to measure a great player is to see the effect she has on her teammates. When she walks on the floor, does she make them better players? When questioned about this very aspect, both players seemed to downplay their importance. This type of humility is certainly admirable. They play the game for the pure joy of it and leave the rest to writers and critics. If you were to choose a couple of area athletes for your daughters or sons to emulate—you couldn't do much better than these two. The bad news for area teams is they are both juniors, as is most of the Reston team. Great job, girls. You are what high school sports should be all about.

Most of the team was sitting together at the same cafeteria table during lunch on the Monday following the Dunbar game. Their classmates were in awe of their accomplishments. A few of them brought copies of Luke's article for them to autograph. People whom B. A. had never seen before came up to her and spoke to her. She had long ago abandoned her philosophy about leading the life of a normal kid. Chasing normal was an exercise that was bound to fail. She knew it was all for the best, as she looked at her new friends laughing and joking around. And the icing on the cake was the fact that she had helped her new best friend accomplish one of her fondest wishes—she was on a good team for once.

* ◆ *

"Hey, daydreamer," hollered Chip across the table.

"What?" asked B. A. as Chip's voice brought her back to the moment.

"Softball started quite a while ago. We're supposed to show up for practice on Wednesday, but I'm going tomorrow. I need to get my shortstop job back."

"I'll probably go tomorrow, too," said B. A. "I just heard that Pops is now the coach. What's up with that?"

"The regular coach is an elementary teacher, like Coach Todd," said Kris. "She's having some problems with her pregnancy, so she asked for the season off."

"Do you think Pops knows much about softball?" asked Lu.

"Are you kidding?" said Chip. "That guy knows more about sports than—than that knucklehead over there." She pointed to Luke, who was talking to one of the pitchers on the boys' team and taking notes. He just looked at her and smiled.

"B. A.," said Kris, as most of the other girls got up to take their trays back, "we've never talked about softball. With that arm of yours, you're not a pitcher, are you?"

Luke's head snapped around when he heard the question, and he looked B. A. right in the eye. His look gave her a creepy feeling.

"Why?" asked B. A.

"Well," said Kris. "It would be ironic if you were. You know, you played Tammi's position in basketball, and she didn't take it very well. I was just thinking if you were a pitcher—"

"I'm an outfielder," said B. A. "I played right field last year."

"Good," said Chip, getting up and following B. A. to class. "Pick me up just before sunset. We'll cruise out to our spot and I'll give you my take on the softball team. We've got a lot of work to do if we're going to be any good."

• ◆ •

The next day Chip and B. A. were hurrying down the hall together. The last bell had rung, and they were heading for their first softball practice. Just before they hit the door, a familiar voice hailed them.

"Hey, superstars," hollered Tammi as she and Darby caught up with them. "I hope you realize that softball will be a lot different from basketball."

"Yeah," said Chip. "The ball is a lot smaller and you get to hit it with a stick. Technically, it's a metal stick, but I think you know what I mean."

"That's not what I'm talking about, short stuff. You're going to be on my turf now, so you can forget about all the grandstanding that you did during basketball. I hope you can adjust to not being the center of attention all the time. It will be painful, but you'll get used to it."

Darby licked her index finger and then acted like she was marking an imaginary point for Tammi. Chip put her head down and raised her arms in the air, saluting Tammi and Darby.

"Oh, goddesses of softball," she chanted. "It will be an honor to carry your equipment onto the field. With your permission, may we at least practice with the team? And if you deem us worthy—put on a uniform?"

"You're one weird bird," said Tammi. "But it's good that you know your place. I'll get back to you on the uniform thing."

With that, she high-fived Darby, and they headed across the parking lot.

When Chip and B. A. got to B.A's truck, Jenny was waiting for them. She had watched the confrontation from across the parking lot.

"What was that all about?" she asked.

"Tammi was just telling us what our jobs were on the softball team," said Chip.

"And what are your jobs?" asked Jenny anticipating one of Chip's rare gems in response.

"We're supposed to back up her awesome pitching with flawless fielding and superb hitting," said Chip, sounding like a college professor. "But the credit for victory must, first and foremost, go to her formidable pitching prowess."

As the girls got into the truck, B. A. and Jenny were thinking the same thing. *Has Chip finally mastered the English language?* They both stared at her for a few seconds as she sat between them without cracking a smile. Then they looked at each other and simultaneously hollered, "No way!"

"Way," said Chip, staring straight ahead. "To the softball field, Barbara Ann."

"At your service, Melinda May," said B. A. as she put the truck into gear.